Praise for Quintin Jardine's novels:

'Perfect plotting and convincing characterisation . . . Jardine manages to combine the picturesque with the thrilling and the dream-like with the coldly rational' *The Times*

'Deplorably readable' *Guardian*

'Jardine's plot is very cleverly constructed, every incident and every character has a justified place in the labyrinth of motives, and the final series of revelations follows logically from a surreptitious but well-placed series of clues' Gerald Kaufman, *Scotsman*

'If Ian Rankin is the Robert Carlyle of Scottish crime writers, then Jardine is surely its Sean Connery' *Glasgow Herald*

'It moves at a cracking pace, and with a crisp dialogue that is vastly superior to that of many of his jargon-loving rivals . . . It encompasses a wonderfully neat structural twist, a few taut, well-weighted action sequences and emotionally charged exchanges that steer well clear of melodrama' *Sunday Herald*

'Remarkably assured . . . a *tour de force*' *New York Times*

'Engrossing, believable characters . . . captures Edinburgh beautifully . . . It all adds up to a very good read' *Edinburgh Evening News*

'Robustly entertaining' *Irish Times*

Screen Savers

Quintin Jardine

headline

First published in 2000
by HEADLINE BOOK PUBLISHING

First published in paperback in 2000
by HEADLINE BOOK PUBLISHING

10 9 8 7 6 5 4 3

ISBN 0 7472 5963 1

Typeset in Times by Avon DataSet Ltd,
Bidford-on-Avon, Warwickshire

Printed and bound in Great Britain by
Clays Ltd, St Ives plc

Headline's policy is to use papers that are natural, renewable and
recyclable products and made from wood grown in sustainable
forests. The logging and manufacturing processes are expected to
conform to the environmental regulations of the country of origin.

HEADLINE BOOK PUBLISHING
A division of Hodder Headline
338 Euston Road
London NW1 3BH

www.headline.co.uk
www.hodderheadline.com

1

He moved towards her. It was dark, but there was no disguising the menace in his eyes.

She stood there framed in the open window, looking down at the incalculable drop to the sea below her, listening to the roar of the water as it pounded and frothed on jagged rocks. I wanted to help her, to leap on his sleek Hispanic back, to slap on a sleeper hold like my wrestler pal Liam Matthews, or simply to spin him round and give him an old-fashioned toeing. All my instincts told me to help . . . she was Prim's sister, for Christ's sake . . . but of course I couldn't. I just sat there, a poor helpless fool, staring at murder about to happen.

Useless, Oz Blackstone, just plain useless.

She sensed him, the lithe Latino, at the last minute; she turned, her eyes widening in sheer terror as she saw him and realised in the same instant, exactly what he had in mind. I expected her to scream, but she didn't. No, as quickly as the fear had flashed across her face, inexplicably it was gone, replaced by a soft mocking smile.

'Just for a second . . .' she said softly.

And there he was, behind the intruder, muscles tensed in his white T-shirt, his long hair flying as he did what I had wanted to do. In a single blur of powerful movement, he kicked the man behind the knee, without warning, sending him spinning, then caught his right wrist and twisted his arm savagely up behind his back.

My eyes must have been standing out like organ stops as I watched, an intruder myself in the darkness. For long seconds, the three figures stood in a frozen tableau, Dawn still smiling, the short struggle between the two men concluded.

And then she stepped aside, away from the open window. Now her rescuer was grinning, his impossibly good looks turned suddenly into something evil. With hardly any visible effort he raised his captive up on his toes and hurled him outwards, over the low sill, into the night. The doomed man's arms flailed wildly as he screamed his way down to the rocks below.

Dawn laughed; a soft, deep, throaty chuckle. I felt a shiver run through me; in that instant she sounded just like Jan. But when she spoke, the accent was different. 'You bastard,' she murmured, as she wound her arms around his neck. 'Just for a moment, I thought you were going to let him—'

He put his hands on her waist, lifted her and threw her backwards, out of the window. It happened so fast that the smile stayed on her face, even as she started on her way down to death.

In the darkness I heard a voice cry out: 'Jesus Christ!' I realised that it was mine.

Miles Grayson laughed as he pushed the remote button. 'Now that, Oz, is the sort of audience reaction any movie director likes to hear,' he said, as his face froze on the big television screen.

Beside me, I could hear Primavera, breathing hard. I pushed myself up from the floor and snapped on a table lamp, then pulled back the heavy, drawn curtains, letting the Glasgow summer evening back into my living room.

'What d'you think?' Miles asked. You two are the first to have seen that, apart from us, the crew, and the technician who helped me edit the final cut.'

'I thought you were supposed to be the good guy,' said Prim.

'That's the hook,' Dawn answered, in her own accent this time. 'Miles is always the good guy, so we figured that when he chucks me out of the window all of a sudden it'll just blow everyone away.'

'Is that the finish?'

A few years ago, *Time* magazine had a poll to choose the most famous human on the planet. The fourth most famous looked up at me from my heavy leather sofa. 'It is at the moment,' he replied in his Aussie-Californian drawl. 'Did you get it?'

I was long past being awed by Miles. All that fame crap aside, he was just my partner's brother-in-law, and just another Equity member, like me. I did a pretty good job of looking down my nose at him; not difficult, since I'm three inches taller than him, when we're standing side by side.

'Do's a favour, of course I got it. Classic sub-Hitchcockesque melodrama; you're the soft-centred, romantic, perennial failure type back from the South Seas and shagging your incredibly rich brother's wife. She sells you this scheme where the pair of you do him in and inherit the family millions . . . except, right at the end she finds out the hard way that you don't plan to share the inheritance.

'Nice one. Kept me right on the edge of my floorboard

all the way through. No kidding.'

'Yes,' Prim chipped in. 'Biased or not, it's the best film I've seen this year. Mind you, it was a bit strange watching you two on screen with you sitting behind me all the time.'

'Did you understand the ending?' her sister asked.

'I think so. You can't help it, when Miles' face suddenly takes on that look.'

The world's fourth most famous human looked at his wife, eyebrows raised. She smiled, and nodded her head.

'Great,' he said. 'Thanks, you two. You've just saved us a few hundred thousand dollars. I was thinking about shooting a few extra scenes, just to bring out the final twist in the tail. But we'll treat you as a test audience and go with what we've got.'

'Maybe you can do a sequel,' Prim suggested. 'Maybe Dawn could have a sister who doesn't believe that she and her husband died accidentally, and turns up to investigate her death.'

Miles grinned. 'You fancy the part?'

'Not me. Better make it an identical twin sister. Maybe you could find a part for Oz, though. He is a member of your profession, after all.'

Miles and Dawn stared up at me. The looks of astonishment which swept over their faces were as dramatically effective as anything we had seen in their movie.

2

'You? An Equity member? You've never done a day's acting in your life.'

'Maybe not, but this is a letter from Equity and it is offering me full membership.'

She looked over her shoulder, with that half-smile, half-frown that only she could pull off, the one that told me when I was being a plonker. She had kept her fair hair long, the way it had gone during her sojourn in Spain. Prim and I don't go back all that far in terms of years, but in terms of shared experiences there was a bond between us tied in stainless steel wire.

Primavera Phillips is the daughter of two genuine eccentrics, whereas my mother, at least, was a normal, feet on the ground sort of woman, even although my Dad is . . . well, he's my Dad. With that sort of genetic inheritance you might have thought I'd only be half as daft as Prim.

Her special sort of daring daftness must be infectious, though, for ever since I met her my life has been stood on its head, and I've found myself in situations that were about as likely . . . and as hazardous to the health . . . as Jimmy Hill walking into the Horseshoe Bar in his England bow tie and asking for a pint of bitter.

All I ever wanted was a nice quiet life as an ordinary, self-employed Private Enquiry Agent, taking enough depositions for lawyers and insurers to keep myself in the modest style to which I'd become accustomed . . . or maybe I should say, in which I'd become complacent.

Not even in my sweatiest nightmare had I ever wanted to become the sort of private detective you read about in mass market novels, or see on telly. Then, one ordinary day, I walked into a flat just off Leith Walk, and came face to face with two bodies. One was dead. The other was very much alive; it was Prim's.

My life changed beyond redemption in that instant. For a start, thanks to Prim's even dafter sister Dawn, she and I found ourselves in mortal danger, from which we escaped only by the skin of our teeth . . . albeit with a big bag of money.

With our riches, the pair of us buggered off to Spain for a while and became involved in an even crazier adventure which ended in death and in the discovery for both of us that while we were deeply in lust, we were not exactly soulmates. In fact, I realised that mine was back in Scotland.

So Prim and I said our goodbyes, and I went home to marry Jan, thinking – stupid bastard that I was – that I would live 'happily ever after'. An imprecise phrase, that; bound as it is round the word 'ever' which has a different duration for every one of us . . . for every two of us.

In our case, Jan's and mine, it meant a few months; time for us to settle down in an eagle's nest in the middle of Glasgow, time for us to discover what happiness really is, before . . . no, that has to stay in the past. I can't avoid the flashbacks, but I won't talk about it again, unless I really have to.

In the wake of that . . . thing, Prim came back into my life, like a strong hawser tethering me to the ground, giving me something on which to focus. With nothing better to do, but knowing from experience that we had to do something, we leased a small office in Mitchell Street Lane, re-established our old business, Blackstone and Phillips, Private Enquiry Agents, and watched the client list expand to bursting point.

Primavera rented a flat, a two-bedroom place in the Merchant City, owned by an Aberdeen lawyer whose older kid had just left Glasgow University and whose younger sprog was still at school.

We kept separate social lives for a while; or tried to. But mine consisted mostly of going for a pint with my copper pal Mike Dylan, and Prim's involved reading a lot and going to the movies on her own. So after a while we started going to the movies together, and sometimes I'd go to Prim's for supper afterwards, or she'd come to mine. In the beginning, neither of us stayed over. We'd been over that course before; and furthermore having a business relationship to protect, we were careful to keep things on a 'good pals' basis.

Then one Friday night towards the end of September, after we had seen *Armageddon*, polished off a couple of steaks and watched *Men in Black* on my video, when Prim picked up the phone to call a taxi, I put a finger on the button and cut her off.

It wasn't the same as before; it couldn't be. We weren't as exuberant as we had been at first, – the truth is, that had gone before we split – but there was a new tenderness there, a new maturity in the way we approached each other. We didn't use any dangerous words, but afterwards, we fell asleep easily enough; at least that hadn't changed.

She gave me one funny look the next morning, when I

came into the kitchen as she was loading her hand-washed underwear and shirt into the tumble-dryer; a slightly apprehensive glance, as if she was searching my face for signs of guilt. I smiled at her, trying to let her know without saying it that she needn't have bothered, that there was no one, anywhere, who would take the slightest exception to she and I sleeping together.

That night, when I came back from my Saturday job, she had moved her clothes into the wardrobe and drawer space which I had made ready for her. Jan's space; Jan, who, everything else aside, had liked Prim enormously.

And that very same night, we won the lottery. Not the mega-jackpot, you understand, only three and a quarter million, but a clear blessing nonetheless upon our new beginning.

It made no difference to us. Honest. We had plenty of money to start with, our business was going well, and my Saturday job was bringing me in even more.

My Saturday job? Oh yes.

About eighteen months back, I had been dropped by my lawyer pal Greg McPhillips into an investigation which involved some extremely crazy gentlemen, and a couple of ladies, involved in the sports entertainment business . . . in other words, wrestlers.

As a cover I had agreed to become the circus's master of ceremonies, or ring announcer, calling the bouts on the Global Wrestling Alliance's television shows. To their surprise, and even more, to mine, a few people thought that I was quite good in the part, and so after the smoke had cleared from the explosive conclusion of the real job which I had been hired to do, Everett Davis, the extremely big boss, had asked me to stay on, and had given me a contract backed up by a few share options in the holding company.

Since then, GWA had gone truly global, and Everett was spending more than half of his time in the States, servicing his recently signed network deal there and completing the take-over of his main rival, Championship Wrestling Incorporated, formerly run by his rogue half-brother. Oh yes, and with the take-over, my share options had gone sort of global also: they were worth around half a million dollars.

Even after all that, I was still taken by surprise when I found out that people other than children and eccentrics watch cable and satellite wrestling programmes. I was in the office one Tuesday morning transcribing an interview with a witness in a constructive dismissal action, when the phone rang. Prim answered, then handed it across.

'Good morning, Oz,' said an easy, slightly smarmy voice. I struggled to place it, but it sounded like most tele-salesmen I'd ever heard, professional, entreating, anonymous. 'I'm Mark Webber, from RHB and F.'

'I don't think I need any of those,' I told the guy.

'Hah! That's what our secretaries think too. But seriously . . .' I tried to take him seriously, but failed '. . . we're an ad agency, in Covent Garden. We're casting for a new commercial for a client in the children's leisure sector.'

Okay, I thought, play along for a bit. 'Children's leisure, eh. Which branch would that be? Smarties, chocolate eggs?'

'Play accessories.'

'Ah. I see. Would they be toys, then? My nephews have a few of them. I must tell them that they're accessorised.'

Mark Webber laughed, as if it was expected of him. For a second I felt like a politician addressing a party gathering. 'I get your drift, Oz; we creatives do tend to fall into line with our clients' corporate language.'

'Indeed? What else do you market? Beverage transporters . . . cups and saucers, like?'

'Touché, old lad. I can hear already that you're just the man for us.'

'I don't know about that, Mark. The only leisure accessories I use these days are limb-extending balata propellants. Mind you, I still can't talk my Dad out of calling them golf clubs.'

The man's laugh took on a manic tone. 'God, that's wonderful. It's a humbling experience for a guy like me to be exposed to a Northern sensibility. Maybe we should ask you to write the script as well.'

'As well as what?'

'As well as doing the voice-over, of course. Listen, this is the story: the client, Roxy Matrix, is launching a new product in October aimed at the Christmas market. It's a power accessory, personal rather than electronic . . .'

'You mean it's a toy, rather than a video game?'

'I suppose so. It allows the child to become actively involved in play and to create fantasies around its persona.'

'You mean it's a doll?'

'Companion, Oz; at Roxy Matrix they call them companions.'

I managed to turn a chortle into a cough without Mr Webber noticing. 'This companion? Is it inflatable?'

'No, no, no. It's solid, powered, and about twenty per cent of life size.'

'Does it have muscles, or tits?'

'Both, in fact; there are two variants. What we're talking about here is a plug-in rechargeable, robotic partnership simulation, alternative humanoids whom the young people can adopt as leaders and role models.'

'You mean like parents used to be? Brilliant idea,' I said in a sudden burst of artificial conviction. 'Ideal for a high achiever partnership in a double-income situation. Buy a couple of these simulated partners for the kids and the carers can devolve young people management responsibility to them, freeing up more time for income generation.'

There was a silence on the other end of the line. I guessed that Mark had finally figured out that I was ripping the shit out of him. (That's like taking the piss, only a lot less gentle.) Or maybe it was the other way around, and he guessed that he had been well and truly rumbled. Across the room, Prim and Lulu, our secretary, were staring at me, each of them just a touch glassy-eyed.

'God!' His voice was suddenly choked. 'What a brilliant concept. We've written the story-board for the commercial already, but I'm sure we can work that theme in; subliminally, of course. It's much too sensitive for us just to go balls-out with it.'

I felt my eyes beginning to glaze over too. 'Mark, can we get this conversation back on track, please?'

'Yes, Oz, of course. I'm sorry; got a bit carried away there. Truly original creative thinking has that effect on me. Yes: the voice-over. Great news for you. Mr Barowitz, the CEO of Roxy Matrix, asked for you personally. Scots accents are very popular just now, but he didn't know that. In fact, his wife,

Ronnie, is a great fan of your wrestling programme, and she insists that you have exactly the right voice for the new commercial. And Mrs Barowitz has great influence over her husband.'

'Let me guess, she's a killer blonde and thirty years younger than him.'

'Maybe twenty years, but you've got the principle right. She's a power in the business. Mind you we didn't just roll over and do what we were told. We at RHB and F are true professional advisers. We watched a couple of your shows before we accepted her idea. She's dead right, you know; your voice and your industry persona are just right for the product. They're called Rick and Ronnie Power, by the way.'

'Mr Barowitz' name wouldn't be Richard, would it?'

'How did you guess that?'

'It just came to me. And how did you come to me? How did you get my number?' There was an edge to my question, I still wasn't anything like convinced by Mr Webber. I thought I detected a strong whiff of bullshit coming down the line.

'I called the GWA. I spoke to Mr Matthews. He's one of the wrestlers, isn't he? He gave it to me.' I made a mental note to have a word with Liam.

'Look, as you said, let's cut to the chase here. We'd like you to do the ad. Your part will take a couple of days; we'll fly you down, and put you up in the Park Lane Hilton . . .'

I decided to play it all the way. 'Not me, Mark, us. My partner comes too.'

'No problem. Now Oz, you're not an Equity member, are you. I couldn't find you on their listing. We have a house rule here that we only use Equity people; one of our directors was a member of the Cabinet and he wants to get back in, and there are still a few dinosaurs in our industry, so we don't want to compromise him by landing him in the middle of a public union row.' The words came tumbling out. 'I can fix that, though. The work you've been doing on television qualifies you for membership, and I have a contact in the Equity office. I'll place you with an agent too; we like to go through them. It'll take no time at all.'

Mr Webber was beginning to lose his audience; the whiff in my nostrils was getting stronger.

'As to the fee, I've looked at the budget and we can squeeze it up to fifteen.'

'Fifteen?' I repeated, a yawn in my voice.

'Yes, fifteen thousand. Sylvester Burr, your agent, normally takes twenty per cent but, in the circs, I'll beat him down to ten.'

The phone almost slipped out of my hand. I took a deep breath. 'I see.'

There was a silence. 'Okay,' said Webber, at last. 'We'll pay Burr's commission this time. That'll leave you with fifteen clear. What d'you say, Oz?'

I did some quick thinking. 'I'll tell you what I say. Put it in writing inside forty-eight hours. No faxes; letter-head, signature in blood, all that stuff.' I gave him the office address.

'And you'll do it?' He sounded genuinely excited.

'If it checks out.' I started to hang up then changed my mind. 'By the way, Mark,' I added, 'if Detective Inspector Mike Dylan is behind all this, tell him from me that I'll have his nuts for desk ornaments . . . they'd be too small for paperweights.'

'Well?' The question exploded from Prim, as I cradled the phone, and doubled over in pent-up laughter. 'What the hell was all that about?'

When I could control myself, I told her. 'You're right,' she agreed, at once. 'It's got Dylan's stamp all over it. He probably recruited a young constable with a posh voice and gave him a script.'

'There's one way to find out.' I picked up the phone and called the GWA office, on the west side of the city. It was mid-morning, so I knew that the superstars would be hard at work. The switchboard operator traced Liam Matthews in less than three minutes.

'Mornin' Oz, me ould lad,' he drawled in his accentuated Oirish, slightly out of breath from his training session. 'What's up?'

'Did you take a call a while back from a guy, looking for me, from an advertising agency called RHB and F or some such?'

'Sure, and I did. Christ was he keen! What was up? Have you got his sister pregnant or something.'

'Not as far as I know.' Interesting. If Mark Webber was a Dylan stooge, he'd wouldn't have needed to call the GWA for my number.

'He seemed harmless to me, Oz,' said Liam. 'I wouldn't have given him your number otherwise. No problem, is there?'

'Not if he checks out. In fact, if he does, I'll buy you a large drink.'

It checked out less than twenty-four hours later, when a special delivery letter arrived at the office, on the RHB and F letter heading, setting out the terms of my proposed engagement and signed not by Webber, but by the former Cabinet Minister himself. At that point, Prim and I began to believe. I replied, accepting of course, by return of post.

The letter from Equity, inviting me to join, didn't arrive until the next day. 'You . . .' Prim exclaimed, astonished. I had forgotten to mention that part of my conversation with the ad lad. 'An Equity member? You've never done a day's acting in your life.'

'Maybe not, but this is a letter from Equity and it is offering me full membership.' I scratched my chin. 'I think it's a condition of employment, so I'd better sign up.' And that is how I came to be a member of the same profession as Dawn and her husband, the fourth most famous human on the planet.

We did the shoot two weeks later. I was given a week to learn my lines; which, as I saw at once, had been written in the same style as my standard ring announcements. The main differences were that I was off camera and that the money was fifteen times as good . . . not that I had ever complained about the grand per weekend, plus expenses, that Everett paid me.

Mark Webber turned out to be a tall, gangling young man in a suit, a silk kipper tie printed with a piece of impressionist art, rimless spectacles, and a pin through his eyebrow: a designer ad-man if ever there was one. He knew his way around the studio, all the same, and knew how to flatter the director of the epic, Ismael Stormonth, a perfectionist with a strong egomaniac streak. If I was on fifteen grand, I wondered what his take was.

My highly paid gig was similar to my GWA role, in that I spent most of the time hanging around, building myself up for my big moment and watching the professionals, in this case the lighting people and the camera person, do their highly skilled stuff. Even after a year, I still thought of myself as an amateur in the television business.

At the end of the first day, I did a first run through of the script, perfecting my delivery so that it was in synch with the rough-cut of the film footage. The second day was spent in the edit suite doing voice-over after voice-over until at last, not just the prickly Ismael, but Richard and Ronnie Barowitz agreed that we couldn't get it any better. Mark told me that it was unusual for the client to attend a shoot, but said that the Barowitzes had insisted.

As for Ronnie, she was much as I had expected, thirty-something, blonde, slightly over-stuffed, a former small-time model who probably had the wrong shape at the wrong time. It had been good enough to catch her toy maker, though. Mr Barowitz, king of Roxy Matrix, was a solemn little man who rarely said a word, other than 'Yes dear.'

'Oz, that was just wonderful,' she oozed at me as we prepared to strike camp. 'I knew I was right in going for you.'

'I'm glad it worked out, Ronnie,' I said. 'I hope the product does as well as you expect.'

'It will, don't you worry. Richard is never wrong. Tell me,' she went on, not giving me a chance to muse on the wee man's infallibility. 'Will your wrestling show be on in the south soon?'

'Yes. We've got a pay-per-view event in the London Arena in a couple of months or so. I'll send you a couple of tickets. Hope you can come; we've got an Irish bloke on the team who'd just love to meet you.'

Prim and I enjoyed a nice couple of nights in London,

courtesy of RHB and F, and that, I thought, would be it. But I always have been wrong more often than I've been right. Less than a week later I was in the office with Lulu, Prim being out on an interview, when the phone rang again.

'It's a Mr Burr,' said the wee one, her hand pressed over the mouthpiece. 'Sounds English.'

I shrugged and took the call. 'Oz,' an exuberant voice exclaimed, 'this is Sly.'

'Too bloody right it is,' I answered, conversationally. 'Who the hell are you?'

'Sly. Sylvester Burr, your agent . . . remember?'

My eyebrows skidded to a halt halfway up my forehead. 'Barely,' I acknowledged, recalling a wee, heavily-bangled man, who had looked in briefly during the second day of the shoot. 'What can I do for you, Sly? Hasn't Mark Webber paid your commission?'

'Course he has, son. It'd be more than his job was worth to hold out on me. No, this has got nothing to do with that young ponce. I've landed another job for you; another Soho voice-over, two days, week after next. The client's Arkaloid Sports, one of the world's major players in leisure wear. I can't get you fifteen this time though; ten's their top whack. That's two for me, eight for you.'

'Plus expenses for Prim and me.'

'I don't know if they'll cover your girlfriend.'

'They'd better not bloody try. No, I just want them to pay for her flight and hotel. That's the deal. Oh yes, and I can only work Mondays to Thursdays. I'm committed the other three days.'

'I'll tell them; they'll roll over for it. The dates ain't a problem either.' He paused. 'You're a quick learner, my boy. You're not Jewish, are you?'

'No, Sly, religion's got nothing to do with it. The fact is that Prim and I have this disease; whenever we're together money just seems to stick to us.'

'Ah, but that's the same as being Jewish,' Burr laughed. 'Whatever, I'll be seeing you.'

He wasn't wrong; even before we recorded the second voice-over, he had come back with a third. In no time at all, I was doing two, sometimes three a month, never for less than five thousand, less commission, plus expenses. Without any conscious effort, I had a third career.

3

'They pay you to do that, mate?'

There was an odd look in Miles' eye as he gazed across at me. On the television screen the last image of my latest commercial was locked in freeze frame. I nodded. 'I'm afraid they do. Not the sort of bucks that you and Dawn are into, but decent enough for humble people like Prim and me.'

A sudden spluttering exploded on my right; the sound of a man choking on a mouthful of lager. Detective Inspector Mike Dylan and his girlfriend, Susie Gantry, had joined us for a drink before dinner at Rogano. 'Humble!' he squawked, when he could. 'You two? Brigands, the pair of you, lunatics and now, bloody millionaires, God help me.'

I smiled at him, as he wiped a trickle of beer from his chin. 'Have you ever thought that God might be helping all of the rest of us here, Michael, but that he might have a different agenda for you? Let's face it, you're the only person in this room who isn't nouveau fucking riche.'

I stopped sparing Mike's feelings on the very day I met him. It was true, though, Susie had surprised the world by steering her late father's property and construction group though a major crisis, and securing in the process her own very healthy financial position. (Actually Susie's Dad, the legendary Jack Gantry, Lord Provost of Glasgow, wasn't late, not in the deceased sense of the word. It was just that he hadn't shown up anywhere for a while.) However it was true also that Dylan would have walked out on her before he would have lived off her. He was fiercely independent and insisted on paying her rent, and on chipping in his half of their holiday bookings.

He and I had survived a couple of adventures, as colleagues and as adversaries; in spite of it all, he had become, after Prim, my best friend. He grinned at me, over the top of his Carlsberg can, and began to sing, very badly, 'He was poor but he was honest . . .'

'And your Master of Ceremonies gig?' Dawn asked me, chuckling at the same time at the man who had wanted, once upon a time, to lock her up for murder. 'That's an earner too?'

'Oh yes, my dear; and the seed from which all the other earners have grown. I've had offers there too. A big boxing promoter asked me a few months back if I would announce his shows. I turned him down, though. It just didn't sound right.'

'Why not?'

'I didn't like the feel of things. I had nothing against the man himself, but some of the people around him made my flesh creep. Anyway, I decided that my first loyalty as a sports announcer will always lie with Everett Davis and the GWA.'

'Do you think we could find a part for Everett in a movie, Miles?' Dawn suggested. 'He sounds larger than life.'

I had to laugh at that. 'He is larger than life . . . life as we know it, Captain, that is. You write a part for a seven foot, two inch black man, and he'll be right for it . . . but no one would ever believe it.'

Miles surprised me by nodding, vehemently. 'Oz is right.

There are a few cast-iron truths in our business, and one is that wrestlers, as actors, invariably suck.' He paused, then looked at me, unsmiling. 'On the other hand, it would be pretty easy to write a part for a six foot, thirtyish Scotsman. Dawn and I are pretty well down the road in planning a project; it's going to be set in Scotland. In fact, we've started shooting some of the preliminary scenes already.

'I'm directing and leading as usual, and Dawn's co-starring; we're pretty well all cast, but there's one part that's been giving us trouble; you fit the profile pretty well. Since you are Equity-entitled, would you like to read for it?'

I'm pretty good at sussing out when my chain's being pulled. I grinned back at him. 'No way am I wrapping myself in scabby tartan and painting my arse blue . . . not for you, not for no one.'

Miles shook his head; he still didn't smile. 'Don't worry, it isn't costume, it's a contemporary thriller. The part we're trying to fill doesn't have much on-camera dialogue, but the story's told in flashback, and he's the narrator. I like your voice, Oz. It's distinctively Scottish, but it's very clear; American audiences will understand what you're saying.

'I'm serious, mate.'

I looked at Prim; a wide, incredulous grin was fixed on her face.

'Tell you what, Miles,' I said, dead-pan.

'What?'

'Speak to my agent.'

4

He did. Two days later we shot a screen test in a private studio in Edinburgh, hired in Prim's name to avoid any possibility of a premature leak to the *Evening News* or anyone else.

Next day, Sly agreed terms; I had warned him not to haggle, but he did anyway. He can't help himself; it's a cultural thing. Three days afterwards, a press release on my signing hit some of the Scottish tabloid press. 'Christ,' I exclaimed to Prim across the breakfast bar, 'they're saying I'm a bloody movie star.'

Filming my scenes was still weeks away, so Prim and I decided to put any thought of it from our minds, and carry on in the meantime with what passed for us as a normal life. Our earlier experience of eating lotuses in Spain had taught us that we are not good at sitting on our backsides watching the world go by, so when the Lottery pointed its great big finger at us, we decided straight away that it would not affect our working routines.

In truth, my weekend job, and my growing Sly Burr business were making it increasingly difficult for me to concentrate on interviewing punters in their offices, homes, and occasionally in their police cells. They were also making it increasingly boring. However that was what Prim and I had chosen, together, to do, so I felt that I had to pull my weight, that I could hardly back out and leave it all to her.

Nevertheless, I felt my ticker give a small jump of pleasure when Mike Dylan called me one Tuesday morning as I was grafting away in Mitchell Lane. 'Have you still got your deer-stalker hat and your pipe?' he asked. He was trying to sound conspiratorially casual, but I thought that I picked up a nervous undercurrent in his voice.

'My Sherlock Holmes kit, you mean? Aye, it's still around somewhere. I'm a bit rusty on the violin though.' Prim was out, or I might have been a bit more guarded. I wasn't sure that she would have been too happy about Mike's call.

'Don't bring that, for Christ's sake. Far too arty for the Horseshoe. There's something I need to talk to you about. Can you meet me there at lunchtime, say one o'clock?'

'Make it twelve-thirty,' I said, knowing that Prim would not be back before then. I didn't want to keep a secret from her if I could avoid it. 'What's the problem anyway?'

'Not over the phone.' He hung up.

It isn't far from my office to the Horseshoe Bar. My curiosity was well pumped-up, so I was bang on time; even so, Mike was there before me; almost twitching with tension, it struck me. He was so agitated he even bought me lunch without a single hint being dropped.

'What's the story, Detective Inspector?' I asked at last, as we set our pies, beans and beer down on a small round table.

'I need a favour, Oz.'

I shrugged. 'I owe you a couple, that's for sure. What's the problem?'

'Someone's after Susie.'

'You're kidding. What d'you mean after her?'

'She's had threatening letters.'

23

'How threatening?'

He looked around to make sure no one was watching us, then reached into the pocket of his light-weight summer jacket and produced a brown envelope. I glanced at it and saw that it was addressed to Ms Susan Gantry, at her office address.

'Is it all right to touch this?' I asked.

Dylan frowned. 'Of course!' he snapped.

'Okay, keep your Ralph Lauren on. I thought it might have been evidence; fingerprints and all that, basic police procedures. Christ, I was only in the force for a few months but even I remember that.'

I took the letter from the envelope, unfolded it and read it quickly. It was brief, and to the point. 'Bitch from Hell. You are going to die with your world in ashes all around you.' It wasn't signed, but it ended, 'A Well-wisher . . . not!'

I nodded. 'Yes, I'd say this was threatening all right. There have been others?'

He took two smaller envelopes from another pocket; they were numbered '1' and '2'. The first letter read simply, 'Your number is up, Ms Gantry.' The second went into more detail. 'You choose your associates very badly, Susie. Now you're going to pay.' Unconsciously, I read it aloud; my voice was barely above a whisper but still, Mike glared at me furiously. 'Shurrup, for fuck's sake,' he hissed.

'Sorry.' I paused and glanced across at him. 'Why didn't you mention this the other night?'

'I didn't like to, not with Miles and Dawn around. The third letter didn't arrive till yesterday anyway; that was the one that really shook us both up.'

'Any idea who this bugger might be?'

'Not the faintest. It's weird, Oz. All three letters were posted in different British cities: Dundee, Birmingham, then London. All three look as if they've been typed on a PC then printed on the same machine. It's the same typeface every time and if you look at it through a magnifying glass you can see the pixels.'

'You don't believe in *them*, do you?' Dylan stared at me blankly; I decided that this was not a time for humour.

'Mike,' I went on, quickly, picking up the eating irons to attack my pie and beans. (The Horseshoe pies are the best in Glasgow. It doesn't do to let them get cold.) 'Why are you showing me these, old son? Surely this is a police job, all the way.'

He threw me another sour look. 'You try telling Susie that: Christ knows, I've tried. But she says that if word got out that she was under threat, it could undo all the work she's done to rescue the Gantry Group over the last couple of years.

'After what happened to her old man, she had to sell off a big chunk of the business at a loss. She's heavily committed to a couple of projects, but she's going to have to borrow big if she's going to see them through. She's worried that if word got out that she was under threat, her bankers might get cold feet. If that happened, it could bloody near wipe her out.

'She's refused point-blank to let me open a police investigation. She says, and she's right, unfortunately, that there are people in the police who make a few quid passing on juicy tips to the tabloids.'

'Er,' I asked, 'haven't you got a duty as a copper to investigate if you know that a crime's been committed?'

'Aye sure, but you know I've overlooked that once or twice

25

in the past. And this is my girlfriend who's involved.'

I frowned and stopped a forkful of pie halfway to my mouth. 'But if this is serious, if it isn't just a nutter . . .'

Dylan shook his head. 'I've taken steps to protect her. I've hired a guy as a day-time bodyguard. Officially he's on the Group payroll as an office manager, but he's ex-SAS, supplied by a personal security firm in London. With him around during the day, and me at night, she's pretty safe.'

I had my doubts about him as a minder, but I kept them to myself. 'So how can I help? D'you want me to fix up a couple of the GWA boys as back-up for your hired gun?'

For the first time that day, he smiled. 'Thanks, but no thanks. My man doesn't need back-up, believe me. Anyway your wrestlers tend to be a bit conspicuous . . . apart from that girl Sally Crockett.'

'You can't have her; she's on maternity leave.'

'Lucky somebody. No, Oz, I'd like you to help me find the bastard behind these letters. For all that Susie's a tough wee cookie, this has her rattled, and I hate to see it. Chances are this is just a disgruntled former employee with a nasty streak and a vivid imagination, but whatever, I want him stopped.'

I hesitated. 'I can't help but recall, Mike, that in the past you've tended to take the piss out of my efforts as an investigator.'

He smiled again; a broad grin this time. 'Aye well, you're the best I've got. Also, you might be a complete bloody amateur, but you've got the detective's greatest attribute on your side.'

'And what's that?'

'You're a jammy bastard. Somehow or other, whenever you

take on one of these half-arsed investigation jobs you always seem to get a result.'

'That's true, but Michael, in the past I've known where to begin. Where the hell do I start here?'

He reached into a third pocket of his designer jacket and handed over yet another envelope. 'That's a list of former employees of the Gantry Group who've been asked to leave or been fired; a bit more than a dozen of them. The name at the top is Joe Donn, the Finance Director Susie had all that trouble with a couple of years back. I've run a quiet PNC check on them all. Two are currently in the slammer, so they're out of the frame. Another three have convictions for minor offences; assault, breach of the peace and possession of marijuana. The rest look like choirboys.'

'All men?' I asked, without looking at the list.

'All but two of them. One of them was a junior, into the petty cash. The other was Joe Donn's secretary; she resigned after Susie caught her smuggling copies of documents out to her old boss. He was trying to make trouble for her by feeding information to a freelance journalist, but a pal of hers on the *Herald* business desk tipped her off.'

'Is he still trying?'

'No. The Gantry Group lawyer put a scare into him. When Donn left for the second and final time, his severance agreement included a standard confidentiality clause. The solicitor wrote to him making it clear that if he broke the agreement again, Susie would sue him for punitive damages.'

'So you think that these letters might be another way of getting his own back . . . by throwing a scare into the wee one?'

Dylan frowned. 'Put it this way. If this was a police investigation, old Uncle Joe would be the first bloke in for interview.'

'Thanks for that insight. Since you lot never get it right first time, I'll probably start somewhere else.'

'Cheeky bastard. You can start wherever you like, as long as you get a result.'

I thought about that as he spoke. I had never met old Joe Donn, but from everything I had heard, he struck me as something of a dinosaur. Not the sort of man who would have written poison pen letters on a personal computer, then printed them out on a laser. No, old Joe would have cut words out of the *Daily Record* and pasted them on to a page from a school jotter, just like he'd seen them do in the movies.

I didn't share this with the detective inspector, though; it would have made me sound too much of a smart-arse.

'I'll do what I can, Mike,' I said modestly. 'There's just one thing, though.'

'What's that?'

'You sure you can afford my fee?'

5

After a spot of haggling, I settled for my lunch as a retainer, and another couple of pints on a successful conclusion. Not that I expected to collect them.

I had some hope that we might have lifted matching prints from the three envelopes, but Dylan knocked that on the head right away. He told me that he had them all dusted by a close-mouthed pal in the Strathclyde forensic department, and had come up blank. There were plenty of prints on the envelopes, naturally enough since the things had been through the Royal Mail system, but the only ones common to all three belonged to Susie herself.

I took them all back to the office anyway, with their contents and with Mike's list of possible suspects. It was time to confess all to Primavera.

She sat in silence as I told her about Susie's stalker. When I was finished, she turned to our assistant. 'Go on out for a coffee for half an hour, Lulu,' she said, quietly. 'Take a fiver out of petty cash and nip along to Princes Square.'

She looked at me across her desk as the door closed, leaving us alone, and leaving me wishing I had gone for a coffee too.

'Does that guy know what he's asking?' she exclaimed.

'Probably not.'

I tried to appease her, but her temper was still on the up. 'Oz, what has happened every time you and I have got involved in something like this? Disaster, and you above all know that. The first time, we got away by the skin of our teeth with our very lives—'

'And with a lot of money.'

Prim shut me up with another look. Best let her get it off her chest, son.

'As for the second time, if we hadn't got involved with trying to authenticate that bloody picture—'

'You might still be living in Spain with your ancient lover.' She winced and looked away. I knew I shouldn't have said it, but sometimes my mouth just goes haywire.

'Yes, exactly,' she said curtly, recovering herself. 'And as for the third time, if Greg McPhillips hadn't volunteered you for that escapade, then—' She stopped abruptly, kinder than I had been, not voicing the truth with which I would have to live forever.

'Mike must know all that, Oz.'

'Not about you.'

'Maybe not, but he was involved last time. He knows what happened, and why. So he must know now what he's asking you to do.'

'No, I don't think for a second that's occurred to him. This is his girlfriend who's under threat, and he's worried sick . . . probably even more worried than he was prepared to let on. To tell you the truth, love, I'm really chuffed that he thinks well enough of me to trust me with this.'

I hesitated. 'And anyway . . .' I began.

She cut me off. '. . . and anyway, you enjoy it, all that private detective stuff. It gives you a buzz, gets you hard. Admit it, you're a sucker for it, and Mike knew that when he called you. He knew you couldn't turn him down.'

'He knew I couldn't turn him down, yes, but that's not why. Two years ago the guy put his job on the line to help me. I owe him; simple as that.'

She frowned. 'Is there anything I could say to make you change your mind? Any threat I could make? Any ultimatum I could give you?'

I sat on the edge of her desk, tilted up her chin and kissed her. 'Sure there is,' I whispered. 'You could tell me you'll leave me if I take this on. That would work. But you're not going to do that, are you?'

She looked me in the eye for upwards of ten seconds; then she shook her head. 'No, I'm not. Because I don't believe in jinxes, and because you're right. Your friends are in trouble, and if you can help them, you have to.' She smiled, gently. 'I love you for it, too. Just be careful, that's all.'

'Of course I will, but don't get this out of proportion. The chances are that all I'm doing is running down a crank.'

'You've got three weeks to do it, then.'

I frowned at her, puzzled.

'Christ,' she laughed, 'have you forgotten already? Your movie career gets under way then.' She pushed herself out of her chair, and picked up Dylan's list from my desk. 'Where are we going to begin, then?'

'We?'

'Sure. You don't really think I'd let you handle this on your own, do you? Lulu's pretty well trained now. It's time she had a promotion and a rise. We'll hire an assistant for her, and she can handle more of the interview workload. With one thing and another you're hardly involved here any more: if I manage the quality of the operation, our clients won't know the difference.'

My reassurances about the safety of Dylan's mission had come back to bite me on the bum, well and truly. They seemed to have convinced Prim, okay; but I wasn't so sure.

'So come on,' she insisted. 'Tell me. Where do we start? With this man Joseph Donn?'

'I don't think so. Dylan thinks he's the bookies' favourite, but he has a recent history of sounding off to the press. This thing has to be done with no publicity, so we'll have to be careful how we handle him. No, I reckon we should begin with his secretary, Myrtle Higgins. She lost her job for doing him a favour; could be she won't fancy doing him any more.'

6

Finding Myrtle Higgins wasn't as easy as we had assumed it would be. We went out that evening to the address which The Gantry Group had on file, only to be told by a student who answered the door that she had given up her room six months before, to move in with her boyfriend.

'Do you have her new address?' Prim asked.

'Somewhere up in Broomhill,' the girl answered. 'She shouldn't be too hard to find.'

'Not much,' I thought. Broomhill was like a rabbit warren; and that wasn't counting all the people who claim to have a Broomhill address, because they don't like to admit that they live in Partick . . . the opposite of Partick Thistle Football Club, which doesn't like to admit that its home ground is really in Maryhill.

There was nothing for it but to check next day with the company to which Susie Gantry had written a reference for her former employee . . . generously, we thought, given the reason for her leaving. Sure enough, Myrtle Higgins worked there, as the Finance Director's secretary, her old job with the group: only now she was Mrs Myrtle Campbell.

She wasn't going to take my call at first, until I told the switchboard that it was to her advantage if she did so. She came on the line all bright and breezy, as if she had won the lottery. I could have told her, that's not how you react; in the moment of realisation you go rigid with shock.

'Yes,' she chirped brightly. 'How can you help me?'

'By keeping you out of trouble, perhaps.' Her tone changed in an instant, to terse and hostile.

'What is this?'

'My name's Oz Blackstone. I'm a private investigator; I need to talk to you about a problem that's arisen at the Gantry Group.'

'Nothing to do wi' me, pal,' she said. 'I left there a while back.'

'Yes, Mrs Campbell, and I know why. Listen, I'm not saying this has anything to do with you, but I need to talk to you all the same. It's important.'

'Fuck off.'

'Not just yet,' I shot back, quickly, before she could hang up. 'Susie Gantry was okay with you, wasn't she?'

'What? Like giving me my cards, d'yae mean?'

'Like giving you a reference for your new job, when she could have had you bombed out with a word. Now you can return the favour: Susie could be in trouble.'

'We're all in trouble, pal, one way or another. I want no more to do wi' the Gantrys, an' Ah certainly don't want you turning up here.'

'Myrtle,' I assured her, 'if I was going to do that I'd be there already. I'd sooner to see you at home, tonight.'

'Listen, whatever your name is. You don't know where Ah live, as far as I can tell, but if you do happen to turn up at my door, my husband Malkie will gie you a doin'. He does martial arts, and stuff.'

All of a sudden, I was glad that Prim could only hear my

side of the conversation: one phone call into our investigation, and I was being threatened with a kicking. 'Is that so?' I said, conversationally. 'Origami's my speciality, actually. What's the address again?'

'Fuck off.' This time she did hang up.

A quick call to a pal at the Registrar's office and a promise of a beer secured me the details of the marriage, four months earlier, of Malcolm Campbell, bachelor, and Myrtle Higgins, spinster, both of an address just off Crow Road. A second, to Mike Dylan, produced the information that Mr Campbell had four convictions for assault, the last of which had earned him six months inside.

A third call fixed me up with a very special insurance policy.

7

Crow Road is one of the nicer parts of the western side of Glasgow. It runs from Anniesland Cross, past the High School, through Jordanhill into Broomhill, and down to Dumbarton Road. You wouldn't call it posh at any point, nearly all of it is very neat and well-looked after.

Malcolm and Myrtle Campbell lived on the second floor of a big red sandstone tenement in a street just off Broomhill Cross. I had heard of a 'wally close' – or half-tiled common entrance, to non-Glaswegians – but in all my time in the city I had never been in one, until then.

Even in mid-evening, the stairway was bright and airy, lit from above by a cupola. As I climbed I guessed that Mr Campbell's time inside hadn't affected his earning power; the building looked moderately expensive.

I turned on to the second floor landing and found the Campbell flat immediately on the right. The front door was freshly painted, in royal blue; that tells you a lot in Glasgow. I took a deep breath and pressed the button which was set in the upper panel, looking like a penalty spot. After a few seconds, it opened, wide enough for me to see a short, slim, blonde girl in denims and an Oasis T-shirt.

'Mrs Campbell,' I began as brightly as I could, 'I'm Oz Blackstone. I—' She slammed the Rangers colours in my face. I sighed, and rang the bell again, taking half a step back. I began to count.

I had reached nine, when the door swung open again, suddenly and violently, framing a stocky, powerfully built man, dark-chinned, with a scar running across the bridge of his nose. He looked to be in his mid-thirties; he was balding and what was left of his hair was cropped very short. He wore jeans, like his wife, and an orange vest, showing off his collection of tattoos and his heavy shoulders. The instant I saw him, he reminded me of someone, someone nameless but nasty. Even if I hadn't known about Malcolm Campbell's record, I'd have treated him very carefully, just on general appearance.

His mouth was narrow and his tight lips barely moved when he spoke. 'You don't take a telling, pal, do you. I'll give yis one last chance. Get down those effin' stairs, or yis'll crawl down them.'

I smiled at him, knowing something that he didn't: that I was going to enjoy the next few seconds. 'Mr Campbell,' I said, evenly. 'All I want is to talk to your wife.'

'Well, she disnae want tae talk to you.'

'She will, though.' I held up my right thumb. 'See that?' I asked him, still grinning. 'You've got no idea what I can do with that.'

He smiled back at me. His smile was even less pleasant than his threatening expression. 'Show us, then.' He clenched and unclenched his fists, rippling the muscles of his shoulders as he spoke, anticipating pleasure.

'You asked for it.' I raised my thumb again, jerked it towards me, once.

All of a sudden the landing seemed much smaller, and darker, as a huge shadow moved up from the staircase, and round the corner, to block out the light.

I remember the first time I saw Jerry Gradi in the flesh. Six feet, eight – tall, wide and deep. Three hundred and eighty pounds, all of them hard as nails. Dyed blond hair cropped short. Nose flattened into his head. Small piggy eyes. Pink ears which looked handmade. I'll never forget that first flash of instant terror.

'This is my pal, Jerry' I said. 'Jerry, this is Mr Campbell. He isn't being very co-operative. He was going to give me a doing.'

'Oh,' grunted The Behemoth.

Malcolm Campbell's mean mouth hung open as he gazed up at the GWA World Heavyweight Champion. For the first time, I was aware of Myrtle, standing behind him. 'I'll get the polis,' he croaked.

'How many you gonna get, and how fast you gonna get dem here?' asked Jerry, in his wrestler voice.

'I don't think you've got many friends down the nick, Malcolm,' I said. 'Now let's get reasonable, while you've still got a friend in me.'

I looked over his shoulder at his wife. 'Come on, Mrs Campbell. A few questions, that's all; there'll be no comeback for you, I promise.'

'Aye, okay then,' she conceded, almost wearily, with a glance at her husband which promised consequences later for his surrender . . . a shade unreasonable, I thought. 'Come on through, but tell your pet gorilla to be careful no tae stand on anything.'

She led us through the square hall and into a big living room. *EastEnders* was on the television and I knew at once who Malcolm's lookalike was. 'Sit down,' she said, then looked doubtfully at Jerry. 'Not you, though.'

I took one of the two armchairs, opposite Myrtle, while The Behemoth stood behind her husband, as he sat on the matching settee. 'I'll bet you're no as tough as you look,' Malcolm muttered. Without a word, Jerry stretched out the tree-trunks that passed for his arms, gripped the back of the heavy sofa at either side, straightened his back and effortlessly lifted it, and its two hundred pound occupant, three feet off the ground.

'Stop that you!' Myrtle shouted. 'Put him down! And Malkie, you keep your mouth shut.'

Both of them did as they were told.

'Right Mr Blackstone,' she went on. 'What's all this about?'

'How do you feel about Susie Gantry?'

'Miss Gantry? I suppose I like her well enough.'

'Even though she sacked you?'

'She didnae sack me, Ah left.'

'After you were caught smuggling photocopies of documents out to your old boss,' I pointed out.

'Aye, but she gave me the chance to resign. She said that if I did she'd give me a good reference. She did too, and two weeks' extra pay over and above my holiday money and wages in lieu of notice.'

'So if you liked Susie, why did you betray her like that? Why did you do that for old Donn?'

'Ah didnae do it for Mr Donn. Ah did it for Stephen.'

'Who?' I looked at her, puzzled.

'Stephen Donn, his nephew. He worked at Gantry's for a while.'

I felt myself frown as I remembered. The young book-keeper installed by Susie's father at the time of Joe Donn's brief reinstatement. He must have worked there for such a short time that his name didn't figure on the list Dylan had given me. It wasn't only my memory that was triggered. In the silence, I realised that Myrtle was staring at me.

'Blackstone, you said your name was. That accountant girl Miss Gantry brought in, she was called Blackstone too. Was she . . .'

'My wife,' I said, not looking at her, avoiding the expression which I knew was on her face, the one I had seen so many times before, the one that always brought it all back. 'So why did you put your job on the line for Mr Donn's nephew?' I went on, quickly.

For the first time, she hesitated. 'He just asked me,' she answered, at last. 'He said that Mr Donn was going to the papers to get even with Miss Gantry, but that he needed some stuff from the office.'

'He just asked you,' I repeated. 'And you just did it? Why, for God's sake? Why didn't you tell Susie?'

'You don't know Stephen.'

'No, I don't. Tell me about him.'

She looked over at her husband. 'He and I had a fling,' she murmured. Malcolm's eyes narrowed to slits. He began to rise from his seat on the sofa, until Jerry's huge hand gripped his shoulder and slammed him back down.

'It was when you were inside,' Myrtle exclaimed, speaking to her husband with a plea in her voice. 'I was really angry with you, remember? Ah told you we were finished, and at the time Ah meant it. It didn't last long, only about a month.'

'So?' I knew I had to keep control of this discussion.

'He threatened to tell Malkie about us if I didn't do what he wanted.'

'And you thought that if he did, Malkie would beat the shite out of him and wind up inside again? Is that it?'

She surprised me by shaking her head. 'No. I was afraid that he would try, and get himself killed. Like Ah said, you don't know Stephen.' She glanced across at her husband again.

'You're a hard man, love, but you'd never really hurt anyone. No' *really* hurt them, Ah mean. It's not in your nature.

'Stephen would, though. He's a real bad bastard.' Her voice tailed off, and her eyes moistened.

'Remember that cousin of Miss Gantry's?' she asked me suddenly. 'The one who came tae a bad end?' Remember him? I can never forget him. I nodded.

'Stephen was palled up wi' him from way back. They were in the same rackets. Believe me, Mr Blackstone, you do not want Stephen Donn for an enemy.'

I decided to leave it at that. Malcolm Campbell showed us to the door, silently. As he was closing it on us, Jerry put a hand on it to stop him. 'Don't you go laying a finger on that little wife of yours,' he murmured, 'just in case I find out. 'Cause believe me, buddy, I can *really* hurt people too.'

8

'I didn't like the boy, Oz. I know I was bound to resent him, given the way my Dad foisted him and his bloody old uncle off on me, after . . .'

She broke off for a second or two. 'All that apart, though, I still didn't like Stephen. He's a good-looking guy, a real ladies' man – I'm not surprised wee Myrtle had a tumble with him – and on the face of it, he's very pleasant. But I always felt that his smile was painted on the outside; that there was something different going on inside his head.'

Prim and I were sitting at the table in the dining room of Susie's semi in Clarkston. She and Mike had been talking for two years about moving into the penthouse flat of the redevelopment of a classic City Centre church which her construction division was planning, but the project was still on the drawing-board. The Gantry Group's influence with the Planning Department was not what it had been in the past.

'What happened when you fired him?' Prim asked, as Dylan topped up our wine glasses. 'How did he take it?'

Susie frowned, as she replayed the event in her mind. 'He was neither up nor down, as I remember. I saw his Uncle Joe and him together; I told them that I was now in total and permanent control of the Group and that I intended to do everything my way in the future.

'That included putting my own staff in charge of financial

management. I told them that they were being replaced by two people I had head-hunted from a major chartered accountancy firm, I showed them the severance terms . . . agreed with my lawyers and watertight, including the confidentiality clause . . . and I asked them to sign letters of resignation and clear their desks, there and then.

'Joe went apeshit; he still thought of me as a wee girl, and thought he could treat me as such. He bawled and shouted that he had given the best years of his life to my Dad and his company, that I was an ungrateful wee whippersnapper, and that I would ruin everything he and my Dad had built up.'

'Wind up with everything in ashes at your feet?' I suggested.

'Not in those very words, but that's what he implied, yes.'

'What did you say?'

'Nothing. I let him shout himself hoarse then I showed him the interim report that Jan did for me. It was very nicely written, tactfully put, but basically it said that Joe was neither qualified nor able to serve as finance director of a major company and listed about twenty different reasons why. When he'd read it I told him that I had shown it to my auditors, and that they agreed.

'Then I showed him his settlement figure. I pointed out that he'd already had a golden handshake the first time I fired him; and now here he was, thanks to my Dad's stupidity, in a position to collect another. But I made it clear to him that if he walked out without signing that letter, I'd tear it up and he'd get statutory terms, which in the circumstances would have been bugger all.

'There was a bit more bluster, but eventually he signed

both the letter and the severance agreement, including the confidentiality clause.'

'And what about Stephen?' Prim asked. 'What did he do while his uncle was yelling the place down?'

'Nothing. He just sat there and let the storm subside. Then, when old Joe was done, he picked up his letter looked at the terms – six months' pay, and he'd hardly been there any time – said "Fair enough" and signed without another word.'

'No threats?'

'Not one. He even shook my hand on the way out, and gave me that wee painted smile.'

I took a sip of my wine, a fairly expensive claret . . . I knew that, since I'd brought it. 'You never thought about firing Myrtle Higgins at that time?'

'Christ no. Myrtle's a good secretary, Oz. On top of that it made sense to have her there to help the new guy settle in. When I did let her go I was sorry, but I didn't have any choice. I could never have trusted her completely after that. Pity. All of it. Even old Joe; if only the silly bugger has decided to go off to a quiet retirement.' She sighed, and in that moment I saw one of Susie's strengths as a boss. She hated firing people, even when it was justified.

'So now Myrtle's saying it was Stephen who blackmailed her into stealing those documents?' she asked me.

'That's right. She did it to keep her husband out of trouble.'

'What's he like, this husband?'

I had to laugh as I thought of the two Malkie Campbells; the one who was going to kick me down the stairs, and one who had come face to face with his worst nightmare. 'Quiet and chastened. Big Jerry has that effect on most people.'

'Er . . . he didn't actually damage Campbell, did he?' Dylan sounded slightly nervous.

I tapped my chest, over my heart. 'Only in here. It had a hell of an effect on him, thinking that he was a hard man, then coming face to chest with someone who put everything into perspective.'

'Maybe you should take him when you go to see Stephen,' said Susie, with a faint grin. 'Not that he struck me as much of a heavy. On the other hand, if he was mobbed up with my cousin . . .'

'It's academic,' I told her. 'The Behemoth's off to the States on Monday, after this weekend's programming. Prim and I will meet Stephen somewhere nice and public . . . if we need to see him at all that is.'

'Why shouldn't you?' Mike asked.

'Because we're going to talk to Uncle Joe first. He's already threatened Susie.'

'I told you I fancy him for it.'

'Sure, and even with your track record, there's a fair chance you could be right. So we have to cover the possibility.' He gave me a mock scowl.

'Those papers, Susie,' Prim cut in. 'The ones Myrtle copied. What were they?'

'Letters. From my old man to the Chair of the Glasgow Planning Committee. Read in a certain way, you could infer that Dad was trying to lean on him for a consent. I guess that Joe was going to pass them to his tame journo and claim that's exactly what did happen.'

'D'you think it might have?'

She grinned across at me over her glass. 'No way. Read in

45

another way, and forgetting who wrote them, they're simple enquiries for the record. When my Dad wanted to nobble someone, he did it in private, without witnesses, and never, ever, in writing.'

'Fine.' I nodded. 'That's how we'll see his old pal Joe as well: in private. If he did write those letters, then he's an even bigger fool than his record says he is, and it shouldn't be too hard to scare him into admitting it.'

9

Although he was well up my 'things to do' list, Mr Joseph Donn wasn't right at the top. I had a Sly Burr radio ad to record in Edinburgh, and a busy weekend, with two GWA shows, one live, one recorded, in Milan – of course, Prim had to come with me – before I could think about tackling the old duffer.

It wasn't until the following Monday morning, five days after our council of war at Susie's place, that we were able to get round to planning our approach to the former finance director of the Gantry Group.

Prim gazed at me across the breakfast bar, her nice, post-orgasmic smile still showing in her eyes from an hour or so before. 'If you think you're keeping all the fun for yourself, my boy . . .' she chuckled. 'It was one thing letting you tackle the Campbells without me . . . there probably wouldn't have been room for me in their flat with Jerry along . . . but there's no risk involved in this visit. Donn's sixty-three, isn't he?' I nodded.

'If there's a chance that he is going to put his hands up and confess to writing those letters, I want to be there to hear it, and to witness his statement when we get it in writing.'

I was slightly concerned that when we confronted the old man we might find his nephew somewhere in the vicinity, but I could see that there was no point in arguing. Anyway, from what I had heard of Stephen, he didn't sound like someone I couldn't handle. I hadn't been a part of the GWA circus for two years for nothing. Everett and Jerry had taught me some knock-down moves, and Liam Matthews, who had become a good friend after an awkward beginning, had shown me a couple of submission holds that he, in turn had learned on the for-real Bushido circuit in Japan. I might have been struggling against an experienced, head-butting thug like Malkie Campbell, but all I knew about the boy Donn was that he frightened women.

'Okay, then,' I said, making a show of grudging concession which didn't fool my partner for a minute, 'you can come on this one. So tell me; how are we going to make sure that the old bastard agrees to see us?'

'I've been thinking about that. I thought I might phone him and pretend to be a journalist, looking into the Gantry Group.'

'What if he tells you to get stuffed? He's got that confidentiality clause to restrain him, remember.'

'I'll charm him, my dear. I'll tell him I only want background information on Jack Gantry, and that I won't quote him. He'll agree to see me, don't worry. Then he'll get a nice surprise when the two of us turn up on his doorstep.'

'Okay,' I agreed. 'Give it a try. The sooner we get it over with the better.'

'You really don't fancy him for it, do you?'

I shook my head. 'I'm not going to prejudge him. I've never met the man, and neither have you. Once we have we'll know better, so go ahead and make that call.'

'Okay.' Prim reached across to our kitchen noticeboard and picked off a yellow sticky with Donn's number, which Susie had given us the week before, then picked up her mobile from the work-surface, and began to dial. She had punched in four numbers when the door buzzer sounded.

She stopped as I picked up the handset, frowning at the small video-screen on the wall, in which the figure of a shirt-sleeved man was framed.

'Yes?' I said.

'Special delivery for Mr Blackstone,' a tinny voice in my ear replied.

'Okay.' I pushed the entry button. 'Come on up. It takes a bit of finding; it's the top flat.'

I went to the front door and waited. When finally he appeared in the hallway, the delivery man was out of breath. 'Jesus,' he muttered, more than a shade grumpily. 'Could yis no' have lived on the ground floor?'

'We like it up here. What have you got for me?' I asked, eyeing a bulky padded envelope tucked under his arm.

'Parcel.' He stated the obvious as he thrust a delivery slip in my face. 'Jist sign, then print your name below.'

'Why print my name? My signature's not that bad.'

He looked at me blankly. 'Jist,' he said, taking back his pen and handing over the packet.

'Have a nice day, now,' I called out to his departing back as I closed the door.

'What is it?' Prim asked as I stepped back into the kitchen.

'Parcel.' I said, looking at it for the first time. Some people open padded envelopes carefully, so they can re-use them. I'm rich, so I didn't bother; I just ripped the thing open. I knew before I looked at the handwritten note on top that it was a revised script for Miles and Dawn's movie.

Quickly I scanned the letter. 'Oh shit,' I whispered.

'What's up?'

'Listen to this,' I told her, holding up the paper. 'It's from your brother-in-law. "Dear Oz. I showed your screen test to our writer when he arrived in Scotland. He thought you were very good. So good, in fact, that he's suggested writing in a couple of new scenes for you, to replace some of the narration. This will mean that we need you on set the Monday after next, instead of on the dates I agreed with Sly Burr. When you get this, gimme a call on my mobile to discuss." ' The number was scrawled as a 'PS'.

Prim's face creased in a sunny smile. 'That's great. How are you placed for next Monday?'

'I hope I'm all right. The GWA shows are in Glasgow next week, so that shouldn't be a problem. With any luck we'll have Susie's stalker sorted out by then.'

'Right let's get to it.' She picked up her phone again and went back to calling Joseph Donn. He took her journalist bait, hook, line, and sinker. The meeting was set for Thursday.

10

Most people beam the first time they see Primavera. The
former finance director of the Gantry Group did too, as he
saw her standing on the doorstep of his impressive villa. It
was a big, brick-built house in Crawford Street in Motherwell,
a town which, until then, I had known only as half of a football
result . . . followed, fairly often, by the word 'nil'.

There was an impressive cherry metallic Jaguar parked in
the drive to the left. Clearly, the bloke had done well from his
years as Jack Gantry's financial yes-man.

'You'll be Miss Phillips,' Joe Donn exclaimed, before the
beam turned to a puzzled frown as I stepped in from the side.
'And you'll be . . .?' he asked.

'I'll be the bad news. My name's Oz; I'm Prim's partner.
We're private detectives working for Susie Gantry.' I didn't give
my surname; it might have led to complications we didn't need.

The man's expression was transformed for a third time,
into one of instant and total consternation. 'Dammit!' It was
almost a moan. 'What does that girl want from me now?
Hasn't she done enough?'

'You've got it wrong, Mr Donn,' Prim answered. 'This is
about what someone's doing to Susie. We need to talk to you
about it. I'm sorry about my deception when I called you on
Monday, but I really didn't want to get into this over the
telephone.'

Donn was a tall man; he was well-dressed, in dark flannel slacks and a green Lacoste shirt, grey hair well cut, and so clean-shaven that his face seemed to shine. As we watched him, he sighed, and shook his head, almost sadly. 'I suppose you'd better come in. If Susie's in trouble . . .' He stood aside, ushering us into a big square hall, then through to a study at the back of the house, which opened into a conservatory.

'Is Mrs Donn in?' I asked.

He laughed, bitterly. 'Mrs Donn hasn't been in for thirty-odd years, son. She left me for someone else; there were no hard feelings, but I gave up marriage as a bad job after that.'

He pointed to a group of heavy bamboo-framed chairs in the sun-room. 'Sit down.' Prim and I took seats close together, looking out into an immaculate garden.

'So what's wee Susie been up to?' he asked at last. 'Who's doing what to her?' He chuckled. 'Trouble follows that lassie, you know. Maybe if her faither had skelped her backside when she needed it, rather than just patting her on the head, she wouldn't have grown up so wilful. Maybe if her mother had lived, she'd have been a bit readier to see the other side.

'I wasn't all that bad at my job, you know, but there was no pleasing Susie, when Jack put her in charge of the Group, then afterwards, when she took over completely.' I had to bite my tongue at that, for I knew from Jan's investigative work just how bad he had been. Yet, Lord Provost Gantry was no fool; the strength of his support for his old pal Joe puzzled me at first. Later I realised that the last thing he had wanted was a competent accountant. 'It wouldn't surprise me if someone was making trouble for her,' Donn went on. 'She must have upset a lot of folk in business by now.'

'You couldn't be wider of the mark,' said Prim, evenly. 'The Gantry Group has better relations with its customers and suppliers than it ever had.'

'Aye, but not, I'll bet, with its bankers, dear.'

'The bank relationship is good too, but the Group is treated like any other business.'

'Which wasn't the case in my day. We had a special relationship then.'

No, you daft old goat, I thought. *Jack had the special relationship. Like he had with everyone.*

'Be that as it may, as far as we can see, Susie doesn't have an enemy in business. Yet someone's been threatening her . . . physically. She doesn't want to make a big fuss over this, since the chances are whoever's been doing it is just plain sick, so she's asked us, as friends, to help her find out who it is.'

'So why did you want to talk to me, Miss Phillips?'

'We've been given a list of people who've left Gantry since Susie took over.'

'People who've been fired, you mean,' said Donn, dryly.

'Or who've left by mutual agreement, let's say,' Prim countered. 'Like you, for example. Over the last three days we've spoken to them all, and eliminated them all as suspects.'

'It's stretching a point to say that I left,' the man growled. 'I was fired to all intents and purposes . . . not once, but twice, as I'm sure you'll know.'

'What do you do for a living now, Mr Donn?' I asked.

'I play golf, son,' he muttered.

'So you didn't walk away penniless from the Gantry Group?'

'No. To be fair to her, the first time Susie lived up to the terms of my contract and more. When Jack re-instated me, it all happened so fast that there wasn't time to sign a contract. And I have to admit that when I left the second time, the Wee One was generous. I suspected at the time that it was hush money; even now I've no reason to think otherwise.'

'So, having taken it, why did you contemplate going to the papers?'

Joe Donn looked at me silently for a while. 'Susie humiliated me, lad. I was angry. I had hoped that there was a closeness between her and me, just as there was between me and Jack. I was fond of her, and when she cut me out, not once but twice, I took it bad.'

'So you got in touch with your journalist pal,' said Prim.

'He wasn't my pal, Miss Phillips. I don't know people like that. No, he was my nephew's mate.'

'Stephen's?'

He nodded. 'That's right. Truth be told, it was Stephen's idea to go to the press. I think he got fed up with me going on about Susie . . . I remember him saying once that I cared more about her than about him, my flesh and blood. Anyway, he suggested one day that there must be some dirt to dig. I said there might be, if we could get hold of a few specific letters.

'Next thing I knew, he'd persuaded poor wee Myrtle Higgins to copy the bloody things. She got caught of course, and she was out too. I put a stop to it there and then. I had a hell of a row with Stephen. We haven't spoken since, as a matter of fact.'

'And you haven't spoken to the press since?'

'Absolutely not. I'm not really angry with Susie any more; just disappointed, that's all.'

Suddenly a couple of loose ends began to tie themselves together in my brain. 'Was Stephen right, about you caring more for Susie than him?' I asked.

Donn smiled, softly. 'Aye, maybe he was.' It was almost a whisper.

'Why?'

'Because I loved her poor mother. Margaret was my wife, see, before she left me for Jack Gantry.'

'Eh?' Prim and I gasped simultaneously.

'Yet you went on working for him?'

'I didn't work for him then. We were friends at that stage. He and Margaret fell in love. People do; sometimes they just can't help themselves. Don't get me wrong, though. I was mad enough at the time. But you couldn't stay mad with Jack Gantry, not forever. When I saw that he loved Margaret as much as she loved him, I began to see that it was all for the best. Then Susie was born, and everything was complete for them.

'Not long after that, Jack asked me to be his finance director, and I couldn't think of a good reason to turn him down.'

'Does Susie know all this?' asked Prim.

'No. I'm sure she doesn't. Margaret, Jack and I decided when she was a baby that there was no need to tell her. She certainly didn't know when Margaret died. Jack and I agreed that there would be no mention of a first marriage at the funeral.'

'And Stephen? Does he know?'

'I couldn't say for sure. I told his father, my brother Thomas, not to tell him. He died when Stephen was only ten, so I don't imagine that he did. I can't vouch for Myra, though; his mother, that is.'

'Where can we find Stephen?'

He frowned across the conservatory at Prim. 'I have no idea: nor do I care after what he did to wee Myrtle. Best ask his mother; most of the time, that is, when he didn't have a woman in tow, he lived with her.'

'Okay, but where can we find her?'

'I've no idea. Myra and I never got on that well: we don't keep in touch. After Thomas died she stayed on in their house in Paisley, but Stephen said on one of the last occasions that I saw him that she was in the process of moving to a smaller place.'

He gave us a sudden sour look. 'You're the detectives. You find her.'

11

There aren't all that many people in Scotland named Donn, not in comparison with the Smiths or the Macs or the Blacks or even the Patels. But there are enough of them to make finding Stephen Donn and his mother seem like a difficult task.

To cut a few corners, I phoned an Edinburgh pal who worked for Telecom. He did for us what he had done on occasion in the past, but for a few more quid this time – he had heard on the grapevine of our being in the money – and ran a check of telephone subscribers.

He came up with five Stephen Donns, two in Glasgow, one in Falkirk, one in Brechin and one in Dundee. Very quietly, Dylan ran police checks on all of them, but none fitted the profile of old Joe's nephew. We checked the Thomas Donns as well; many widows can't bring themselves to remove their late husbands' names from the phone book. There were three of those, all very much alive.

Another Monday morning had come around when my pal Eddie came back with his trawl of the M. Donns; first initials only, since women's forenames are never listed in the directory. They hold them on computer, though. 'Sorry, Oz,' our informant said. 'Two Marys and a couple of Margarets, but no Myra Donns. The closest I can get is a Meera.'

'What?'

'Aye, it's spelled M-I-R-A. My mother knows someone in Manchester with that name.'

'M-I-R-A,' I repeated. 'You could pronounce that Myra, couldn't you?'

'There's nae law against it, Oz;' said my cheerful chum.

'Okay, let's try her. Where does she live?' He read out an address in Barassie, in Ayrshire.

As soon as I had hung up, Prim called Joe Donn to check the spelling of his sister-in-law's name, but there was no reply, other than a message inviting us to leave a message. She looked across at Lulu. 'Fancy doing that interview for McPhillips this afternoon?' Keen as mustard, our newly promoted executive nodded.

'That's good,' Prim smiled. 'I fancy a trip to the seaside.'

We thought phoning Mrs Donn and asking her straight out if she had a son called Stephen, and if she knew where he was. Sure, it was the obvious thing to do, but we decided that if she was the woman we were after, and was concerned for her son, it would be too easy for her just to say 'no', and stop us in our tracks. Eyeball to eyeball was surer, and anyway, I fancied a walk on the beach too.

Barassie is no more than a village to the north of the town of Troon, on the Ayrshire coast. Even without our street atlas we would have had no trouble finding the address Eddie had given, or rather sold us, in a newish block of flats set in immaculate grounds in a small crescent just behind Beach Road.

We had the afternoon in front of us, and it was a beautiful day, so we decided to take a walk on the sands before getting down to business. I had something in mind; as it turned out, so had Prim.

'If the weather was always like this in Scotland,' said she, as we stood, holding hands and looking across the wide, calm Firth of Clyde at the spectacular and wholly unexpected skyline of the Island of Arran, 'we'd never think of going anywhere else.'

'Maybe, but it ain't,' I pointed out. 'In a month or two on this very spot we won't be able to stand up straight for the wind and the rain.'

'So what, if we've got each other?'

'So it's just as good to have each other in Spain, or in Barbados, or in California, or in Singapore, or in Sydney, or in any other place where the rain doesn't hit you horizontally. What d'you say to the idea of leaving Lulu to run the business, once she's got a bit more experience, and taking a sabbatical this winter, a couple of months maybe?'

She looked at me, curious. 'I'd say it sounds like a great idea, but what's brought it on?'

'Ach I'm not sure. Maybe it's the old Oz trying to get out. What with the business, the GWA gig, the Sly Burr stuff, and now Miles' and Dawn's movie, I'm feeling more than a bit hemmed in. Just when I should be more in control of my life than ever before, it's all gone crazy; I'm not in charge any more. This thing we're doing for Dylan's a welcome break, I tell you . . . yet we don't need to be doing any of it, neither of us.'

'It isn't Glasgow that's difficult for you, is it? The flat, and all its hard memories . . .' She was frowning now, concerned.

'No, love. I can handle all that, honest.'

'It's not me, is it?'

Her big brown eyes were wrinkled as I looked down at her.

The sun glinted on the natural highlights; the skin of her tanned shoulders glowed with health. I put my arms around her and kissed her.

'Oh, no, my love,' I whispered. 'It's not you. If not for you, I really would be crazy. I'd have come apart, back then, if you hadn't been around to hold me together. I don't know what to call what you and I have between us; there's nothing conventional about it, that's for sure.'

'No, there isn't; is there.' She put her head on my chest. 'I should have hated you when you left me there in Spain. When we talked it through, I was very rational, trying to be as mature and considerate as I could, laying my own sins alongside yours, and agreeing that what we were doing was right for both of us. But all the time I was trying my best to hate you, trying to find the anger I felt should be there.

'I couldn't though, because I realised that you couldn't help what you were doing. So after you left, I went back to real work, built up a new circle of friends, slept with a bloke just for the hell of it, and got on with my life.

'Then you showed up in Barcelona, and there was the awful coincidence of me being there when you heard about . . .' She paused for a second or two.

'I didn't know what to do; whether to be around for you if you needed me, or whether to steer clear for good, in case you thought I was trying to step back in there. Then you asked me for help; in the circumstances you might have been seen as cruel and insensitive, but, my dear, you've never struck me as either of those things.'

'And now?' I asked her. 'How do you feel now? Are you

really happy, or just enjoying yourself like we did the first time?'

'Both. There's just one worm that gnaws at me from time to time, but I can live with it.'

'What's that?' She shook her head. 'Come on,' I insisted.

'Okay. It's the notion of being second best.'

'You're not. You're different; you're you. There are no degrees. My first life is over. You're my life now, and I love you.'

Primavera looked up at me and smiled. 'Marry me, then.'

'Funny you should ask me that,' I said, reached into my pocket, took out a small box, and pressed it into her hand. In it was a diamond; a very large diamond, set in platinum. She took out the ring and slipped it on to the appropriate finger. Of course, it fitted. Dramatic gestures have to be well planned; I had established very casually that Prim's third finger left and my pinkie were almost exactly the same size.

The stone caught the sunlight and sparkled, but it was nowhere near as bright as her smile. 'Too many people about for us to celebrate properly,' she chuckled. 'But wait till I get you home.'

'In that case, let's go and see Mrs Donn. With any luck she'll be out, and we can go straight back to Glasgow.'

She wasn't, though. Within ten seconds of my pressing the buzzer next to her name at the apartments block's entrance, a voice crackled from the speaker. 'Yes?'

'Mrs Donn?' I asked, my voice raised. It's a reflex, isn't it. Standing before one of those things you always feel the need to get as close as you can and shout.

'Yes. You don't have to yell. I can hear you.'

'Sorry. My name's Blackstone. Your brother-in-law Joseph suggested that I should speak to you. My associate and I are trying to contact your son, Stephen. It has to do with the time he spent working for the Gantry Group.'

'Has it now,' said Mrs Donn, metallically. 'You'd better come up, then. I'm on the top floor.'

The block was as well looked-after inside as out, better than our own, in fact. We climbed two carpeted flights of stairs, to reach the third-storey landing. She was waiting for us at her front door, a slim, well-dressed woman, with close-cropped brown hair and fine angular features. It was difficult to place her, age-wise, but I guessed that she was in her mid-fifties.

'I'm Mira Donn,' she announced, pronouncing the name 'Meera'. Clearly, she and Joe hadn't spoken much. 'Come in and tell me what this is all about.' I had been expecting her to sound like a Paisley Buddy, but her accent, no longer filtered through the intercom, was smooth and cultured, as if she had really worked on it.

I introduced Prim as she showed us into her living room, which had a small balcony looking out on to the beach. The twin glass doors were open, and a copy of the *Herald* lay on a folding chair outside. I glanced around the room; it was conventionally furnished, but in the corner opposite the television, there was a small desk with a lap-top computer.

'I was watching you on the sands,' she said. 'You were a picture, you know. And then you walked right up to my door. Not many people out on a Monday, are there, now that the schools are back in. I'm lucky; as a college lecturer I have another week.'

'What do you teach?' Prim asked, as we eased ourselves into two more chairs. The small terrace seated three, just.

'Communication skills. At the local Technical College. Before, I lectured in Glasgow, but I decided to move down here a couple of years ago.' She smiled, 'Preparation for retirement.

'So how is my brother-in-law?' she asked, suddenly. 'A strange man, Joseph. Empty, I've always thought. Empty of everything, including pride. Imagine, that he could work for the man who stole his wife. I only met Jack Gantry three times; he was hypnotic, I'll grant you, but even so.'

'Mr Donn seems very well,' Prim answered her. 'He's retired completely.'

'He always was. My husband was an accountant too. Unlike his brother, he was fully qualified, yet when he died, he was only a senior manager in his firm. He worked under the most tremendous pressure and eventually it killed him. Joseph, on the other hand, failed his finals and wound up making a small fortune working for Gantry. I'd be bitter if it wasn't so ironic.

'Tell me. Did the Gantry daughter ever find out about her mother?'

'Not as far as we know,' I said. 'We're friends of Susie, so now we're in a bit of a quandary. We don't know whether to tell her or not.'

'I would tell her. It was Jack's idea to keep it a secret; he bullied Margaret and Joe into agreeing.'

'Why?'

She looked at me and made a face. 'Who knows for sure, young man? But Jack always had to be seen in new things. New suits, crisp shirts, the latest model car; and he insisted on the same for Susie when she was a child. I always suspected that he was trying to gloss over the fact that his wife was secondhand.'

'Does Stephen know that Susie's mother was his Auntie?'

'Not from me,' Mira Donn answered, shaking her head. 'Since Tom died, I've barely even thought of the Gantrys. I had no reason to tell him, and I'm sure Joseph wouldn't; Jack's word was law to him.'

'How can we get in touch with your son?' Prim asked quietly.

'Why do you want to?'

'Because someone's been sending Susie threatening letters.'

'Threatening?'

'Threatening her life.'

'A lunatic, surely.'

'Quite possibly, but there are a number of people we need to talk to, just to be on the safe side, and Stephen's one of them. Can you give us his address, or a phone number?'

'No, my dear, I can not. Stephen flies in and out of my life like a migrating bird. Right now he's off with the flock.'

'What does he do for a living these days?' I asked her. 'He worked as a book-keeper at Gantry's, we understand.'

'He only did that as a favour to Joseph. Stephen has a book-keeping qualification from FE College, but he never wanted to do that for a living. Instead he chooses what he sees as the glamorous life. He travels the world; every so often I will have a postcard from an exotic place. He tells me that he has interests in nightclubs, and such things, but I never hear any details. One day he will grow up, I'm sure, but there's no sign of it yet.'

'When did you hear from him last?'

'Around two months ago.'

I handed her a business card. 'Perhaps you'd ask him to call us next time he gets in touch with you.'

'I'll do so, but I make no promises. Stephen is a law unto himself.'

'I hope he can carry on like that, Mrs Donn. So far this isn't a police matter, but if these letters don't stop, I can't see it staying that way.'

12

We cut it fine, that night. On the way back to Glasgow, Prim called Susie and invited her and Mike for supper. But, once we were home, we caught up with celebrating our engagement and rather lost track of the time.

Fortunately, like many independent young people, we are fairly accomplished high speed cooks. 'Dab hands wi' a Wok,' as they say in Glasgow and Shanghai. We had just finished preparing our ingredients when the buzzer sounded.

Naturally, Susie clocked Prim's diamond as soon as she opened the door. If she was miffed that it was bigger than hers, she didn't show it at all. 'Congratulations,' said Mike as he shook my hand. 'I didn't realise you were pregnant.' Entirely the wrong thing to say to me, but once it had escaped from his mouth there was no hauling it back, so I laughed it off. If anything showed in my eyes, he didn't notice.

We spent the best part of the next hour drinking champagne . . . or three of us did, since it was Susie's turn to drive . . . and looking out on the city below.

Eventually, Prim and I disappeared into the kitchen and set to work with the wok. We dished up our stir-fry with a couple of interesting bottles of Austrian red wine . . . guaranteed free of anti-freeze . . . which Prim had found in our local off-licence. She has a great eye for these things.

'When are you getting married?' Susie asked, as she cleared the last prawn from her bowl.

As Prim looked at me, I could only shrug. 'This year,' I supposed. 'Once I'm through with Miles Grayson's movie.'

Dylan's mouth dropped open. 'Once you're what?' he gasped. Susie looked as flabbergasted as he did. 'You mean Miles wasn't kidding at Rogano's the other night?' she squealed.

'No, he wasn't as it turned out. Och it's nothing, though,' I protested, with a show of modesty that was completely fake. 'It's nepotism, really. What I'm doing is just an extension of the work I do with the GWA, and from the voice-overs.'

'How many careers are you planning to have?' asked Mike.

'After this, just one: husband.' I found myself smiling. 'Okay, I might keep on the GWA stuff because I like the people so much; and the money for these commercials is just too silly to turn down.'

'Jesus, man, how much more do you want?'

I looked at him, severely. 'Money is money, Michael. You ask Susie. I could do these jobs for free, but the advertising people wouldn't understand. Neither would Sly Burr: he knows that twenty per cent of anything is better than one hundred per cent of fuck all.

'One thing, although I haven't talked this through completely with Prim. There'll be no more sitting in grubby rooms interviewing people to help bloody lawyers get even richer than us. It's time to move on from the Private Enquiry business.'

I sensed my fiancée grinning at me. 'I was getting to like it.'

'Then you keep it on, my dearest, if that's what you want. As you say, you and wee Lulu virtually run it between you already. But I'm going to concentrate on the things I enjoy most . . . I might even play a bit more golf.'

'And what about the Private Eye-ing?' Susie gave me a mischievous look over her glass of sparkling mineral.

'I gave that up a couple of years back,' I assured her. 'The stuff I've been doing for you two is strictly a one-off, with Prim's permission.'

'So how's that going?' asked Mike, serious all of a sudden.

'That's the other thing on tonight's agenda. We've been looking at everyone on your list, spoken to them all, and, we think, eliminated them all. We're left with one name, though, the one you didn't include: Stephen Donn. He was behind the bother you had with his uncle. Joe was angry with you at the time, and Stephen seems to have taken advantage of that. The old fella swears blind that he didn't know about Myrtle copying those documents.

'Joe has nothing against you, Susie. He was very hurt when you fired him, but for a reason that you couldn't help.

'Let me ask you something. When you were wee, and your mother was alive, was he close to your family?'

She took a few seconds to answer. 'Yes, I suppose he was. He did have a sort of special place; I called him Uncle Joe when I was a kid, and every time he came to the house he'd give me pocket money. I was closer to him than my real Auntie; and I saw much more of him than I did of her. Truth is, I never could stand her.'

'And how was he with your parents?'

'He was my Dad's best pal. The three of them always got on

together. My Mum was very fond of him, I remember.' She paused and stared at me. 'Here, you're not suggesting that he and my Mum had an affair are you? That's ridiculous; she loved my Dad. He was the only man in the world as far as she was concerned.'

'Not always,' said Prim gently. 'Joe Donn was your mother's first husband.'

Susie stared across the table at us, in sheer disbelief, her eyes moistening. 'You're kidding,' she protested, at last. 'Who told you that?'

'Joe did. And his sister-in-law confirmed it. It seems to be true, Susie.'

She was crying now, tears rolling down her cheeks. 'But why didn't they tell me? Why keep something like that from me?'

'It was your father's idea, apparently,' I told her.

'We could speculate all night about his motives,' said Dylan, grimly, 'and never get anywhere. The Devil alone knows some of the things that have been hatched in his mind.'

'But I wouldn't have cared,' Susie wailed.

'No, but clearly your father did,' I told her. 'I reckon the easiest way for you to look at this is for you to accept that he thought that keeping your mother's past and her relationship with Joe Donn from you was in your best interests.'

She shot me a quick scornful look. 'Then it must have been in his too, otherwise he wouldn't have done it. No one's interests ever ranked above my Lord Provost's, not even mine.'

She paused. 'Mike,' she asked. 'Would you be okay to drive home if you stopped drinking now?'

Dylan nodded. 'In a couple of hours, yes. Why?'

Susie drained her mineral water and held out her glass. 'Guess,' she said. 'I'll have some of that Austrian stuff, Oz, if I may. No, on second thoughts, I'll have a lot.'

I filled her glass as she asked, right up to the top. 'I'm sorry, Susie,' I offered. 'Maybe we should have kept the secret, like your old man wanted.'

She shook her head, firmly. 'No way. The very fact that he wanted it that way is reason enough for you to tell me. And I'd have expected no less of friends.'

'So where does this leave us with the letters, Oz?' asked Dylan.

'Unless you've come up with another suspect, I'd say it leaves us wanting to speak to the boy Stephen, wherever he is.'

'What d'you mean, wherever?'

'I mean that no one bloody knows. Young Mr Donn seems to be a night person. His Uncle Joe cast him out after the Myrtle incident, and he only goes to see his Mammy every so often. He's not on the phone anywhere, and he doesn't seem to have a known address.'

'A real mystery man, this. Does no one know anything about him?'

'His mother said something vague about him having interests in nightclubs. That could mean anything, though. Susie's cousin; that's another connection we have. Myrtle said that they were in the same racket . . . and we know what that was.'

The Detective Inspector growled. 'That gives me an excuse to lift the boy when he shows. Meantime I'll run a PNC check; that might come up with something.'

'But why, Oz?' Susie moaned, her glass empty already. 'Why should he pick on me?'

'Maybe he's still fighting what he sees as his Uncle Joe's battle. Who knows? Listen, you haven't had any letters since the last one, have you?'

'No. Fingers crossed, they've dried up.'

'Yes,' Mike chipped in. 'Let's not get this out of proportion; it's long odds that this is a crank thing and that the guy's got bored with it, having caused a degree of alarm.'

'And everything at work is normal?'

'Too right, with the new office manager around.'

'Ach, well. It's probably all over, like you say. Prim and I have taken it as far as we can, that's for sure.'

'Yes,' said Susie, 'and thank you both very much. I'm grateful for everything you've found out . . . and I mean everything.'

I opened another bottle of the fine Austrian; and then another. For most of the next three hours or so, Susie agonised over whether she should approach Joe Donn to bring their unorthodox connection into the open.

'Wha'd'y' think, Mike?' she asked him over and over again. 'Nothing, love,' he replied consistently. 'You have to work that one out for yourself.'

Finally, at around the twelfth time of asking, he slipped an arm round her waist and lifted her out of her seat. 'I think, my dear,' he announced at last, 'that it's time for you to go to bed.'

'Yesh pleashe,' she giggled. Night had fallen as we drank and talked. The moon shone down upon us, and the lights of Sauchiehall Street shone up at us.

'Why don't you crash out here?' I suggested.

71

Dylan shot me a look. 'If you think I've spent the last three hours drinking Strathmore and watching the Wee One get pished, only to decide to stay the night, you have another think coming, pal.'

So we saw them to the door and all the way down to the main entrance. Susie's car was backed into one of our block's visitor places, off-street and hidden from those entrepreneurs who make their living through dealing in expensive alloy wheels. The term 'Hot Wheels' has a different meaning in Glasgow.

We followed, watching with some amusement as Mike walked the love of his life down to the front door, then strode across to their car and slid behind the wheel, thinking that she was on his heels. But Susie had stayed put, saying her extended goodbye to us.

'So sorry,' she slurred, as she threw her arms around Prim's neck, for support as much as affection. 'So sorry. We've spent all fuckn' night talkin' 'bout me, 'n it sh'd have been your night all along. You two be happy now.'

I couldn't help grinning as I looked across at Dylan, as he switched on the car's ignition, then left the engine running as he jumped out and came across to retrieve his scooshed girlfriend.

He was half-way towards us, when the car exploded. There was no big bang as such, just a soft 'crrummmp' sound, followed by a fireball, and then another so violent that it threw all four of us off our feet, and so hot that it seemed to draw all the air from our lungs.

13

By some miracle, none of us was seriously hurt. The only casualty was Mike's red Lacoste wind-cheater, the back of which was melted by the heat.

No longer just a foursome, we sat upstairs in our apartment, with medics buzzing around us, fire officers asking us questions about the sequence of events, and uniformed policemen hanging around in the background.

Downstairs, in the car park, the sleek silver sports coupé in which Susie and Dylan had arrived was now a blackened skeleton, as was the vehicle next to it, a Mazda owned by a ground floor neighbour. Prim and I were lucky; our cars, a BMW Z3 and a Freelander, had been far enough away to escape the flames.

It would have been an exaggeration to say that the experience had sobered Susie, but it had quietened her, that's for sure. She sat on our two-seater with her head on Mike's shoulder, looking totally confused and whimpering quietly. The ambulance team had wanted to take her to the Royal, but she had panicked when they produced a wheelchair so, for the sake of peace and quiet, they had left her in Mike's care.

None of us said much, not for a while. We just sat there, sipping black coffee, exchanging looks. It was as if we were waiting for something to happen. When it did, it came in the form of a middle-aged Chief Inspector and a slightly older man, a Divisional Fire Officer, both of them wearing the heavy uniforms and looking as if they owned the place, as they burst into our living room.

'A word in private, DI Dylan,' barked the policeman.

'No.' My friend Mike is rank conscious, normally, but a fiery enema is liable to make anyone unco-operative. The Chief Inspector, clearly not programmed for that response, stared at him, his mouth hanging slightly open and his heavy moustache twitching.

'I'm not leaving Susie. You want to talk to me, you do it here.'

Mr Senior Plod glanced at Prim and me, in an attempt to be meaningful.

'What's your name, Sir,' asked Dylan.

'Chief Inspector Brown,' he replied, then nodded towards the fireman. 'This is Mr Callaghan.'

'Well, Mr Brown, this is Mr Blackstone and Miss Phillips. They're friends and they've had their eyebrows singed too, so they have an interest in this. We'll talk here.'

Chief Inspector Brown folded his cards. 'Pull up a chair from the table,' I offered.

They settled themselves in front of us, but Brown managed still to behave as if Prim and I weren't there. 'What are you working on just now, Inspector?' he began.

'I can't tell you that.'

For the second time in as many minutes, the policeman was stuck for a word. So he simply repeated the question, more emphatically this time. Dylan repeated his answer.

'Look,' snapped Brown. 'Do I have to get your senior officer to order you to tell me?'

As I looked at Mike, I saw something in his face I'd seen only once or twice before. 'Just you fucking try it,' he said quietly.

'I'll do just that. Where d'you work from?' The Chief Inspector's mouth was set in a tight line.

'Headquarters. Pitt Street.'

'Right. Use your phone, Mr Blackwood?'

'There's one in the kitchen, Mr Brown,' I told him. He stood and stomped off, leaving Divisional Officer Callaghan sitting in an awkward silence.

When he returned, almost five minutes later, his face was distinctly red. I always feel sorry for people who blush. It's like wearing a sign round your neck reading, 'I've been a dickhead.'

Brown settled awkwardly on to his dining chair. 'You might have told me you were Special Branch,' he mumbled.

I stared across at my pal. 'You might have told me too,' I said. 'If I'd known that our nation's security was resting in your buttery grip I might have felt differently about staying in this country.'

Dylan grinned. 'Need to know, Oz. Need to know. I was transferred four months ago.' He turned to Brown. 'Now, can we forget about all that silver braid on your uniform and assume that I'm in charge here?'

Not waiting for a reply he turned to the fireman. 'What have you got, Mr Callaghan?'

'Someone doesn't like you, Mr Dylan,' the DO replied. 'There were two seats to this fire; the car's petrol tank and another source. I think someone followed you here and when you were inside, secured a firebomb device close to the fuel tank, beside the exhaust. It had a small explosive charge, and a quantity of petrol in a plastic container. I'd say it had a trembler trigger and that the vibration from the silencer was enough to set it off.

'The heat from the first blast was enough to blow the vapour and fuel in the main tank. If you'd still been in that motor, son,' said the grizzled fireman, grimly, 'you'd have been done to a fuckin' crisp.'

'Yeah.' Mike nodded. 'That's what I thought.' He looked at Callaghan, then at Brown. 'But as far as your reports go, it was a wiring failure. A tragedy averted, but an accident nonetheless.'

Brown drew in a deep breath and shook his head. 'I don't know about that, Inspector.'

'Well I bloody do, Chief Inspector. That's how you'll write it up, and if anyone says anything different to the press, I'll bloody have him. Police or fire service, it doesn't matter, his carcass will be mine.' I hadn't realised till then that Mike was turning into a Glaswegian; his Edinburgh veneer was being worn away. He went on, 'Oh yes, and one other thing; neither my name nor Miss Gantry's will feature in your reports.

'You can go and make another phone call if you like, but I promise you that is how it will be. I'm not having the world knowing that some bastard thinks he can kill an SB officer. I'm damn sure you'll find that the Chief Constable will feel the same way.

'Now, maybe you'd do us a favour and send for a traffic car to give Susie and me a lift out to Clarkston.'

Brown nodded and left, meek and dismissed, Callaghan following in his wake. As soon as they were gone, I turned to

Dylan. 'What's happening here, man?' I demanded. I was confused, probably still a bit shocked from the blast, and just a touch impaired by the fine Austrian red. 'What do we make of that?'

He shrugged, but only with one shoulder since Susie had fallen asleep, immobilising the other. 'I don't know for sure, Oz. I haven't been in SB all that long. I can't tell you what I'm doing there, but I suppose it's possible that what happened tonight was connected to that rather than to Susie's letters.

'I doubt it, though. Most of the people we target assume that they're under surveillance and let us get on with it. As the new boy, I'm still on the routine stuff; I doubt if any of our customers even know I exist.

'I don't like even thinking it, far less saying it, but I fear that the letter-writer wasn't kidding.'

' "You are going to die with your world in ashes all around you." ' Both of us looked round at Prim as she spoke. 'That's what the last letter said, wasn't it. Looks as if we should have taken it literally.'

'When I catch this bastard,' Mike muttered, looking more thunderous than I had ever seen him, 'I'll . . . I'll . . . What's worse than reducing him to ashes, Oz?'

'How about a really good kick up the arse?'

He nodded, grimly. 'That's where I'll start, then.'

'That's where *you'll* start?'

'Oh yes. This is a different game now. Office bodyguard or not, I never really thought that those letters were meant to be taken literally; I always guessed, just like you did, that they were only the ravings of some crank. I'd never have exposed you to real danger, pal.'

I scowled at him. 'You mean apart from the real danger of a kicking from Malkie Campbell?'

'Ach, I've got faith in your ability to handle the likes of him . . . as you did.' He looked up at the ceiling, with a sudden, tension-relieving grin. 'Christ, I wish I'd seen the look on his face when he clapped eyes on your big pal.'

'So,' I said, 'what you're telling us is now that we've done all the hard work and identified your number one suspect, we're off the case.'

'Exactly. Thanks for all you've done up to this point, both of you, but this belongs with the police now.'

'But what about Susie? What about the effect on her business? What about your reasons for involving her in the first place?'

'Not a problem any more. There's no danger of publicity now. Chief Inspector Chocolate there, he'll write up his report like I told him, and that'll be that as far as the official side is concerned. This'll be a Special Branch inquiry from now on.

'I'll take this to my boss first thing tomorrow morning, and I'll tell him about the car thing. I'll mention the letters at the same time, and tell him that it was because of my Special Branch involvement that I asked you to look into it informally, rather than make an official police complaint. He'll buy that all right. He'll also agree that on the off-chance the explosion could have been job-related, our lot should investigate it.'

The un-Dylanlike grim expression returned. 'I tell you, Mr Stephen Donn . . . if it is him . . . has no idea what he's bitten off.'

I couldn't help it: I wasn't ready to believe completely in the new Mike. 'Oh aye?' I asked. 'You think your outfit can find this guy, if his own mother doesn't know where he is?'

'You sure she doesn't?' he shot back. 'Look at the sequence of events. You go to see Mira Donn this afternoon asking her about Stephen. A few hours later, Susie's car blows up.'

'No,' I protested. 'No way would she be involved in this.'

'She doesn't need to be. She only needs a mobile number that she didn't bother to tell you about. She only needs to have phoned her son to ask him what the hell's going on.'

I had to admit that it sounded plausible.

'If you find Donn,' I asked, 'what will you—'

'DI Dylan,' Chief Inspector Brown's voice barked from the doorway, cutting off my question in mid-ask. 'Car's here for you. Don't keep them waiting now.'

His shout woke Susie. She looked around, moist-eyed, dazed and confused. 'Whrr . . .?' she mumbled.

'You're on your way home, love. Let's go now.' Mike half-lifted her to her feet and walked her to the door, his arm round her waist.

'Keep us in touch won't you,' said Prim as we followed them to the front door.

'I'll tell you all about it when everything's sorted,' Dylan replied. 'But not before. Meantime you just forget it and concentrate on the boy Oz's acting debut.'

14

'Tell me, boy. Have you ever given any thought to the possibility of planning your life?' Mac the Dentist gazed at me over the top of his pint. 'Thinking beyond the next few days, I mean.'

Prim and I hadn't slept much after our flat was finally cleared of police and firemen. We had lain wide-awake for most of the night, as the truth of our friends' narrow escape had come home to us.

'Oz, you do know that Mike's right, don't you. We've got to leave Stephen Donn to him from now on.'

'Sure, I know that. After what happened tonight it would be crazy to try to stay involved. No way would I put you in danger.'

'Nor I you. Except . . .'

'. . . except nothing. But I know what you mean.'

'It's frustrating having come this far. And you've always said . . .'

'. . . that Mike as a detective couldn't find his arse with both hands? I know, but I suppose—'

'Suppose nothing. Mike's right.' A giggle in the dark. 'Mind you it'll be the first time . . .'

In the end though, we had agreed that difficult as it might be to suppress our mutual curiosity, we would have to make the effort. I had to prepare for a weekend GWA trip to Holland by learning a few words of Dutch, read up on my part in Miles' and Dawn's movie – working title *Project 37* according to my script – and Prim had the business to run. By Thursday, though, we were going crazy, frustrated at not knowing what was going on. I tried calling Dylan on his mobile during the day, but came up with the 'unavailable' message every time. In the end, we had decided to give ourselves a complete break by driving up to Anstruther that afternoon to see my folks and flash Prim's sparkler at them.

We took them by surprise. Mac the Dentist had just ushered the day's last patient out of his surgery, and Mary, my stepmother, was still in her going shopping clothes. They congratulated us as we had expected, even if I did detect a split second's hesitation on Mary's part; understandable in the circumstances. Two hours later we were sitting in the bar of the Ship Inn in Elie, having a drink while we waited for our table to be prepared in the restaurant next door.

I looked back at my Dad. 'What do you think Prim and I are doing now, if not planning our lives?'

'Ah, that's not what I mean and you know it. You're still the same bloody mayfly you were when you were a kid. I never know what you're going to be up to next; and how can I when you don't bloody know yourself.' He grinned at Prim. 'As for this one here, she's your partner in crime.

'Christ, look at you, the pair of you. You've got all that money, and what are you doing with it? Not a damn thing. Okay, you bought our Ellie a house, and that was good, but you've still got a fortune. You could be investing it in a proper business and running that; or you could just be living on it and getting your golf back to a decent standard. But no, not you two. You're still tearing about interviewing hooks and crooks for lawyers, introducing wrestlers, selling bloody toys on telly, and now acting, for any sake.'

Suddenly his grin vanished; he reached out grabbed one of my hands and one of Prim's and squeezed them both. 'Still, I'm glad you've made up your minds about the most important thing. You've had enough hurt in other ways; you're right to grab each other now. I don't know anyone who won't be happy for you. Isn't that right Mary?'

Next to him, my stepmother nodded and smiled. 'Of course it is. The world goes on, and we all have to go on with it. This afternoon is history already, gone with everything that has passed before. You have to live with your memories, but it is possible to live happily with all of them.' She linked her arm through my Dad's. 'We're proof of that, aren't we, Mac.'

'We sure are, my dear. So just you two follow our example. And remember to stop and smell the flowers . . . for as long as you like. Take some time for yourselves. Have a couple of kids. Find a direction and stick to it. Most of all, steer clear of the private detective business. That's brought you nothing but grief.'

We hadn't got round to telling them about Mike and Susie's problem; at that moment we decided that we wouldn't bother. Instead we nodded and promised them that we would think about curtailing things in the future and about keeping our activities on more of a straight line.

We allowed ourselves to be talked into discussing wedding plans, of which in truth, until that time we hadn't even begun to think. Mary was all for Prim turning matters over to her mother, but that seed fell on stony ground.

'My folks are Churchy,' my fiancée explained. 'I'm not. And all that apart, there's no way I'm letting anyone stick me in a white frock and parade me through the town in a Roller.'

'Hey, what about me?' I protested.

'You can wear the frock if you like. I'm just not into that sort of show.'

Eventually we hit on the proposal that we would get married on our own turf, in the Registry Office in Glasgow, and that we would have a reception in the Hilton, within sight of our flat. The hard part about that would be selling the idea to Ma Phillips, when we saw her on the following Sunday. Dad wouldn't be a problem; he never was where Prim was concerned.

Mac the Dentist was pulling teeth next morning, so he kept a check on his intake. Nevertheless, by the time our taxi came to collect us, he was fairly relaxed. 'What age are you now, son?' he asked, as he stood on the narrow pavement outside the Ship, watching the girls slide into the back seat of the cab. 'Thirty-two, isn't it?'

My Dad is the great pillar of wisdom in my life. Whenever I've been worried, confused, uncertain, bewildered or just downright scared, he's been there for me. Most times he's just laughed, given me a figurative cuff round the ear, told me not to be daft, and everything's been all right. But on occasion, he's gone all serious; that's just about the only time he ever calls me son.

I nodded, trying to ignore the sign. 'You should know as well as I do,' I told him. 'Maybe better. After all I hadn't a bloody clue what age I was until I was at least three; so you've known what age I was for longer than I have. Understand?'

'Daft bugger,' he grumbled. 'However many years it is you've been kidding folk along on this planet, there's never been one of them when you could put anything over on me. Even when you and Jan split up, and both of you really thought you had, too, I knew better.'

He tapped me on the chest. 'Just like right now. I know there's something going on you're not telling me about, and it makes me suspect that you've been up to your sleuthing tricks again.

'If I'm right, you remember this. Those of us who are lucky enough to be given a second shot at happiness have to do everything in our power to make sure that we don't . . . fuck . . . it . . . up!'

15

There can be few greater contrasts in Scottish humanity than that between Prim's father and my own.

Where Macintosh Blackstone is effusive, outspoken and self-willed, David Phillips is reserved, understated and compliant. Where my Dad practises the skilled but muscular science of dentistry, David is an artist. He built his furniture design and cabinet-making business into one of the most noted and successful in Scotland, then retired in his early fifties to pursue his hobby, carving and painting wooden soldiers. Thanks to Prim's enterprising mother, this became a second career.

David frowned, appraisingly, as he eyed Prim's engagement ring across the dinner table, then nodded. 'Craftsmanship,' he said. 'Anyone can set a stone in metal, but only a craftsman can set it as well as that. Look after it, in time it'll be an heirloom.'

'David!' Elanore Phillips' bell-like voice rang down the length of the table. If there is anyone in Prim's family who's a match for my Dad it's her Mum. Elanore was a social worker . . . and a very caring one, her daughter assures me . . . but she chose to retire at the same time as her husband, to pursue her own secret passion, writing stories for children. Between them they turned their big Gothic house in Auchterarder into a unique, private, arts centre.

Mum Phillips tends to take the lead in any family discussion. I heard Dawn groan beside me as she looked directly at Prim, and said, 'Now, about the wedding.'

I kept my fingers crossed. I had already done the big church performance once, with Jan. Much as I love Prim, there was no way I wanted to go through that scene again, but because I love her, I would have if she'd given in to her mother.

Fortunately that hasn't happened since Prim was around fourteen. 'I promise you, Mum,' she answered. 'When it happens, you'll be among the first to know.'

'Oh come, come, Primavera. Dawn's already done me out of one big day by marrying in California. You don't have any excuse.'

A confrontation between the two strong women of the Phillips family is something to see. I'll swear I noticed David begin to smile, then bite it off, hard. Next to him, Miles, who wasn't used to the domestic fireworks display, took a sudden interest in his place-mat.

'Excuse, Mother?' said Prim, slightly lowering her voice, as she does when she's about to level someone. 'I don't have to excuse myself to anyone . . . other than Oz, every now and again.

'Now listen up. You've had your wedding. Okay, it was thirty-five years ago, but you'll have to make do with it. This one's ours, and we're calling the shots. If you behave yourself then Oz and I will let you be there, but we'll be making all the arrangements and we'll be doing it our way . . . which will be quiet. You and Dad can pick up the tab . . . I'll give in to that tradition . . . but that'll be it.'

Most people would have had the sense to cave in and drop

the subject, but Elanore is made of sterner stuff than that. She's a romantic, too, and there are few things less shakeable than a determined romantic. She glowered along the table at her husband, but Dad Phillips, almost imperceptibly, shook his head.

And then, for God's sake, she turned to me. 'Oz, talk some sense into her!' she appealed. I felt like the House of Lords.

'I've done so already, Elanore. I know I'm crazy to risk a fall out with my future mother-in-law, but when Prim said "we" she meant it. She and I are agreed on this.'

She gave me a long hard look; then, to everyone's huge relief, she smiled. 'At least you're well matched, the pair of you. I remember the first time Primavera brought you here. She said, "He's crackers, but I think you'll like him." She was right on both counts.'

'Give your mother a clue, at least, my dear,' David Phillips asked, unexpectedly; I guess he judged that it was safe to speak. 'When?'

'That depends on Miles,' Prim answered. 'Once Oz is finished with his bit of *Project 37*, we'll get round to doing the deed.' She turned to her mother. 'It's no big deal, Mum,' she said, giving Elanore back a piece of the ground she had just cut from under her. 'We're living together already; all we're doing is formalising things.'

'*Project 37*?' I couldn't remember the last time I'd heard Prim's father ask two questions on the trot.

'I'm a shade paranoid about my movies,' Miles explained. 'I like to keep a degree of security around them; that includes giving them working titles which don't give any clue to their content. The one we're shooting just now happens to be my thirty-seventh. Simple as that.'

'What's it going to be called?'

'We're probably going to call it *Snatch*. It's about a kidnapping. Dawn's the female lead. She's a Scottish heiress who's taken from her father's estate on Deeside and held for ransom. I play her boyfriend, who happens to be a Special Branch cop.'

'Christ,' I gasped. 'Art mimics life.'

'Eh?'

'Sorry. Shouldn't have said that. The fact is, you've met one of those.'

'Mike?'

'Yes, but don't mention it when you meet him again at our wedding. Here,' I wondered, 'won't that title make some punters think it's a porno job?'

Dawn spluttered, and Miles grinned. 'So what? It's all bums on seats, Oz . . . or asses, as we say in the States. I wanted a one-word title, and since someone else used *Ransom* a few years back, and Dawn and I were in Stevenson's *Kidnapped* three or four years back, this was the best we could come up with.'

'What part will Oz play?' asked Elanore. 'A lunatic?'

'No. He plays Dawn's brother. My character spends most of the story trying to find her, but the whole thing's seen from Oz's point of view. We've written in some simple scenes to give his character some depth.

'Towards the end I work out that Dawn's being held on an abandoned oil platform in the North Sea, and I try to rescue her myself. Having Oz as narrator leaves open the possibility that I might not survive.'

'Where's the twist at the end? I've noticed that there always is in your work.' I glanced at David. I've always known that there's a shrewd mind under that reserved crust of his. He set me wondering too. I'd read the script: there was no big surprise ending, only a shoot-out, then happy ever after.

Miles laughed out loud. 'Nice one, Dad. Maybe it isn't written yet,' he replied, intriguingly. 'We've done all the outside shots on the rig we're using, to ensure consistent weather. The scenes on Deeside and Aberdeen will all be done on location too, in a mansion and in offices we've rented for the purpose. But the stuff at the end, and all the undercover scenes on the rig, will be shot on a mock-up in a major studio just south of London.'

'So,' said Elanore, 'to return to the original question. When will these two be clear to get married?'

Her official son-in-law glanced at me in a way which set me wondering. 'That'll depend on some late changes we might make, but maybe mid-October; early November, for sure.'

I raised a mock eyebrow. 'Should I be talking to my agent about this?'

Miles laughed. 'Maybe you should, mate. Maybe you should.'

It had been niggling at me that I might have been a shade blasé about *Project 37*, that I wasn't as nervous as I should have been in the circumstances. At that moment, my excitement switch was thrown, and my old friend the hamster began to do its familiar laps of my stomach.

My cellphone was switched on too. I had forgotten, so I started in my seat when it rang. 'Sorry,' I said to the rest of the table as I stood and stepped through to the living room to take the call.

'Where are you, Oz?' said Mike Dylan. 'I thought you'd be back from your GWA travels by now.'

'I am. We're up in Auchterarder, with Prim's folks. Miles, Dawn and I are going up to Deeside in the morning to start work on this movie. Where are you right now? Spying on Commies?'

'There's none of them left. They're all called Social Democrats now. No, I'm at home with Susie.'

'How's she doing?'

'She's okay. She was shocked for a couple of days after the bang, but she's back to normal now.'

'What about you? Still mourning for that jacket?'

'Claimed that on my insurance, son. I've been too busy looking for that bastard Donn to think of anything else.'

'So it wasn't work-related?'

'Nah, definitely not. My boss is still keeping the investigation in-house though, and he's letting me handle it.'

'So how are you getting on?'

'That's just it. I'm not. The fucker seems to have vanished from the face of the earth. I've been checking around the city nightclubs, and I've found a couple where he's known. I've been leaning on known drug-dealers, since we think he was involved in that racket with Susie's wayward cousin. Some of them admitted having heard of him: I even picked up a whisper that he might have been the trigger man in a heroin execution in Paisley three years ago.

'But nowhere, Oz, have I picked up the faintest sniff of him. If anyone knows where he is now, they're too scared to say. Even as I speak, my nose is right up against a brick wall, and our SAS guy is still on the payroll, on a twenty-four hour basis, now, just to be on the safe side. I wondered . . . and it hurts my pride to say this . . . whether you've got any ideas?'

I'm sure he must have been almost able to hear my smile on the other end of the line. But I left it at that: this was too serious for triumph. I thought about his question for a few seconds. 'Only one,' I told him, eventually. 'Given the link that you pointed out between our visit to his mother and the explosion, can you put a tap on her phone? The boy's bound to phone his Mammy sooner or later. Maybe you should bug Uncle Joe too, and all the people who know Stephen.'

Dylan whistled. 'Jeez, Oz,' he said, 'I don't know. Wiretaps are supposed to be for exceptional circumstances. If we ask for too many, eyebrows are raised.'

I could not help but laugh. 'What happened to Dylan the Decisive, the bloke we saw last Monday? Some guy's trying to kill your girlfriend, Michael. Isn't that exceptional? I suppose you could always take Mrs Donn down to headquarters and give her the rubber hose treatment, but I can't help feeling that a phone-tap would be more discreet. Don't bother with the rest if you're worried; concentrate on her.'

As he might have sensed my smile, so I saw him frown. 'I suppose, since we don't have anything else . . . I'll ask my boss.'

'You do that. Keep me in touch too. I've got an interest in this after all; the bugger melted a big chunk of my car park.'

16

Although most of my scenes were to be shot in the mansion on Deeside, the first of them were set in the rented office space in Aberdeen. Miles took me straight there next morning, to pitch me head-first into the movie business, as he put it.

He, Dawn and I left Auchterarder at sparrow-fart. I was excited, yet sad, too, as I kissed Prim goodbye, and headed for the bedroom door, with one last look over my shoulder at her sleepy, smiley face on the pillow. It felt strange to be going somewhere on my own. For more than a year she had travelled virtually everywhere with me, to London for my Sly Burr gigs, and all over Europe with the GWA shows; but on this occasion she had decided that Lulu was just a bit short of experience to handle the business on her own, and that she had to go back to Glasgow to give the girl her support.

We travelled to Aberdeen in a limo, complete with chauffeur. I hadn't got used to the business of being rich; it struck me as extravagant. However Miles assured me that the last thing an actor needed was the hassle of driving when he should be getting his mind in tune for the day's work. In his case, this was direction. He had no scenes himself; all the scheduled action was dialogue between me and the eminent Scots actor who was cast as my father.

'We shoot in the afternoon, Oz,' Dawn explained as the

long black car pulled out of her home town. 'We'll spend the morning rehearsing.'

'That's right,' said her husband. 'You'll be on camera, just to let you get used to your surroundings, but they won't be rolling. Film stock is expensive, mate.'

'And you don't want to waste any on me fucking up?'

Miles chuckled. 'I wouldn't have put it as bluntly as that. But yes, that's what I mean.'

I frowned. 'You two are really taking a chance on me, aren't you.'

'We don't think so. You don't have any formal training, that's true, but neither had I when I started out. Christ, I got my first part in Australia by answering a newspaper ad, just after I came out of the forces. What you do have is a great voice, and your experience in commercial work means that the narration side of the project will be easy for you. On top of that you're great performing live on camera in your GWA shows; pro wrestling is a form of acting after all.

'The only thing we don't know is how quickly you'll take to dialogue. I don't have any worries there though. The people you're working with, Dawn and me, and Scott Steele, the guy you're with today, we're all top-notchers; you'll be able to feed off us.'

'I've done dialogue, of a sort,' I pointed out. 'Live on air too. In-ring interviews with performers are a big part of my GWA work, and they're all rehearsed.'

Miles' eyes widened. 'Hey, I never thought of that, but you're right. If you can work with those stiffs, you'll have no trouble acting with Scott and the rest of us.'

I was big-headed enough to agree with him, yet I was still

a jangling bag of nerves when I walked on stage, in make-up and wearing a new Armani suit fresh from the costume department. Our studio for the day was a whole floor of the office block. It had been stripped out and a set built in one corner. In another, makeshift dressing rooms had been built. There were no stars on the doors; Miles is an ordinary guy at heart and doesn't allow any airs and graces on his sets. There was something odd about the windows, I noticed. I asked the assistant camera operator what it was; she told me that non-reflective film had been applied to both sides of the glass.

Working on camera in television and in movies are wholly separate experiences; for example, movie lights are much hotter, the cameras are bigger and much more threatening, and there are people crowding around the performers. The biggest difference, though, for me was this: performing on television in the way that I had done up to then, most of the time, I had to look directly into the camera, while, in the movies, that is absolutely the last thing you must do.

This more than anything else was what Miles drummed into me during rehearsals. He was right about Scott Steele, too; my co-star was a real professional. He was stocky, silver-haired and a bit wrinkled under the slap, but there was an assurance about him which put me at my ease right away. There was nothing complex about my lines to begin with, but the way Scott delivered his seemed to draw them smoothly from me. His relaxation relaxed me, and when the time came in the afternoon for the cameras to roll, I had almost forgotten that they were there.

Miles was a pro too, his direction was light and easy. Basically, he left Scott Steele to do his own thing and ease me through our scenes. Still, when it came time to wrap up for the day, I felt like a wet rag. 'How did I do?' I asked Miles, as the lighting people began to break down their gear.

'You want to see? We monitor everything on video, so have a look.' There was a monitor in the furthest corner of our studio. He plugged a lead from the video camera into the scart socket and switched it on. I couldn't really believe it as I watched my first movie scene, for the first time. 'Hey,' I gasped, 'it's okay, isn't it?'

'Yeah,' said Miles, in his familiar, balloon-pricking drawl. 'Scott's terrific, ain't he.'

'You're not too bad either,' Dawn chuckled, taking my arm.

Normally the main performers had accommodation on Deeside, in the rented mansion, or in a country house hotel in Aboyne, but for the next two nights, because we were due to film some street scenes next day in Aberdeen, and more studio stuff on the day after, we were all booked into the Treetops Hotel, not far from the city centre.

Scott came with us in the limo, having changed out of the conservative Austin Reed suit which he had worn on camera, into jeans and a sweatshirt, the same gear as me in fact.

'You're a lucky bastard, young Blackstone,' he said, sincerely but not unkindly, as the driver pulled out into the evening traffic. 'I had to slog my guts out for twenty years in theatre companies, bit parts on telly, Edinburgh Festival crap, and dodgy pantos all over Scotland, to reach my present standing in the profession. You do a couple of years as an MC and a few voice-overs, and here you are getting equal billing with me.'

He shot me an ironic smile. 'The world's fuckin' ill-divided son, is it not?' I noticed that off-screen, he had a Glasgow accent.

'It is that, Scott.' I agreed, returning his smile. 'Did Miles tell you I won the fuckin' lottery as well?'

He stared at me for a few seconds, then realised I was serious and exploded with laughter. 'Ah,' he spluttered. 'It was bribery, was it? That's okay. I can live with that.'

'Not at all,' Miles protested. 'He hasn't got enough to bribe me. It was nepotism; he lives with Dawn's sister.' He paused. 'That and the fact that he's damn good.'

'Aye,' said my co-star. 'That's the saving grace, I'll grant you.'

At the Treetops, the old actor and I showered off our make-up in our rooms, then met downstairs in the bar to top up our fluid levels. Our denims drew a slightly disapproving look from the barman, but we ignored him. 'Scott,' I asked after a while, sat beside him on a high stool, 'am I doing someone better out of a job? Should I be feeling guilty about all this?'

He laughed. 'Not for one minute, son. This is the most cut-throat business in the world . . . apart from the law, that is. You are where you are by sheer random chance, so accept it.' He paused. 'The truth is that there are two other young Scots actors who, I would say, could have played your part better than you, and who have names that would mean something in the billing. One's working on another movie and the other one's agent was daft enough to turn the part down because Miles wouldn't bill the boy above the title.

'You at least have a recognisable face through your grappling work, and a known voice from your commercials.

The part's no' too difficult either, so you were a reasonably safe choice.'

A short hoarse laugh sounded behind me. 'Now is not that an ironic thing for someone to say about you, Oz.'

I couldn't help it, I gasped with surprise, even before I turned round towards her. 'Noosh,' I heard myself exclaim, astonished. 'What the hell are you doing here?'

She hadn't changed a bit in the three years since last I'd seen her. She was still dressed in the inevitable formal business suit, which seemed to highlight the austerity of her features: the high Slavonic cheekbones, the ash-blonde hair with the odd grey streaks, the silvery look about her eyes.

'The same as you, I guess. I often drop in here for a drink after work.' The accent was still the same, slightly East European.

'Last I heard, you were working in St Petersburg.'

She nodded. 'I did, for a while. I was transferred back to Scotland a year ago, to head the Aberdeen office.'

I remembered my manners, and turned back to my pal. 'Sorry, Scott. This is Anoushka Turkel, a friend from Edinburgh. Noosh, this is Scott Steele, a prince among actors.'

The veteran slipped off his bar stool, shook her hand formally, with a short, classic bow. 'Delighted to meet you. Now I'm going to be rude and bugger off. I like to dress a bit better than this for dinner.'

As he left, Noosh climbed up on his vacated seat. I ordered a white wine for her and another pint of lager.

'So . . .' I said. Now that we were alone, the awkwardness returned. It had always been there between the two of us –

inevitably, since we had both been Jan's lovers, and in turn, she had left each of us for the other.

'Yes, so indeed.' She paused and her gaze, usually rock-steady, faltered, and lowered. 'I heard, of course. But . . .'

'No point in talking about it,' I said, trying not to be abrupt. 'We'll never compare notes, you and I.'

She laughed, short and brittle. 'Indeed not.' Then her eyes caught mine once more.

'So now you are an actor. It doesn't surprise me, you know. You were always a crazy guy, and always playing a part, I thought.'

'Which one was that?'

'The part of the young, free and single; as if you thought that was how you should be living your life and were determined to do it with style.' She snorted again. 'I mean, having a bloody iguana as a pet in your flat.'

'Loft, please, Noosh.'

'You see? Another part of the act. Everyone else lived in a flat, but you had to live in a loft. How is your old loft-mate these days? Did you put him in a zoo when you and Jan got married?'

'In a way. He lives in St Andrews with Jonathan and Colin, my nephews.'

'And where do you live now?'

'Glasgow.'

'Let me guess. In another loft?'

I laughed. 'No, in an old church tower actually. We have a great view of the centre of the city.'

'We?'

'Primavera. She came back from Spain. We're together, in

business and in life; we're getting married in a few weeks, once I'm finished with this gig.'

There was an awkward silence as Noosh sipped her wine. 'I see. Maybe this time it'll last.' If there was a trace of bitterness there, she snuffed it out at once. 'What you doing in Aberdeen? Is it your movie?'

'Yes. Scott and I filmed some scenes today. Tomorrow morning we're doing some scenes in Union Street. Just me, walking along the pavement through crowds of pedestrians. We've got an army of extras standing by from seven o'clock.'

She chuckled. 'Crazy boy,' she muttered. 'Hey, can I be an extra? I've always wanted to be in a movie too.'

'Sure,' I told her. 'If you can get yourself to Union Street for seven, I'll see that you get on camera.'

She drained her glass and gave me a long cool smile for the road. 'It's a date,' she said, as she turned to leave. 'Thanks for the drink. I'll see you there.'

17

When the phone rang in my room at five-thirty a.m., I suppose that was my real introduction to the world of movie-making. On most days when production is in full swing, it really does involve early starts and late finishes.

It was fun though; the whole crew had eaten at a long table in the hotel, where I was made to feel, for the first time, not like a curiosity but like a fully fledged member of the team. One or two of the technicians even turned out to be GWA fans, and talked themselves round to asking the inevitable question. 'Can those guys really fight?'

I had never thought of Mike Dylan as a creature of habit, but for the second night in a row he managed to interrupt my dinner. I was in the middle of explaining to the Best Boy, who was in fact a girl, that Jerry Gradi really was so tough that he could crush walnuts with his arse, when my mobile trembled in my pocket. I had called Prim from my room, so I knew it couldn't be her, but still, I was surprised when the intrepid detective inspector spoke.

'I've got it, Oz,' he began.

'What? Paranoia? Social dysfunction? Genital warts?'

'No you daft bastard. I've got a tap on Stephen Donn's mother's phone. My boss signed the application this morning and we were in place by this afternoon.'

'Congratulations. Does she have a mobile as well?'

'No, but no problem if she does. They're simple to tap; MI5 do it all the time.'

'Comforting to know that,' I said into my cellphone. 'I don't suppose you've got anything yet?'

He laughed. 'Well, we know that the principal of her college fancies her. He called her about six o'clock and asked her if she'd go to the Lakes with him this weekend. She said she'd only go if the guy's wife called her to say it was all right.

'Other than that, she didn't have many calls. Just a couple from women friends, organising a theatre night. We might have to wait for a month before the guy calls her . . . but he will. I'm sure he will.'

'Just a thought, Mike. Does this guy pay income tax? Did it ever occur to you that the Inland Revenue might know where he is?'

'Teach your granny, Blackstone. Stephen Donn hasn't paid PAYE since he worked at Gantry's. He's self-employed and his papers all go to an accountant in Paisley. We checked there: the bloke told us that Donn comes to see him once a year with his records, then comes back once the calculations are done and gives him enough cash to cover his fee and tax due. It's a common practice among dodgy people who don't want to be easily traced.'

'When's he due to show up there again?'

'Not before next April. For my money, the guy's involved in something illegal; probably the drugs trade, that's what most criminals are into in Scotland these days.'

'Ah well,' I said, sincerely; I could still feel the heat of the explosion. 'I hope you get a result from the phone thing sooner rather than later.'

I was still thinking of Mike's phone call as I stepped out of the hire car into Union Street just before seven a.m.. For all that I was amused by Dylan behaving like a real policeman for the first time since I'd met him, I was worried for Susie. She's a good-hearted girl, and she didn't deserve to be persecuted by any nutter.

Aberdeen's City Council was bending over backwards to help us. *Project 37* was the first major movie to have been shot in the Granite City in more years than anyone could remember, so nothing for us was too much bother. Union Street, the city's main drag, was ours until eight-fifteen, when the temporary traffic diversion would end. We had been promised that if the weather was bad, they would do it again another time, but the morning was fine and sunny.

The cameras and lights were all in position by the time we arrived, and a mass of extras were waiting. Miles went straight to work, grabbing a megaphone and giving them instructions. It was a simple job; some of the crowd were told to walk along Union Street east to west, others west to east. A few were cast as public transport passengers, a queue boarding a bus which was drawn up at a stop. We had volunteer motorists too, ordinary drivers who had brought their cars and cycles along to join in the fun. Their instructions were simply to drive along the street, turn and drive back again.

As he split the extras into groups, all of them volunteers recruited by an advertisement and an editorial piece in the *Press and Journal*, I looked around the sea of faces until I spotted Noosh. She gave me a cool smile and a wave. I beckoned her over and strolled over to Miles.

'This is Anoushka, a friend of mine,' I told him. 'She'd like to be in the movie.'

'No problem, mate.' he said. He pointed along the road a little. 'Anoushka, Oz will be walking along there, east to west, past that shop. You just come in the other direction. Don't look at him, don't look at the camera, but just stick to the outside of the pavement and you'll be in shot.'

'Thank you very much. I've always wanted to do this.' I'd never seen Noosh Turkel looking like a schoolgirl before.

'No problem.' Miles went back to his megaphone. The 'pedestrians' were in position, and the car-owners were standing by their vehicles. 'We don't have a lot of time here, folks,' he yelled, 'so I want to get this shot right first time if I can. We'll have a rehearsal, then go straight into a take.'

We did our rehearsal walk-through on Miles' call of 'Action', and must have convinced him that we all knew what we were doing, for we went quickly for the real thing. I was impressed by the smoothness of it all, as I walked the line which had been chalked for me on the pavement, through and past the people. The idea was that I was looking for someone in one of the Union Street shops, so every so often I would pause, peer through a doorway, then move on. My stopping points were marked with big chalk crosses, but I told myself that I was out for an ordinary walk in an ordinary street and it worked. The camera was following me, out of my line of sight, and our volunteer motorists were cruising past me, so it was easy to maintain that illusion.

I was only vaguely aware of Noosh coming towards me. She was following Miles' instruction to the letter, walking so near to the edge of the pavement that I was almost on the road. At that moment, I became aware of the noise too; one that hadn't been there on the run-through; the sound of a motorcyclist revving his engine hard. I couldn't help it; I looked along the street and saw him in the distance, a biker in heavy black leathers and a sparkly red brain-bucket with a dark visor.

As I looked at him he let in his clutch and sped away from the kerb, heading in my direction, accelerating hard. There was something wrong, I knew; no way was this in the script. The gap between us closed, and as it did, I saw him reach inside his leather jacket. He had levelled off his speed when I saw the pistol in his hand. I should have been scared shitless, I suppose, but I've had a gun pointed at me before, and I knew that this one was being aimed at someone else.

No, unmistakably, the rider was homing in on Anoushka, as she walked along, her back to him, unawares. *This has to be part of the movie*, I told myself. *Some fucking stunt Miles chose not to tell me about*. Whatever it was, I decided on the instant to play it for real. I broke into a run, heading for Noosh.

'Look out,' I yelled as the gap closed between us, sending a pedestrian extra sprawling sideways. Her eyes widened and they caught mine as I dived for her. I saw the gun levelled at her head as I hit her, saw the muzzle flash as I bore her to the ground, saw the biker swerve to avoid us as we lay in the roadway, and saw the fumes from his exhaust as he speeded up and roared away, swinging into Market Street and out of sight.

As we lay there panting, gasping for breath, a shadow fell across us. 'That was great cinema, mate,' Miles drawled, with a touch of wonder in his voice, 'but what the fuck was it all about?'

I glared at him as I got to my feet, helping Noosh up too. 'I thought you'd be telling me that. You mean you didn't set it up?'

'Set what up?'

'The arsehole on the bike!' I shouted at him. 'He took a shot at Anoushka.'

Miles is a damn good actor, but he can't fake the sort of astonishment that showed on his face.

Anoushka looked as bewildered as he did. 'He shot at *me*?' she gasped. 'Are you sure?'

'Dead bloody certain,' I snapped. 'As dead as you'd have been if I hadn't taken you down. The guy was out to kill you. Now, what's it all about?'

She was trembling and looked tearful as she shook her head. I was sorry at once for my show of temper. 'I don't know,' she murmured. 'I suppose it could have been something to do with my time in St Petersburg. There were bad people there; a lot of them.'

'Okay,' said Miles. He called over to his assistant. 'Bernie! Call the police. Get them here fast!'

'Does that blow the shoot?' I asked him, a professional to the last.

'Not necessarily. I may have enough in the can. I didn't tell anyone, but I ran the cameras during the rehearsal.'

'You may have something else in the can too,' I told him. 'Like a shot of that biker.'

18

For a while, it looked as if the police might have to impound Miles' film, but eventually they settled for a print.

The team who turned up was led by a Detective Super-intendent: Miles Grayson is an important man, after all, and he was spending a lot of money in the Grampian force's area.

The head man – his name was Alex Francey – interviewed Noosh and me himself, back at the Treetops, in the bar where we had met the night before. His sergeant and two detective constables were left in Union Street, taking statements from the few extras who had seen anything.

We sat at a low round table, with coffee and biscuits which, considerately, I had put on Miles' tab. 'When did you first become aware of the man on the motorcycle, Miss Turkel?' he asked.

'That is Ms,' she corrected him, stiffly. She was back to her normal ice-maiden self; she had left her fear behind in the city. 'I wasn't aware of him at all, not until almost he ran into us, after Oz had knocked me to the ground.' She threw me a quick glare, making a show of flicking dust and road debris from her long skirt.

'Then all I saw was the back of his bike, from ground level.'

'Did you get his registration number?'

'I wasn't exactly thinking about that at the time, having

just been rugby-tackled by a large man.'

Detective Superintendent Francey grinned. 'So the day hasn't been all bad,' he said. I winced as he spoke, hoping that he would see my face and know that he was on dodgy ground.

Noosh chilled him, froze him solid, with just a stare. For a moment, they looked like two Batman villains: she Ms Freeze, he Jack Nicholson's Joker, with his smile painted on his face.

'Right,' he went on quickly. 'Can I ask you to think back now? Just try to picture the scene again, and tell me everything that happened.'

Noosh loosened up, just a bit. 'I was simply walking along on the outside of the pavement,' she replied, 'as I'd been told to do by Mr Grayson. Then I saw Oz running. I was surprised, but I remember thinking that this must be a part of the movie they hadn't told me about. When I realised that he was coming at me, I didn't have time to do anything about it.'

She paused, her eyes closed for a few seconds as if she was picturing the scene inside her head. 'He reached me, and pulled me to the ground. As I fell, there was a bang. Yes I remember that now. Then the noise of tyres on the road, and of the bike speeding up once more.

'I looked up at the man. I saw his back as he drove off, and his shiny crash helmet. But I don't remember his number plate.'

'He didn't have one,' I said. 'I remember that now. I saw him from the front and the rear; the bike didn't have a number plate. I'm sure of that.'

'Okay, but you got a good look at the man?'

'Sure, dressed from head to foot in black leather, with a

damn great black-visored, crimson thing covering his head.' I frowned at the detective. 'It could have been you, for all I could tell.'

'Did you actually see the gun being fired?' Francey asked.

'Yes, definitely. Flash, bang; that's how it goes, isn't it?'

'Are you sure it was being fired at Ms Turkel?'

It was my turn to run a play-back in my head. 'Yes, I'm certain,' I told him, once the sequence was over. 'He accelerated from way back up the street. My attention was attracted at first by the noise he was making. We were recording wild sound, and I thought it might screw up the take. Then I saw him ease down his speed, line himself up behind Noosh, and pull the gun from his leathers.'

'Can you describe the firearm?'

'Small and black. It looked like an automatic. Mind you, I've only seen two real, unholstered pistols in my life, so I'm no expert.'

'What about the bike? What make was it?'

I shrugged. 'Two wheels, handlebars, painted mainly yellow: that's it, I'm afraid.'

'It was a Kawasaki,' Noosh blurted out, looking at me, rather than at the detective. 'I know about motorcycles, remember.' I did. For a while, when she and Jan lived together, Noosh owned a Honda.

Francey coughed. 'What about the man, Ms Turkel? Have you any idea about him? You said you're a lawyer,' he added helpfully. 'Have you got any disgruntled criminal clients who might be bearing a grudge?'

She shook her head, sending her sleek hair swinging. 'I'm a corporate lawyer, officer. I don't do criminal work.'

'Well, how about your private life? Is there an ex-boyfriend who might want to hurt you?'

'I don't have ex-boyfriends,' she said, abruptly. 'I have ex-girlfriends, but none of them ride motorcycles.'

'Well maybe one of them has a boyfriend who does?' the Superintendent suggested, with a touch of desperation.

'Only one of my ex-girlfriends has ever had a boyfriend,' Noosh retorted. 'And he is not a biker; not at all.'

'Still, if you could give me his name . . .'

'I'd rather not.'

'You don't have that choice.' Francey shifted in his chair, as if he was flexing his shoulders. 'You may not be not a criminal lawyer, but I don't have to tell you about the penalties for withholding information.'

'That's right, you don't, because there are none. I'm not obstructing your investigation and I'm not under oath.'

'The Fiscal might not share your view about obstruction, and the Law Society might disagree with you too. I can make a lot of trouble for you, Miss Turkel.'

I didn't want to go any further down this road, but I couldn't let this go on. 'I'm the man she's talking about, Super-intendent,' I said, a wee bit more aggressively than I'd intended. 'Noosh and my late wife lived together for a while. They parted on good terms and neither Jan nor I ever held any grudges. You'll need to find another line of inquiry, I'm afraid.'

He gave me a policeman's look; it came right over the top of his nose, boring into me. 'Any ideas, then?' he asked, dryly.

'Only one,' Noosh intervened. 'I spent some time in my firm's St Petersburg office. While I was there I had a client who turned out to be Mafia, so we ceased to represent his company. He was unhappy; threats were made, so my firm decided it was time for me to come back to Scotland. But as we all know, such people can have long arms.

'That is the only help I can give you. Now, what are you going to do for me?'

'What do you mean?' Francey looked puzzled.

'I mean,' Noosh chilled him again, 'are you going to give me police protection?'

He recovered his composure, just a little too late to be convincing. 'Of course, ma'am. I'll see to it right away.' Seizing the excuse, he hurried out of the room.

19

The rest of that day would have been a complete wash-out in filming terms, had we not scored enough usable footage before Noosh's disaster.

As it was, with some hard work by the crew, we were able to bring our schedule forward and shoot the studio scenes which had been pencilled in for Wednesday. It was a long day, but I was happy; it meant that I could catch a flight to Glasgow next morning, back to Prim. I'd been missing her, especially in the aftermath of the Union Street incident.

I had another visit from the Old Bill in the evening, just as the crew were striking our set, from a detective sergeant and a constable sent along by Francey to take a formal statement. It made me feel that I was back at my old job, even though I was on the other side of the table.

The sergeant's questions laid heavy stress on the gun. I didn't tell him much more than I had told his boss; small, black thing, didn't appear to have a revolver chamber so I guessed that it was an automatic. Mind you, I could have told him that it was a Walther. I've had one of those pointed at me, not once but twice, and when you've looked down the barrel of a gun you can almost remember its serial number. I kept that detail to myself, though; those were incidents which I definitely did not want to discuss with the police.

Instead, I asked him, 'Why do you need to know?'

'We pass it on to police intelligence.' I bit my lip; it wasn't the time for the old gag about contradictions in terms. 'They can sometimes give us a steer about other crimes where that type of gun's been used. We're still looking for the bullet, of course; once we find that it might tell us whether that specific weapon's been used in another incident.

'It's a bugger not havin' it.' He sighed in a way which hinted that, sod it, his life would have been much easier if they'd been able to dig a slug out of Noosh or me, or one of the extras.

I let it pass and waved them goodbye, then took a taxi out to the address in the west of the city which Noosh had given me. I wouldn't have felt right if I had left without checking that her protection was in place.

Detective Superintendent Francey had been as good as his word. There was a car parked just across the street from her small granite bungalow; two guys were sat in it, and I guessed that they weren't looking for unlicensed television sets. I gave them a cheery wave as I opened the garden gate, before they could start worrying about me. I don't suppose many hitmen arrive by taxi, but I didn't want anyone to get nervous.

In a way, stepping into that living room was like a trip into the past. I recognised the sofa, the two recliner armchairs, upholstered in soft grey fabric, and the low coffee table. They had all been in the flat in Castle Terrace, in Edinburgh, which she and Jan had shared. Noosh's manner, too, was the same as it had been then; not unfriendly, but cool and appraising.

'You all right?' I asked her.

'I've been better. I have a sore bum, for one thing.' She

smiled. 'But at least it doesn't have a bullet in it.'

'You're safe now, anyway. Those guys across the road are pretty obvious.' I looked around the room. 'Do you live alone?'

'Oh yes.' She nodded, pausing for a moment. 'I don't think I'll live with anyone again,' she ventured. 'Too dangerous. There can be too much hurt involved.'

Suddenly she looked vulnerable, and I thought of her in a way I never had before. 'Noosh,' I said, 'I'm sorry. I never meant for that to happen.'

'I know you didn't, Oz. Nor did Jan. But the two of you, you didn't really know what you were doing then. You were afraid of commitment, both of you; it was as if you had decided that there were wild oats you had to sow before then.' She chuckled, sadly. 'I guess that I was the field; and so was Primavera.' With her faintly European accent she pronounced the 'v' softly, almost as an 'f'.

'When you came to Castle Terrace with her that day, looking for help, at first I thought, "This is great. He's getting out of Jan's life at last." That lasted for a few minutes, until I realised that it would have the opposite effect. There was something in the way you and Jan looked at each other that day, that told me how it would end.'

'You might have told me, then.' The words burst from me; I couldn't keep the bitterness from my voice.

Her hand flew to her mouth. 'Oh Oz, my dear, I didn't mean that. I could tell that you had to be together, that's all. Even when you went off, all lusty for Primavera, I knew better than you did.'

'You've changed a lot, you know. You were just a boy then, an irresponsible, crazy boy. But now you've grown up.' She smiled at me again, as she never had before. 'Now you're a crazy man.

'Seriously, after all that's happened, I'm glad that things have worked out for you and Primavera. Like I said, she and I had something in common back then; we were both ditched. She must have loved you all along.

'Just you two be lucky from now on.'

'If you only knew the half of it, Anoushka. The way it's been lately, lucky's my middle name.' I glanced out of the window, at my waiting taxi.

'Look,' I told her, 'I'm dining with the gang tonight, so'll need to be going.' I took a card from my wallet and handed it to her. 'There are all my numbers, home, office, mobile and e-mail. The boys outside will look after you, I've no doubt, but if you have any more trouble, or threats – or even if you just feel a bit nervous – get in touch with me any time.'

She walked me to her front door. Holding the round brass handle, she raised herself up on her toes and kissed me lightly on the lips. 'Be good,' she whispered. 'I wouldn't want anything to happen to you. Luck doesn't last for ever; but then, I suppose *you* know that more than most.'

20

'Did the Grampian guys say anything to you? Did they tell you whether they had any leads at all?'

'They told us bugger all, Mike. They just asked questions, that was all.' Dylan had a day off, so he and I were in the Horseshoe for a Thursday lunchtime pint, pie and beans.

I had said nothing at all to Prim about my Aberdeen adventure, after making sure that the press hadn't blown it up. There had been some local coverage, in the *Evening Express* and on *NorthSound* about the police being called to the scene, but the force press office had written it off as a false alarm. Kiki Eldon, Miles' unit publicist, had done a good job too, spreading a few tenners around among the extras just to emphasise the point, as it were.

I had told her about meeting Noosh, on the off-chance that she did phone, or send me an e-mail. She had been interested, and pleased that there were no hard feelings, but that had been that.

Nevertheless, I was still suffering after-effects from the incident – like waking up in the middle of the night in a cold sweat – so when Dylan had called proposing a Horseshoe session I had jumped at the chance; not because I'm a great lunchtime boozer, but because I needed to talk to someone.

He had sat there quite calmly as I told him the story. I was a bit huffed; I had expected him to be more impressed.

'They would ask questions, Oz,' he mumbled, indistinctly, through a mouthful of pie. 'It's their job; I just wondered whether they'd told you what they were thinking.'

'I got the impression that they weren't thinking too hard. All they really did was ask us what we thought.'

Dylan nodded. 'Standard procedure; more often than not the victims will tell you who did it, even if they don't know themselves, or if they do but are trying to protect someone. See you, Oz, you're a romantic when it comes to criminal investigation. You think the answer always comes in a flash of brilliance, like a revelation from God, or your Uncle Bob, or somebody.'

'You mean that isn't what happens?' I asked him innocently. 'That's how it's always worked for me.'

'Sure,' my friend countered, 'after you've picked your way through a pile of casualties. Your blinding light always strikes you too late.' A flash of uncertainty in his eyes told me that he knew he'd dropped a clanger, but he decided, rightly, that the best way to deal with it was to blunder on to the next outrage. 'I'm a detective, pal,' he continued. 'You're a chancer.'

I couldn't let that one past. 'Is that right, Detective Inspector? In that case, which of us has the better clear-up rate?'

'Clear-up rate? You, what have you cleared up, except the empties from the night before and the Durex from under the bed?'

'Well,' I countered, feeling my eyes narrow a bit, 'for a start there was the guy two years ago. I got him, didn't I.'

'He was barking mad, Oz. Christ, he was banging your enormous pal's wife; that's how nuts he was.'

'Nonetheless, I got him; you lot didn't.'

'We might have, if your pal had reported it as a crime long before he did.'

'There were reasons for that. And that business with the painting out in Spain that Prim and I were involved in. We got a result there too; and what a result.'

'The way you tell the story, the guy confessed to you.'

'Sure, but we'd worked it out by then. Anyway, what about the wee stockbroker in Edinburgh, the one who was found dead in Prim's flat? That's still on the unsolved list, is it not, despite you and ex-Superintendent Ross being hot on the trail?'

Dylan frowned. He always does when I bring that one up. 'We reckoned the wife did it; you know that. The Crown Office wouldn't prosecute, that was all.'

'That's balls, Michael, and you know it. Your boss Ricky thought that Dawn did it. He even had me in the frame at one point; or so you told me. As for Linda Kane, no way did she do it.'

'You still let us arrest her, though.'

'Well? The cow did try to kill Dawn, Prim and me. Too effing right we let you arrest her.'

'You know, Blackstone,' Mike growled; he only calls me by my surname when he's on a fishing trip. 'I think you're hinting that you got a result there too.'

'We got a large reward for the money we recovered.'

'That's not what I mean. I think you know who killed Kane. What if I was to pull you in – you and Prim – and ask you that, under caution?'

I laughed. 'A rubber hose job?'

'Something like that.'

'Greg McPhillips would have us out of there in two minutes, and you know it.'

'Aye, I suppose so. But come on, Oz, give us a clue, between friends. That one's always niggled at me.'

I looked at him for a while. Then I put part of my life in his hands. 'You can close the book on it, Mike. The guy who killed Willie Kane is dead himself.'

'Accident?' he asked, quietly. 'Natural causes? Or did someone do him?'

'Accident. Sudden, bloody and very, very fatal.'

'Not in Geneva, by any chance?'

My eyes, formerly narrowed, widened suddenly, giving him his answer.

'I wondered about him when I heard about the accident report from Switzerland. I even had a look at it. At the time the Swiss police were a bit puzzled by the fact that the guy had two bullets in his chest and he was as high as a kite on heroin, but a street full of witnesses saw him run right in front of the bus, so that was that.'

I left him staring at the table while I went up to the bar for another round of pints.

'Dawn wasn't involved, was she?' he asked, when I returned.

'No way.'

'That's all right then. Now, back to your bother in Aberdeen. I'll ask my SB colleague up there if he can find out anything for me. I'll check the network too, just in case there's been an alert about Russian gangsters coming into Britain.

'Mind you, that sounds like clutching at straws to me.'

'What way?'

'Ach, you've always had a taste for the exotic, but in the real world, where we're faced with an alleged crime like this, the first thing we do is look for a domestic solution. We usually find it too.'

I shook my head as I sipped my pint; no mean feat, that. 'You won't find it here. I promise you.'

'Oh no? You mean it couldn't have been a jealous boyfriend, because of Ms Turkel's preferences?'

'Something like that.'

'So who says it was a man on the bike? What was the rider wearing?'

I described the biker's outfit, in detail.

'And was his cock hanging out of his leathers?'

'No. Mind you, it was cold that morning, so if it was it'd have been pretty shrivelled up, and I might not have noticed it.'

'Somebody would have. I can see the headline now: "Motorcycle flasher in Union Street gun drama". No, Oz, for all you know your gunman could have been a gun person, a hellishly furious, scorned, et cetera, former woman friend of the lesbian lawyer. Tell me different, go on.'

I couldn't.

'That's if there was a gun person at all. Are you dead sure of what you saw?'

'Of course.'

'Who else saw the gun?'

'Only me. The rider was coming right in behind her, but I was in the line of fire. Noosh heard it, but only I saw it.'

'She could have heard a backfire from the bike. You could have seen something else; the biker could have slowed down

119

because his mobile phone rang. Maybe that was it.'

I leaned across the table. 'Michael,' I asked him, straight-faced. 'Do you remember your first shag?'

He looked at me as if I was daft. 'Of course; everyone does.'

'Well, having a gun pointed in your general direction is just as unforgettable, and you don't just remember the first time.'

'Maybe so, but I suspect that my colleagues up in Furry-boots City are a bit sceptical, nonetheless.'

'They're giving Noosh protection.'

'Of course they are. She asked for it, and she's a lawyer, so they're playing it by the book. Let's see how long it lasts, though. Like I said, I'll ask some questions tomorrow, and find out what their thinking is.'

For the next few minutes we ate in silence, doing justice to the Horseshoe pies. When we were finished, and the last bean scooped up, I looked at Dylan again. 'Any progress on your own stalker?' I asked him.

To my surprise, he beamed back at me. 'I was saving that. We got a result off the wire-tap on Tuesday. Mrs Donn had a call from her baby boy; we managed to trace it all the way to a call-box in Amsterdam. Bugger's in Holland.'

'Did he say anything significant?'

'Not as far as I could see from the transcript. He was just asking after her, that was all. She asked where he was, but all he said was "Moving about". She asked when she'd be seeing him again, but he was vague about that too.

'Still, at least it gives us something to go on, we can keep an eye out for the boy coming in on the Schiphol flights and the ferries.' He paused. 'Of course there's a problem with that. We don't actually know what Stephen Donn looks like. Susie's given me a general description, but we don't have a photograph of him, for the people at the airports. The thing is, we don't want to tip our hand here, so I'll probably just give them a photofit.'

'Why don't you pull Prim and me back on to the case. We'll get you a photo.'

He gave me his best sarcastic look. 'How will you do that? Break into his mother's house while she's at college?'

'I suppose we might. But no, that'd be too risky; there are too many retired people in the block she lives in. No, I thought we'd just go back to Uncle Joe.'

I knew that I didn't have to make the offer, but what else could I do? Mike was going to check out Aberdeen for me to make sure that Noosh was okay; he was good at extracting one favour for another.

'Okay,' he agreed. 'See if you can do it tomorrow morning.'

I waved my empty glass at him. 'In that case,' I suggested, 'on balance, the last pint's on you.'

21

This time, there was no need to pull a stunt to get to see Joe Donn. Prim called him and asked if we could visit him again. He must have taken a shine to her, for he agreed without a murmur.

We took the Z3 out to Motherwell; it's a bit of a toy, that car. How many times in Scotland would anyone actually want to drive one with the top down? Very few indeed, but that Friday was one of them; as I drove along the M74, past Strathclyde Country Park with its fun fair and its rowing course, the wind sent Prim's hair flying out behind her and tried to find its way inside my wrap-round shades.

Mr Donn was polishing the Jaguar when we drew up in front of his house. He looked at our car, nodding approval. I repositioned the electric hood, locked it and the car – okay, it was a good neighbourhood, but you can't be too careful when you drive a flash motor like ours – and followed him into the big brick house.

He was as well-dressed as he had been before; still casual, but Calvin Klein, this time, from head to foot as far as I could see.

'So what is it this time?' he asked as he showed us into his study. 'Will I save you the trouble by confessing now?' I stared at him.

'Okay, I admit it,' he chuckled. 'I once went to a conference, met a woman and charged her dinner to the firm on my expenses. There you are, you can shop me to Susie; then I suppose I'll have a visit from her polisman boyfriend.'

'No, Mr Donn,' said Prim. 'That won't happen. Everyone fiddles their expenses a bit – even Oz.' That wasn't true, but I let it pass.

'Last time we were here,' she continued, 'we told you that someone had been threatening Susie. It's a bit more serious now; there's been an attempt on her life.'

In a second, Joe Donn's face seemed to turn as grey as his hair. 'You what . . .?' he gasped.

'Someone torched her car,' I said. 'She was meant to be in it at the time, but by pure chance, no one was.'

'Do the police know who did it?'

'The police wrote it off as an accident,' I lied, technically. 'We're still handling this thing, and we're still looking for your nephew. Have you seen him since we were here last?'

He shook his head. 'No. Nor, as I said, do I expect to. Stephen's a bad lot. I had hopes for him, but he's let me down all along the line. My last words to him were something about not darkening my door again.' He glanced at Prim. 'Only I didn't quite put it like that.'

'Do you have a photograph of him?' she asked.

Donn nodded. Some of his colour had returned, I noticed, but he was still pale. 'I should have. Hold on a minute; I keep my photographs upstairs.' He hurried from the room.

We wandered into the conservatory as we waited, admiring his big, immaculate garden, amused by the practice golf net in the far corner. 'Nice place this,' Prim murmured. 'D'you think we should buy something like it?'

123

'What, in Motherwell?'

She give me her 'Daft bastard' look. 'I was thinking of Florida, actually.'

'We've got two houses already.'

'But neither of them has a garden.'

'Exactly.'

It's a thing about Prim. She'd really love to have green fingers, but in fact she's death to anything with roots. Last December, my sister Ellie gave us a poinsettia, and Prim announced that she would look after it. A week before Christmas, the one remaining red leaf fell off.

We were so busy admiring the place, we didn't notice or care that Joe Donn's minute had stretched out to fifteen. It was only when he coughed behind us that I glanced at my watch and realised how long he had been gone.

'That's a funny thing,' he said, looking slightly puzzled. 'I thought I'd plenty of photos of Stephen, and yet I can't find one. Come back through here though; there's one thing I do have. After we both left Gantry's, I took him on a golfing trip to Portugal. I had my video camera with me and I shot some footage, with Stephen in it. If I lend it to you, maybe you could have a print taken off that.'

We followed him back into the study, where he opened a cupboard, revealing rows of neatly labelled Super 8 tape cassette boxes. I watched him as he pointed his way along the second row, until he came to a box labelled Portugal. He took it out, and flipped it open; it was empty.

'What the hell?'

'Could it still be in the camera?' Prim asked.

'No chance. I never took out the tape I used last time I was in Spain. It's still there. I'm meticulous about my tapes. This one's been pinched.'

'In that case, Mr Donn,' I told him, 'it looks as if your Stephen's a shy lad. He doesn't want anyone to have his photograph. I appreciate that you've fallen out with him, but does he have a key to your house?'

'Yes he has. I never bothered to have it off him; he's my own flesh and blood all said and done. He could have nipped in any time I was at golf.'

I glanced at Prim. 'Only one thing for it then, love. We're going to have to go back to Barassie.'

22

As it happened, she had to go to see Mira Donn on her own. The Global Wrestling Alliance circus was in London that weekend, and I had to head for Hillington to join up with the team before we caught the plane south. The Barassie trip was no problem for us, though, since I was travelling alone for once, Prim having decided that she had too much work on her hands.

I was looking forward to the trip, since Daze was back. Everett Davis, the Big Man himself, had signed himself off from the States for a few weeks to appear in the European shows.

He was at the front door of the headquarters building when my taxi arrived, all seven feet, two inches of him, supervising the loading of our team bus. 'Hey, Oz, my man,' he boomed in his deep, dark chocolate voice. 'So how's the movie business?'

'Fascinating,' I told him. 'I've been shot at once this week already.'

'You'll have a quieter time this weekend,' he promised me. 'You got no action this time.' I was relieved about that. A few weeks before, Darius Henke and I had staged a mock confrontation in the ring, which had ended with me being choke-slammed by the Black Angel of Death, as the marks knew him. There is a public belief that when wrestlers are slammed down hard on to the ring floor, or when they slam other people, somehow it doesn't hurt. This is wrong: it does.

As usual, the roadies had gone ahead of us. When we arrived at the London Arena just before six p.m., it was set up and ready for us. The dressing-room accommodation there isn't bad, better than most in fact, but for a troupe as big as ours it's a long way short of one for one.

So when the doorman brought in the bouquet as the guys were changing for the Friday evening run-through, and brought it straight to me, I didn't half take some razzing, I can tell you. At first, I assumed that it was Prim's way of telling me she wished she was there, but I was wrong. When I glanced at the label I saw that it read, 'For Oz, love Ronnie.'

Mrs Barowitz, the blonde toy doll who had started me on my voice-over career. I had arranged to send her the tickets I had promised her, and then I had forgotten all about her; ungrateful sod that I am.

'Hey Mr Announcer,' Bret Austin called out. He was one half of the current tag team champions. 'Whatcha going to do wiff them?' Bret's a Londoner and his real name is Phil Mitchell; but he could hardly use that for wrestling, could he.

'I haven't a bloody clue, mate,' I told him, honestly. 'Why don't you give them to your wife?'

'I was 'oping you'd say that,' he grinned. 'I could use the brownie points.'

I handed him the flowers. 'Don't forget to bin the card.'

He glanced at it and frowned. 'Who the 'ell's Ronnie? You got a poofter admirer, Oz?'

'Very far from it, my friend,' I assured him. Even then I didn't quite realise the truth I spoke. I found out, though, when I checked into my hotel suite after the rehearsal. I took my bag straight into the bedroom, and unpacked it carefully, hanging my ring suit in the wardrobe and putting the rest of my things in a drawer. I was closing it when I heard a sound from the bathroom; a soft, splashing sound.

Even then, I really did think when I opened the door, that Prim had decided to surprise me. But no, there she was in the bath, all of her, none of it covered discreetly by bubbles like you see on telly; Ronnie Barowitz.

'Hello Oz,' she simpered. 'Surprise, surprise.'

'Jesus Christ,' I exclaimed. 'How the hell did you get in here?'

She smiled. 'It's amazing what you can do with fifty quid and a porter. Even in a place like this.' And then she stood up.

Most people look far better with their clothes on, no doubt about that. No doubt either that Ronnie belongs in the minority, even though she's a fake blonde. She stood there, Venus risen, and I have to admit that I felt myself rising too.

She beckoned to me. 'Come on in—'

'Don't say it, Mrs Barowitz – the water's lovely.' She laughed, but I heard it die in her throat as I turned and walked out of the bathroom. I was in the small sitting room, looking out over the Thames when she appeared in the doorway, draped in a hotel dressing-gown; it was unfastened.

She stepped close to me. 'I'm sorry, Oz. Maybe this was too much of a surprise for you.'

'You can say that again.'

'Okay.' She looked up at me, blatantly, and let the dressing-gown fall to the floor. 'But now you've got over it, what do you say?'

I bent, taking care not to bump into any part of her pink

body, picked up the robe, and draped it around her once more.

'I say thanks for fixing me up with that voice-over, Ronnie; but now I'm going to dinner. Please don't be here when I get back.'

I turned as I reached the door. 'You don't know how lucky you are. Any other weekend, my fiancée would have been with me. If she'd walked in there and found you in the bath, she'd have fucking drowned you in it.

'Give my regards to Richard.'

Before I joined the team in the bar I paid a call on the duty manager and told him that it would be a good idea if he fired one of his porters. When I went back upstairs two-and-a-half hours later she was gone; save for a small present in the toilet, she might never have been there.

I said nothing to anyone about my groupie. Actually, they aren't unusual around the GWA. Quite a few of the lads have girlie fan clubs, and Sally Crockett, the ladies champ, used to have hordes drooling after her before she married big Jerry. Everett has a simple rule on job-related sex; don't do anything that could draw down flak on the GWA; I didn't think for a moment that Ronnie could have, but I was quietly pleased with myself for the way I'd handled it. The truth is that the old Oz Blackstone, the one from three or four years back, would have been right in there. Noosh was right; I'd grown up.

I looked for Ronnie at ringside next night. just before our live event went on air. There was no sign of her in the block where she should have sat, although all the places seemed to be taken. The show itself made me forget all about her. The GWA is a very professional outfit and its standards are consistently high, but the London Arena show was a cracker, highlighted by the return of Daze Everett in his new-look gold outfit, reclaiming the European Title after a spectacular battle with the Black Angel, one of the very few guys in the business who is big enough to look convincing against him.

As always, the crowd was pumped up to a frenzy by the end, and took a while to clear the Arena. We have a cute way of helping them. As the house lights go up, several of the performers appear in the foyer, and invariably are surrounded by autograph hunters, speeding the flow out of the hall. Sometimes I join them, but that night, all I wanted to do was get on to the bus and back to the hotel for dinner.

I changed quickly and stepped out of the stage door, my suit bag over my shoulder. The bus was parked at the top of an alley: a long dark alley. I was about halfway towards it when a man stepped out of the shadows, looking right at me; somehow I knew he wasn't going to ask me for a light – not that he'd have been on; I don't smoke.

He stood there blocking my way, then began to move towards me. I glanced over my shoulder and saw, fleetingly, that there was another guy behind me, with the same determined expression on his face. I realised that I was the meat in a particularly nasty sandwich. I backed off from the first man, letting my bag slip to the ground, trying to think myself out of this situation. No one said anything; we all knew what was on the agenda.

I kept backing off, until I felt the man behind me grab my arm. Still I didn't turn, but dropped my right shoulder, leaned back into him, and swung my elbow into his gut as fast and as hard as I could. I felt as much as heard his gasp, and had a good look at him for the first time as he started to double up.

I had been taught several wrestling moves by the guys, but I had never used any of them for real. In a more confined space, I'd have been dead, but there was room to move in the alley. I picked the first hold to come to mind; clasping my hands behind the guy's head as it came down, I jammed my shoulder up under his throat and dropped into a sitting position on the ground, pulling him down with me. That is the patented finishing manoeuvre of a very famous wrestler. He knows how to do it without hurting people: I don't. My sudden stop and the man's momentum drove the hard corner of my shoulder into his windpipe, putting him out of action for the foreseeable future.

The heavy in front of me hesitated for a second. I guess he'd been told that this job would be a milk run. While he was thinking, I ran at him and smashed a stiff-arm across his chest. He was a bit bigger than me, but then so is Liam Matthews and I knocked him over with that move once. The difference was that Liam meant to fall; this bloke slipped and sat down hard, but he bounced straight back up. I sensed trouble, for I was running out of tricks. He didn't know that, though, so, while he was still trying to size me up, I poked my fingers into his eyes, then dropped my right shoulder and hit him with another stiff-arm, upwards, straight in the balls this time.

As the bloke hit the deck with a whimper, I felt another hand on my shoulder; God, I hadn't noticed the third one. I had worked through my repertoire, so I simply spun round and threw a punch. Fortunately, Liam Matthews has seen my right-hander before and he has good reflexes, so he swayed out of the way.

'Christ, Oz, we should have had the cameras out here,' he drawled. 'That was pretty impressive.'

'How long have you been here?' I demanded.

'Long enough so's you wouldn't have been hurt. Who are these guys anyway?'

I looked blankly at him. 'No idea.'

'Let's find out then.' The guy with the sore throat had also bitten into his tongue. Given that he was choking and had blood pouring from his mouth, he wasn't going to be saying anything for a while, so Liam stepped up to his pal, who was on his knees trying to think about legging it, and kicked him in the ribs. 'What're you doin' here?'

'Just lookin' for someone to mug, mate,' the heavy wheezed.

Liam thought this was hilarious. He roared with laugher, then slapped the man hard across the face. 'As a general rule, friend, muggers tend to avoid GWA shows.' He dug his thumb hard into the side of his neck. 'Now, who sent you after my friend Oz here? Tell me and you can walk away from here. Any more bullshit and you won't.'

'I don't know who sent us,' the man protested. 'It was a bloke in a pub, this lunchtime.'

'What did he look like?'

'I dunno. Just an ordinary bloke. About thirty, I s'ppose; wore a black shirt and jeans . . . sunglasses, a pair of them Rayban jobs.'

'So what did he say to you?'

'He told us that a pal of his wanted this geezer duffed up, 'cos 'e'd done something 'e shouldn't. He'd heard we 'andle that sort of stuff. He gave us two hundred quid, and promised us another two once the job was done.'

'And how was he going to know that?'

'He'd have known when the guy didn't show up on the telly. We were meant to break both 'is arms, like.'

'Sure, 'n you mean like this?' Quick as a flash, Liam grabbed his right wrist, pulled it up, and twisted it, hard; I heard a crack. The man screamed in pain, as the muscular wrestler pulled him to his feet by his collar. 'That's the hardest two hundred you've ever earned, pal,' he murmured, then amazingly, took a ten pound note from his pocket and shoved it into his good hand. 'You and your mate, get yourselves a taxi to the hospital, and don't even dream about my pal again.'

As the two hooligans dragged themselves painfully out of the alley, Liam turned to me. 'So what have you been up to, Oz?' he asked, with a smile. 'What have you been doing that you shouldn't?'

At that moment there was only one thought in my mind. I told him about Ronnie Barowitz's ambush in my hotel room, and about me giving her the bum's rush. 'Maybe she told Richard, her old man, and he took offence; got someone from his factory to find those two clowns.'

'What? He sent those guys to cripple you for *not* shafting his wife?' He bellowed with laughter again.

'Okay, it sounds weak, I admit. But from what I've seen of the two of them, whatever Ronnie wants, Ronnie gets. If she went home and told him that I'd made a pass at her, he'd have believed her, no question. And if she'd said she wanted me sorted, he'd have done it.' I scowled at him.

'Anyhow, whatever the truth is, we've blown the chance of finding out. If we'd got the name of the pub from those two I could have had it staked it out and caught their client if he came back.'

'Fat chance of him coming back. Here, how did that fella know you're on telly?'

'No trick there. It's not just kids who watch us.'

Back at the hotel, I opened the door of my room cautiously, just in case there were any more surprises waiting for me. It was clear, but nonetheless, I spent the rest of my time in London looking over my shoulder. By the time we had finished recording the Sunday show, I was feeling pretty paranoid.

In fact the Ronnie incident preyed on me so much that it wasn't until I was almost home that another possibility dawned on me.

23

At first I hadn't intended to tell Prim about my exciting weekend, but I have this belief that the first secret in a relationship can be the seed of a disease which can destroy it in time. So I blurted it all out as she drove me home from Glasgow Airport in the Freelander.

She was far more worried about the two hooligans than about Ronnie. I was pleased at first, until she told me why. 'She's a man-eater, dear; I knew that the moment I saw her. She's a predator, and you're insecure when it comes to aggressive women.'

I felt myself pouting. 'I'd prefer to say that I like to make my own choices rather than being chosen. I chose to think of you and showed her the door.'

'I'll express my gratitude later,' she promised. 'Now about these thugs. Were you hurt at all?'

'I've got a bruise on my shoulder, that's all.' I laughed. 'When Liam told Everett about it, he wanted to put me in a match.'

'What?'

'Don't worry, I told him to forget it.'

'We won't see those men again, will we?'

'No danger. They were hospital cases; I'm pretty sure they'll be retiring from the thugging business. Now, tell me about Mira Donn. Did she give you a photograph of her boy?'

Primavera grinned. 'Now that's an interesting story too. I went to see her on Friday evening, as we agreed; I didn't tell her about the firebomb, just that we still needed to speak with him. I told her it would help us if we knew what he looked like. She told me that as she was sure he had done nothing, she was quite happy to give me a photo.

'Then, just like Uncle Joseph, she went to look for one, and came back a few minutes later looking puzzled. She said that she couldn't find any, that all the pictures with Stephen in them had disappeared. I asked if she could lend me a negative so I could make a print; she had another look through her box, but the negs were all missing too.'

'Do you think she was just kidding you along?' I asked. 'Trying to get out of giving you one?'

'No, the woman was genuinely surprised, embarrassed and a bit rattled too, I think. I got the impression that she was beginning to believe that her Stephen might have had something to do with Susie's letters. So at that point, I asked her straight out if she had heard from him. She said that she hadn't – but of course we know from Mike that he called her last week. She was covering up for him.'

'Was she indeed? Did you tell her that we'd been to Joe's looking for a picture?'

'Yes.'

'In that case, I reckon she's figured out that Stephen knows we're on to him and that he's been back to her place, and to his uncle's, to make life a bit more difficult for us.'

'If she wasn't covering up for him before, she is now. Let's see what else she's been up to.'

As Prim swung the car on to the Kingston Bridge, I could

see our flat. But I was buzzing; I couldn't wait until we got there. I took my mobile from my pocket and dialled Susie's number. I was pleased when Mike answered, for I didn't know how much he'd told her of his operation.

'Hello mate,' he said cheerily. 'You back from London?'

'Nearly. I'm on my way in from the airport. Listen sunshine, we've drawn a blank on photos of young Mr Donn.' Quickly I told him of the missing family snapshots.

'Jeez,' he whispered. 'If there was ever any doubt that he's our man, that seals it.'

'Sure, but there's something else I'm wondering about him. A couple of guys tried to do me over in London on Saturday night.'

'They what?! You all right?'

'Sure, Liam and I sorted them, no problem.' I laughed. 'You don't mess with the GWA, mate. I thought I knew who sent them, but now I'm not so sure. I don't want to say too much on this thing, but did you pick up any traffic from Barassie on Friday evening?'

There was a short silence. 'No one's reported anything to me, but I'll check up, and let you know.'

'Thanks. While you're doing it, bear this in mind: it occurred to me on the plane. The lady in question's a lecturer in communications, and she has a computer. I wonder if she uses e-mail?'

'Good thinking, Oz. I'll let you know. I'll try to get back to you tonight.'

24

As it happened, I didn't hear from Mike until next morning, and rather earlier than I had hoped, at that. I had a one-day voice-over in Edinburgh on the Tuesday of that week, then two days' filming on Deeside on the Wednesday and Thursday, before heading off to Dublin with the GWA on the Friday, so I had decided, reasonably, I thought, that Monday would be a day off.

That's why I was in bed when the front doorbell sounded at five past nine: not the buzzer from the street entrance, but the doorbell itself. It rang three times before I was fully awake, and twice more as I stomped downstairs, tying the belt of my dressing gown and wondering which of my effing neighbours had been foolish enough to interrupt my rest.

'Jesus, Oz,' said Dylan, grinning and resplendent in a tan Dannimac raincoat, as I swung the door open. 'I've seen people in Casualty on a Friday night looking in better nick than you, son.'

'And I've seen better dressed postmen,' I growled back at him. 'How'd you get in?'

'I bumped into Prim on her way out just as I was arriving; she let me in. Have you decided to retire, then?'

'Bloody hell, Michael,' I barked. 'In the last few days, I've acted in a major movie, done two international television shows, found a naked lady in my bath, been shot at – or nearly

– by a helmeted motorcycle assassin, and set upon by two second-division heavies with instructions to break both my arms. I think I'm entitled to a wee lie-in, don't you?'

I stood aside to let him come in. 'You know where the coffee and stuff is. Make us some, while I get dressed.'

It took me just under ten minutes to shower and throw on some clothes. By the time I ambled barefoot into the kitchen, still running my electric shaver over my chin, Mike had made not just coffee but two bacon rolls for each of us. 'HQ canteen shut, is it?' I asked. 'I'm not sure I want any of those.'

'Come on, pal,' he grinned, 'you want to play at being a polis, you have to act like one. Hope you like brown sauce on your bacon, by the way.'

'I'll slum it with you,' I grunted, finishing my shave. I glanced out of the window; it was a grey, damp morning, a reminder that winter was only a couple of months away.

'This is elevenses for me, you realise,' said Dylan. 'I've been in the office since just after seven checking up on Mrs Donn. She didn't have a call from Stephen on Friday; that I know for sure. Nor did she phone him.'

'Dammit.'

'Ah, but . . . your wee flash of intuition worked out. The woman is on e-mail. When did Prim visit her?'

'Just after five.'

'Thought so. That got me excited, because about two hours after that, Mrs D connected to her internet server and sent a message down the line.'

'Can you read it off the server?'

'In theory we could. What we have is a burst of digital information, that could be decoded, but that would take cleverer people than we have. But anyhow, we don't need to do that. I had a word with the service provider and persuaded him to give me the name of the addressee. The message went to S Donn at Hotmail.'

'Hotmail?'

'Yes, it's an international e-mail clearing house that anyone can subscribe to. You tap into it through the Web, and you can access it from anywhere. So, I went on line and I accessed the boy's mailbox.'

'But doesn't he have a password? I thought everyone had.'

Dylan nodded. 'Sure, but that's not much of a barrier. Have you any idea how many people use someone's Christian name? Have you any idea how many use their partner's or their mother's? I just keyed in M. I. R. A. and, open sesame, I was right in there. Stephen picked up his mother's message less than two hours after she sent it.'

'Have you got the message?'

'No, he'll have stored that on his own terminal; it's been wiped from Hotmail. His log's there, though, and it shows the time of transmission and collection. You don't have to be a computer genius to work out what it said, though. "Dear son, Why is this man Blackstone and his girlfriend asking after you, and why did you nick all your photos from my house and from your Uncle Joe's?" Or words to that effect.'

'Do we know where he was when he collected it?'

'No, it couldn't tell me that.'

'Still,' I said, 'now you can monitor his e-mail traffic, wherever he is.'

Dylan shook his head, even as he ripped a chunk off one of his rolls. 'Not exactly,' he replied, when he could. 'I'll have left a trace on the log this morning myself. If I go in regularly, he'll twig for sure. Even doing it just once, there's a chance he'll notice the entry and know from the time that it wasn't him. If he does that, then straight away he'll change the password to something we'll never guess.'

I had to agree with this. Finding the mailbox was a bonus, but it wasn't going to unlock the secrets of Stephen Donn's world, or even tell us where he was.

'So, Oz,' Mike asked, once we had finished breakfast, 'what's your interest in all this?'

He was so chuffed with himself over his computer trickery that he'd missed the bloody obvious.

'Remember the naked lady I mentioned earlier? The one I found in my bath? As the Sunday tabloids say, I declined her offer and left – well actually I told her to bugger off. When those two hard men showed up twenty-four hours later I assumed straight away that she or her husband was connected to it.

'But suppose, just suppose, Stephen Donn was sufficiently annoyed by his mother's message to want to put me out of business for a while. Even if he was in Amsterdam he'd have had time to get over to London, source some hired muscle and put it on my trail.'

'Why should he even know about you?' Mike protested.

'For openers, my surname must be familiar to him; Jan worked at Gantry's before him, remember. Also he blew up Susie's motor in my car park. If he's been stalking her, there's every chance he knows me and how I relate to her.'

'But how would he know where to find you?'

'Anyone who's watched the GWA in the last couple of

years knows I'm part of their set-up. Anyone who's watched satellite sports promotions in the last month would have known I was due in London last weekend. Anyone who can read a newspaper could have known I'm in Miles's movie, as did the person who hired those gorillas. They said that my pulling out of the film was to be the trigger for the second half of the payment for the job.

'I tell you, mate, the more I think about it, the more I'm convinced that Stephen Donn put me on the spot, rather than Richard Barowitz or his wife.'

'So where are these heavies now? Have the police got them?'

'No, they were a bit damaged, so we let them go. The GWA doesn't need that sort of publicity.'

'Great! That's another possible lead to Donn gone down the pan. This guy's trying to kill my girlfriend, Oz. You have a couple of guys who might have met him and you let them swan off into the bloody night!'

His sudden show of irritation took me by surprise, but I had to admit that it was justified. 'I'm sorry man,' I said. 'The Donn connection didn't occur to me at the time.' Then I had an afterthought. 'You could always check the hospitals. One of them had damage to his throat and a lacerated tongue, and the other had a broken forearm, or wrist.

'Even if you do find them, though, you won't get much of a description out of them. All they could tell us was that the bloke who paid them was ordinary looking and that he wore Raybans.'

'Fuck the description. The next time Donn sees you on telly and realises that you're in one piece, he might go looking for his money back. If he does that I'd like to have some people of my own there to meet him, as well as your two damaged Cockney pals.'

25

Maybe I should have been, but I wasn't too bothered about the London episode being repeated. If Stephen Donn had sent me a message, effectively it had been received, since Prim and I were no longer involved in the search for him, and wouldn't be visiting either his uncle or his mother again. If Richard Barowitz had been behind it – well, I'd already decided that I wouldn't be doing any more voice-overs for Roxy Matrix and their alternative bloody humanoids.

Happily, my schedule for the rest of the week was so busy that I was able to forget all about the London experience. The Edinburgh voice-over was a piece of cake – literally; it was an ad for a Scots bakery chain – but my two days on Deeside introduced me to some new aspects of movie-making.

Miles had said that my scenes would be simple, and he was good as his word. The most difficult thing I had to do was to walk in on an argument between him and Dawn, and deliver the deathless line, 'Hey, leave me out of this!' – with style, mind you. All the same, it was fascinating to watch, in another setting, the care and precision with which the operation was run. There were close-ups, two-shots, three-shots, and the positioning and backgrounds had to be right for every one of them.

The mansion was even bigger than I had expected, with a long, south-facing drawing room which was big enough to accommodate actors, production crew and equipment; a major cost saver as opposed to replicating it on a set, Miles assured me.

My first three-way scene took up a whole day; Miles and Dawn had always struck me as a happy relaxed couple, but there, in the office as it were, sparks flew all day as he fought for perfection in the scene. They were meant to be arguing on screen, but there were moments off-camera when I wondered if they were keeping it up simply to preserve the mood, or were really going at it.

I had a room in the house for the three nights I was up there. At the end of that difficult, but ultimately rewarding, day's shooting, Dawn went off for a bath while Miles and I sloped off to the study for a soothing gin and tonic. 'I didn't realise you could be such a bastard on set,' I told him, settling back into a big, over-stuffed armchair. 'If I talked to Prim like that I'd have the imprint of her engagement ring in the middle of my forehead.'

'I'm a perfectionist, mate,' he said, his accent becoming noticeably more Aussie, as it always did in private. 'I direct most of my own movies because I'm lousy at taking direction myself. I could name half-a-dozen people in Hollywood – and you'd know them all – who won't work with me. If I see something that I know would make a movie better, then I tell them; most LA egos can't take that.

'Dawn's made the same way. She has her own ideas and won't keep them to herself; that's why I fell for her in the first place. When she was cast in *Kidnapped*, she had only a tiny little part, no more than a week's work. Yet on her second day on set when I was laying down the way I wanted the scene played she said in her little Scots voice, "Excuse me, but don't you think it would be better if . . ."

'If she wasn't so fucking gorgeous I might have fired her there and then – my ego's as well-developed as any of those guys I mentioned. Instead, I thought about what she had said, and took part of it on board. We never looked back from that moment on; now when we work together I know that she's going to say what she thinks. I might not always agree with it, and when I don't we go at it hammer and tongs, yet at the end of the day she makes me a better director and I make her a better actor.'

He grinned as he got up to mix us two more G and Ts. 'If it didn't work that way we'd have gone the way of most movie couples long ago. As it is, we'll last for ever. She doesn't know this – don't you tell her, either – but when this project is wrapped up, the director credits will be Miles Grayson and Dawn Phillips.'

'Hey, that's great,' I told him. 'Can I tell Prim?'

'If you think she'll keep it to herself, sure you can. Don't mention it to Elanore, though. She'd burst her girdle.'

I studied him as he gazed out of the window. Somehow I knew that he was contemplating an evening shot, making use of the spectacular effect of the sinking sun as it washed the trees which bounded the mansion. 'You really love your work, Miles, don't you,' I said.

'Sure,' he replied. 'I can't imagine it any other way. Don't you?'

'I would if I knew what my work was. I know I'm past my sell-by date in the job I started on, acting as a lawyer's leg-man. Prim's keeping that business going, but I've reached the stage when I don't enjoy it any more. The truth is it was never any more than okay; it paid the bills and gave me a lifestyle, but there was never any fulfilment. The only time it gave me a buzz was when I found myself involved with real detective work, and that only ever happened by accident.

'My GWA work is different, though. Bizarre as it may be, I'm doing something creative there. In my voice-overs too, and now here, even though it's a one-off. But always I have the feeling that I'm just stumbling along.'

'Then take control, Oz. You're privileged; thanks to the lottery you can decide what it is you want to do and go for it, shit or bust. You say this movie is a one-off, but there's no reason why it should be. You ain't going to win an Oscar, but you're competent in what you're doing. I'd cast you again, and so will others.'

I had to laugh. 'You saying I should become an actor?'

'No,' he shot back. 'I'm saying you could. I'd recommend a little formal drama training, but it's open to you as a career option.'

'If I want a career.'

'Of course you do. You're a young guy and you're full of energy. You can't sit still.'

He was right; I tried that once, and it was a near-disaster.

'I don't know what I'd be doing now if I hadn't found this business. I'd have played cricket for a while, I guess. I can't bat worth a light, but I was a pretty quick bowler. I might have managed a few one-day games for Australia. But after that, I'd probably have wound up selling cars, or maybe insurance.

'Every day I say a little prayer of thanks that twenty-odd years ago, I answered a newspaper ad looking for young guys to work as extras or minor players in a movie. I've been hooked on this business ever since. It's the breath of life to me, and I'd die as a person without it.'

'Do you have any ambitions left, then?' I asked. This had turned into the deepest conversation I'd ever had with Miles. I'd known him for going on three years, but I hadn't learned much about him that I couldn't have found out in a newspaper.

'Sure I have,' he replied 'and it'll go on for as long as I do. I want to make my next movie better than my last, and so on. It's nothing to do with money; that just happens, and it doesn't have a hell of a lot to do with art. I'm not Bergman, or Bresson; I'm trying to be the movie equivalent of Robert Louis Stevenson; a great story-teller and entertainer.

'My motivation is constant improvement; that and trying to reach as many people with my work as possible. There's nothing I wouldn't do if it was in the interests of one of my movies.'

'Including his own stunts.' Dawn's voice came from the door of the study. We stood – gentlemen to a fault, both of us – as she came into the room; she was dressed in a simple blouse and skirt, and the ends of her hair were still wet from the shower. 'I warn you now, Oz. If you ever work with us again, and there's action involved, make damn sure there's a clause in your contract that says he has to use a stand-in.'

'Don't worry,' I assured her. 'After last weekend, I don't need to be told that.'

26

For the next couple of weeks I settled into what most people would call chaos with just a dash of organisation; for me it was a normal life. Most of my time was booked, Sly Burr having worked a couple of London voice-overs into my movie schedule, but I managed to go into the office on a couple of occasions, just to make sure that Prim, Lulu and the new assistant were running Blackstone Phillips Investigations to my satisfaction.

I realised very quickly that they were doing a far more disciplined job than I ever had, and were providing just as good a service, but no way would I ever have admitted that to them.

Primavera came with me to Dublin with the GWA, and to Copenhagen the following weekend. She was popular with the wrestling team, most of whom remembered her first appearance among them, on a dramatic night in Barcelona – a night I will never forget either, but for a different reason.

By the end of the following week, my filming in the North was over; next on the schedule were two weeks in the studio in London for my off-camera narration, and for a few more scenes that Miles had mentioned, casually over dinner, on my first night in the Deeside mansion.

I'm pretty fit, but the action was catching up with me. I was knackered, and so I was pleased that the GWA had a weekend off, thanks to a big golf tournament which was dominating the satellite television channels. Prim and I decided that we would get out of Glasgow, and spend a couple of days in St Andrews with my sister, my nephews, and of course Wallace, my old flatmate.

They were all pleased to see us when we arrived at the freshly decorated bungalow, with its view across the links; none more so, it seemed, than Wallace. Green iguanas are reptiles, right, and generally reptiles have very small brains, capable of focusing only on catching and crunching insects, or in the case of crocodiles, any large mammals which are daft enough to drink from the wrong river. I doubt if they even think about sex; although . . .

My point is that when I gave him to my nephews on a permanent basis I didn't expect my old chum to have a memory which stretched back beyond his last bowl of Wonder Wienie Iguana Superfood, yet every time I walk into a room and he's there, no matter how many other people are around, he ambles across to me, climbs up my leg and settles across my shoulders. He has five strong talons on each foot, so I have to be careful what I wear when I'm seeing him. The first time we visited Ellen and the boys in their new house, he did for a new silk shirt as well as leaving some choice scratches.

The performance was repeated when I went into the boys' playroom, soon after we arrived at St Andrews that Friday evening; I'll swear that as he secured himself on my old denim shirt he even rolled an appraising reptilian eye at Prim. After all, he played a significant role during the first night we ever spent under the same roof.

Ignoring his presence, and with Jonathan and Colin

following, we wandered through to the kitchen where Ellie was preparing a meal. When I'd called her to ask if we could come, I'd told her we'd go out to eat, but she wouldn't hear of it. Very few people are capable of throwing a chilling look down a telephone line, but my sister is.

'You can take him with you, back to Glasgow, if you like, Oz,' she said. 'Didn't you ever try to house train him?'

I felt my nephews' eyes settle on me. They weren't taking their mother's threat seriously; they were used to the sparring between us and were waiting for my counter-punch. I raised an imperious eyebrow. 'Of course. When he lived with me in the loft he used to climb up on the roof and crap in the guttering. Try leaving a window open.'

'The insurance company would just love that. Ach, the truth is the old boy's not that bad. Most of the time he goes outside to a corner of the garden, or he does it in his cage. I don't give him the run of the house like you used to.'

I ruffled wee Colin's hair. 'What about these two?' I asked. 'You got them trained yet?'

'In the bathroom department, yes. But in terms of general behaviour . . .' She pointed to Colin; it was enough to make his face redden. 'That one there, he's six now; you'd think he'd know better than to get himself locked in someone's cellar.'

'You what?'

'Aye! He was playing with a bunch of his pals the other day, where they shouldn't have been, in the garden of a big old house down the street. It belongs to an old man who's retired from business. This one climbed in a wee window, then fell to the floor and couldn't get out. The place was dark and the door was locked, so he starts screaming. His pals were afraid of the old boy, so they came running to me.'

I whistled. 'Jesus, what an error of judgement on their part.' Beside me, Jonathan, the older wiser, brother, nodded agreement.

'As they found out,' said Ellie grimly, with a glance at Colin. 'The upshot was that I had to ring the man's doorbell and ask him if he could let my son out of his cellar. He wasn't very pleasant about it either; chuntered on about getting the police.'

'That's right,' Jonathan chuckled, 'until Mum ripped into him about leaving his window open in the first place. "It's an invitation to curious children", she said.' I looked at him, astonished. Although he was only ten, he had picked up about five years' worth of maturity in the two since his parents had split up; on top of that I realised that he had become a terrific mimic. I felt slightly sorry for the old man with the big house; even if Ellie hadn't been there, he'd have had to deal with Jonathan.

My sister glowered at her younger son. I sympathised with him; as a kid I'd been on the receiving end of that stare. 'He's into everything, that one. I've told him that next time he gets himself locked in somewhere I'll leave him there overnight,' her eyes fixed on mine, 'just like Dad did with you once.'

The boys stared up at me. 'True,' I admitted. 'When I was about your age, Colin, I used to climb up the step-ladder into our attic. I had a one-man gang hut up there. Parts of it weren't floored, so my mother was always telling me not to, but I kept doing it, until one day your Grandpa took the ladder away.

'I thought it was a game until it got dark.'

Prim squeezed my elbow. 'Pity we haven't got an attic,' she said.

'You can shut up for a start,' I retorted. 'Elanore's told me all about you as a kid. Watering the plants, indeed.' She shut up.

We had a good evening, the six of us. Wallace spent most of it on my shoulders, Colin spent most of it enjoying having a man at the table, and Jonathan spent most of it chatting Prim up. Once they were banished to bed and the iguana to his cage, us adults settled down to catching up.

As a dutiful brother, I made a point of asking Our Ellie if everything in her life was okay. 'Not bad, son,' she assured me. 'My divorce went through without a hitch. Alan's being very good about the maintenance money for the boys; comes through by bank transfer on the first of every month. He comes over to see them every couple of months, and they spent the first half of August with him, but of course you'd know that, since they were in your apartment.' In fact the boys had spent all of the school holidays in St Marti, with their Mum during July and with their father for the rest of the time.

'Everything's fine on the job front, too,' Ellie went on. 'I got a promotion last week, I like the people I work with, and the school roll keeps going up.'

'And on the other front?'

She grinned at me; an un-Ellie-like grin, shy around the edges. 'On the other front, I'm getting enough of the other, thank you very much, and that's all I'm saying. I'm happy as I am, especially since I learned that a woman doesn't have to wake up to the sound of a man snoring next to her to live an enjoyable life.

'I've got a lot to thank you for, both of you.'

'The house is nothing,' said Prim. 'You'd have done the same if it was you who won the lottery.'

'I didn't just mean the house. I was in a real rut out there in France with Alan, all on my own in that museum village. I was bloody miserable, in fact. Then you two showed up out of the blue, footloose and fancy free, in the middle of an adventure. Right then I saw what my life was compared to yours, and I realised that I didn't have to put up with it.

'For a good part of my life, Oz, I tried to set an example for you, as my wee brother. It was a real culture shock to discover that I should be following yours. But you taught me that very important thing when it really mattered.' She looked at me and said the most tender thing I'd ever heard from her. 'You saved my life, brither, in a very real sense.'

I grinned at her. 'You've got it wrong, Ellie. I did follow your example; what I became is what you made me, as much as Mum and Dad. After Mum died, you lost yourself for a while, that was all. Not that those years with Alan were a total loss: far from it. See those two through there? Go back twenty-five years or so and they could be us.'

We killed a dozen cold Buds as we sat there looking out of the big bay window at the darkening night across the Old Course, and eventually, at the moonlight on the Eden Estuary beyond. We brought Ellen up to date with our business, with my movie-making and with our wedding plans, which had changed since Prim had laid down the law to her mother in Auchterarder. To be fair to everyone in terms of travel we had decided that we would do everything in Gleneagles Hotel: wedding, reception, first night, the lot.

'And after that?' asked Ellie.

'Somewhere sunny,' said Prim. 'We've never been to Asia; there maybe.'

We were so relaxed come bedtime that we almost forgot to plan the next day, but eventually we agreed that the girls would go shopping in Dundee and that I would 'do something nice' with my nephews, as long as it didn't involve taking them among bawling, swearing men at a football match.

Next morning, I decided that Ellie's conditions would allow me to take them to see Raith Rovers, in Kirkcaldy; the only bad experience they were likely to suffer there was loneliness. But before then, the big city of St Andrews was ours to explore, with its crowded golf courses, its wind-blown, chilly North Sea beaches, its shops – none of them with the slightest attraction for a ten-year-old, far less for a six-year-old.

Fortunately there's always the Castle. St Andrews is rich in Reformation history; bloody history at that. I walked the boys along to the Martyr's Monument on the Scores, erected on the spot on which George Wishart, the unfortunate who gave the thing its name, was burned at the stake. I toned down the details of the story as far as I could, but my nephews eyes were still gleaming as we reached the old ruin further down the road . . . kids are sadistic little buggers, aren't they?

It was still only mid-morning, so the Castle wasn't busy, with only a few visitors dotted around. 'See that big window there?' I said, as we stepped through the entry kiosk. 'That's where Wishart's pals took their revenge. An army of them, with old John Knox among them, took the place by storm, and hanged Cardinal Beaton right there in that very window, for everyone to see. Then they occupied the castle, until it was recaptured by the King's troops.'

'Who was John Mox?' wee Colin piped up.

'A Reformer,' I told him. 'Not a very nice man either, by all accounts. No one was very nice in those days, on either side. In this very castle there's a thing called the Bottle Dungeon. It's no more than a hole in the ground, hollowed out of the rock. They used to drop prisoners in there; the walls are smooth and they slope out on the way down, so that they couldn't climb out, or stand up straight either. The lucky ones had food dropped in; the unlucky ones . . . didn't.'

'Want to see it, want to see it!' Colin clamoured.

'All in good time,' I told him. 'There's something else I want to show you first.'

During the siege of the Castle, after Knox's, or Mox's, lot had topped the infamous Cardinal, the occupants had an ingenious idea. They would tunnel out under the walls, give the King's forces a right doing, and disappear in the confusion. What they didn't know was that the besieging commander was thinking along the same lines.

As it happened, the rock on which St Andrews Castle is built was too tough and too difficult to excavate, so neither side made it all the way through, but the aborted tunnels are still there. For me, they're the most interesting part of the place, and they're always my first port of call. The tunnel to the outside is as you'd expect low and narrow, and so we had to slide in.

'Follow me, now,' I told the boys. I felt a hand gripping the leg of my jeans.

'Didn't they hear each other tunnelling Uncle Oz?' asked Jonathan.

'No one really knows. Maybe they did; maybe that's why they both stopped.'

'How did the siege end?'

'The Reformers were starved out in the end. They surrendered; Knox was sent to the galleys for his pains. He was lucky he didn't go the same way as Wishart and Beaton.

'You all right, Colin?' I called back. There was no answer. 'Colin!' I shouted again.

'He's not here Uncle Oz,' said Jonathan. 'He was here to begin with, but he's not now.'

'The wee sod! Come on, let's back out of here and find him.'

'He'll have gone to find the Bottle Dungeon. That's what he wanted to see first.'

'He'll have a close-up view of the back of my hand,' I muttered. 'Come on.' Jonathan, impressed by my threat, trotted along at my side as I set off across the open castle green to the seaward wall, beneath which the Dungeon was hollowed out. I expected to find the wee chap waiting for me, wearing his patented guilty look which he knew always softened me up, but there was no sign of him. In fact there was no one to be seen.

The old familiar tension in my stomach began as soon as we reached the old cell. Naturally, Historic Scotland, which manages the place for the Nation, doesn't want to put the punters in peril, so there's a protective grille over the hole through which the tenants were dropped in.

The grille had been removed; it was lying at the side of the entrance. Jonathan ran over to it and picked it up, as if to replace it. He's a strong wee lad, but I could see that it was heavy for him.

'Put that down,' I snapped. He isn't used to having me speak sharply to him, so he did as he was told, at once. I dropped to my knees beside the Dungeon, and looked down, but it seemed pitch-dark. I moved around to the other side, allowing as much light in as possible, and leaned into the narrow opening.

'Colin!' I shouted, but there was no reply. I peered into the enclosure, and gradually my eyes became accustomed to the light.

There was, indeed, a figure down there: a small figure, maybe ten feet below me on the floor of the old Bottle. And he wasn't moving.

I turned to Jonathan. 'Run to the kiosk. Tell the man there that there's been an accident, and that I want him to close the place and get over here fast.'

My nephew's young face twisted with anxiety. 'Is Colin all right, Uncle Oz?'

'That's what we're going to find out, pal. You do what I tell you and it'll help. Oh yes, and ask the man to bring a torch, and a ladder.' As Jonathan sprinted off towards the entrance, I took out my cellphone and called the emergency services, asking for an ambulance to the Castle, full speed.

I didn't wait for the man with the ladder; instead I gripped the edge of the hole and lowered myself in, pushing myself off and jumping the last few feet, taking care not to land on the wee chap. I knelt beside him in the gloom. He was lying on his left side; very gently, I stroked his cheek. 'What have you been up to now, Colin, my wee man?'

Never in my life have I been so glad to hear a child whimper. 'Sore,' he moaned.

'Where, son?'

'My shoulder.'

Remembering the first aid that my Dad had taught me, I held Colin's wrist and found his pulse. It was fast, but strong and steady. 'That's good,' I told him. 'Do you hurt anywhere else?'

'My head, Uncle Oz,' His whisper sounded fuzzy and dazed, 'and my neck.' He stirred slightly, then cried out in pain. I guessed that he must be lying on the damaged shoulder, so, as carefully and slowly as I could, I put both hands under him and turned him on to his back. His eyes were almost closed, and I could see a lump and a big graze on his left temple.

'There,' I murmured. 'That'll be easier. Now I want you to lie very still until the ambulance people get here. Don't even talk, if you can manage that. God, fella, your Mum said you were into everything, but I didn't think you'd go this far. She's going to murder me, I tell you.'

'What's going on down there?' The shout came from above.

'You've got a six-year-old prisoner,' I called back. 'The ambulance is on its way. You got a ladder?'

'Aye, and a torch.'

'Slide the ladder down here, leave me your torch and go and wait for the ambulance.'

The attendant did as he was told. 'Is the wee boy all right?' he asked as I climbed a few rungs to take the light from him.

'No,' I told him, a bit roughly, I'm afraid, 'He's quite badly shaken up and he may have broken his collar-bone. You're going to have to explain to me how he came to fall in here.' His mouth opened as if in protest. 'But not yet,' I snapped. 'Go and wait for the ambulance.'

There is no group of health workers whose members are more professional and skilled than the paramedics . . . I'm glad to say. The ambulance team was on the scene within ten minutes of my call. I explained what had happened, then climbed out of the Dungeon as they began to fit my nephew with a neck brace and to strap him, slowly and tenderly, to a lifting board.

The attendant was with Jonathan as I emerged into the sunshine; the few other people who had been in the Castle were standing around, looking on.

'Okay,' I said to the man. 'Why the hell wasn't that grille in place?'

'It was, sir, I'm sure,' he protested, in a light Highland accent. 'The janitor goes down into the Dungeon every morning to clear up the rubbish that folk have dropped down the day before. He wouldna' leave it uncovered. The wee boy must have lifted it off himself.'

'The wee boy is six years old, and as far as I know neither of his parents come from the planet Krypton. He could no more lift that than he could fly, see through walls or leap tall buildings at a single bound.'

'Well he must have dragged it then.'

'Crap!' I said, tersely, my anger fuelled, I must confess, by my fear of having to face my sister. 'Did you see the Dungeon after your janitor had finished here? Did you, personally, see that cover in place?'

Reluctantly, the man shook his head. 'No, but—'

'But nothing. I want to talk to the janitor.'

'He's on his break, sir.'

The man was behaving very reasonably, but that cut no ice with an angry Blackstone. 'Well put him together again and get him here,' I barked at the poor sod.

Relief came his way in the form of one of the paramedics, who tapped me on the shoulder. 'Excuse me sir, but first things first,' he said. 'I need a hand to lift your nephew out of there. My colleague will stay down there to steer, like, and make sure he doesnae get another bump on the way up.'

I nodded. 'Sure. How do you think he is?'

'He's broken his shoulder right enough, and he's dazed. They'll have to check for a possible skull fracture, but I'd say he'll be all right.'

Relief flooded through me as I helped the green-suited ambulance crewman lift wee Colin, secured on the board, out of his temporary prison. 'Since it's a child, we'll need you to come to Ninewells in the ambulance with us, sir, or follow right behind in your car.'

'Jonathan and I will come with you,' I told him, then turned back to the attendant. 'I want you to report this to the police.' I took out a business card and scribbled Colin's name and address on the back. 'Those are his details, and my mobile number's on there too.'

27

There was a moment when I thought that Ellie as going to take my head clean off at the shoulders, and that the Ninewells Accident and Emergency department was going to face its biggest ever challenge.

'How the hell could you have let him do that, Oz?' she shouted at me. I just stood there like I had when I was a kid, when she had me in a corner, knowing that a smart answer – or like now, any answer – was the short route to a smack in the mouth.

It's at times like those that you find out who your real friends are. 'But Mum,' said Jonathan, without the slightest sign of flinching, 'you did the same thing yourself the day that Colin got shut in the cellar.'

She glared at him, but he stood his ground. 'God,' she gasped, eventually, 'you two! You're like peas from the same pod, so you are.' Then, to my great relief, she smiled. 'And you're right too, son. There's no holding that wee so-and-so when he's determined to do something.'

Thankfully Colin's skull wasn't fractured; nothing was broken other than his shoulder, which was reassembled under anaesthetic and immobilised. Partly because of his concussion, and partly to give the delicate bones a chance to knit, the casualty registrar decided to keep him in hospital in Dundee for a few days, and decreed that school was out for at least a fortnight. Ellie was worried about work at first, but that problem was solved by a single telephone call to our stepmother, who had retired from teaching a year earlier. She volunteered at once to look after the convalescent Colin, and to keep him up with his school work as well.

'Can I stay off too, if Grandma Mary's coming?' Jonathan asked. 'She could teach me as well.'

'Don't push your luck, wee man,' I whispered to him.

Back in St Andrews I called in at the police office. The duty sergeant knew about the incident; he told me that the janitor had been interviewed and had insisted that after he had cleaned the Dungeon, he had put the grille back in place as usual. None of the bystanders were any help; not one of them had noticed the Dungeon or had seen Colin near it.

'As far as we're concerned, sir,' the uniformed policeman told me, 'the incident is closed. If your sister wants to sue Historic Scotland, that's up to her, but we cannae help her. Are you sure your wee nephew didn't move that cover himself?'

'We'll ask him when he's well enough,' I said. 'But unless he's been doing a lot of weight training for a six-year-old, there's not a chance.'

That evening I really did insist that there was to be no cooking. Ellie put up not a moment's argument, and Jonathan chose the takeaways, which inevitably meant pizzas, with chips on the side. We maintained a certain standard though, by eating at the table rather than from trays.

'What do you think, Oz?' Ellen asked me, at last. 'Do you think the people at the Castle are lying?'

I shook my head. 'Not for a minute. The sergeant told me that he knows the janitor well, and that he would vouch for him personally. There's only one person who can tell us what happened. Maybe tomorrow we'll be able to ask him.'

28

I hate seeing children in hospital; I hated the experience as a child too. It only happened once, after I fell out of a tree and broke my arm, but I still remember how lonely I felt, lying there sleepless in the half-light of that crowded old ward, listening to other kids crying.

For my nephew Colin, though, everything in life is an adventure. When we went in to visit him next morning, there he was, sitting on his bed with his back to a mound of pillows, wearing the Winnie the Pooh pyjamas which we had bought him the day before, happy as a Piglet in excrement, and eyeing up everything that was going on around him in the small ward.

His left arm was bound securely to his chest, and the graze on his temple looked less vivid, although it was surrounded by a big dark bruise.

'Hello, Mum,' he said as we approached the bed. 'Hello Uncle Oz. Hello Auntie Prim.' He gave the three of us a superior look, as if he was enjoying his wounded soldier status, and was determined to make the most of it. Yet, to my surprise he ignored his brother.

Ellen leaned down and kissed him, taking care not to touch his broken shoulder. 'How are you, my wee man?' she asked, laying a bag of assorted chocolate miniatures in his lap. Prim put a bag of apples beside it, and I gave him a new Game Boy, winning Most Favoured status in that instant.

'I'm all right, Mum,' he answered, proud and brave. 'My shoulder doesn't hurt. They give me pills for it, and last night they gave me something to make me sleep.'

'The nurses look nice,' Jonathan ventured. Colin shot him a look of pure disdain. There was to be only one centre of attraction, I guessed.

I sat on the edge of the bed. 'About yesterday, son,' I began. 'Tell me, how did you manage to get the cover off the Dungeon?'

He looked at me as if I was daft. 'The cover was off, Uncle Oz. I never touched it.'

'Are you sure about that?' I asked gently.

'Yes,' he protested. 'It was there beside it.'

'Did you see anyone take it off?'

He shook his head, then winced, from a flash of pain in his shoulder. 'Leave it for now, Oz,' said Prim.

'No, I can't,' I told her. 'This wee rogue was in my care yesterday. I need to know everything that happened. And I'll tell you this: if that sergeant's been covering up for his pal the janitor, I'm going to have him.'

I turned back to my nephew. 'Come on, Colin. Tell me how you got down there. Did you try to drop in the way I did? Was the Dungeon deeper than you thought? Look, it's okay; I'm not going to be angry with you. I brought you a Game Boy, didn't I?'

He smiled at me, but it was fleeting and uncertain. 'I tripped up,' he whispered.

Something was wrong with that picture. I couldn't help it; I frowned at him. 'What did you trip over, Collie? It's all smooth around the Dungeon. I looked around the edge, there was no ground scuffed up or anything.'

'My lace was undone. I tripped on that.'

'That sounds likely enough, Oz,' said Ellie. 'I'm always chasing after him to do his laces.'

I ignored her. 'No you didn't, son. Your laces were tied tight. I did them myself, remember, and when I found you I checked to make sure they were still secure. Then later, in the ambulance, I undid them and took your trainers off. There's something you're not telling me. Isn't there?'

He looked at his lap, and picked up the Game Boy. I took it from him. 'Not until you tell me, Colin.'

His face had gone white, making the bruise on his temple seem even more vivid. As I stared down at him he glanced at his brother. 'Jonny shoved me,' he mumbled.

'What?' Ellen and I spoke together.

'It was Jonathan. He pushed me in.'

'No!' my older nephew protested, his knowing eyes suddenly frightened. 'Uncle Oz . . .'

I laid a hand on his shoulder. 'It's okay, son, it's okay.' I looked back at his brother. 'Colin, Jonathan was with me all the time. He didn't push you. What on earth made you think it was him?'

'He's mad at me.'

'Why's he mad at you?'

'Because I started a fight at the school wi' a bigger boy. He was bashing me and Jonny saw him and bashed him up, and a teacher saw him and he got lines to do, and he was mad at me . . .' The wee chap's voice tailed off, and a big tear ran from his right eye down his cheek. I looked at my sister, and she at me; Colin had described an identical incident from our own primary schooldays. Ellie was the best fighter in the school.

'I can well understand him being mad at you,' she told her son, 'but he didn't push you into that Dungeon.'

'But somebody did, Colin?' I asked. 'Is that what happened?'

He nodded, then winced again. 'Yes, I was standing on the edge of the Dungeon, trying to see in, and I felt a hand in the middle of my back, and then someone shoved me. I remember falling, but I don't remember anything after that, till you and Jonathan and the ambulance man.'

'Before then,' I asked him. 'Did you see anyone?'

'Just an old man and an old woman, but they were on the other side of that green bit. I didn't see anybody else.'

'But you're sure someone pushed you?'

'Yes,' he said, firmly. I gave him back the Game Boy.

'You might have to tell this to the police, wee man. I'm going to see them as soon as we get back to St Andrews. I promise you, when we catch this character, he'll be for a dungeon himself – for a lot longer than you.'

29

Mac the Dentist is a formidable sight on the very rare occasions when he gets angry. Prim and I had called in at Anstruther after leaving Ellie and Jonathan in St Andrews. He had listened with mounting fury as I had told him Colin's story.

'What sort of animal would shove a wee boy down a twelve-foot drop?' he barked. 'If I could get my hands on the bastard, I'd give him a free root canal job – no anaesthetic, though.

'What did the police say?'

'Just about what I expected, Dad. I blew out the sergeant; I insisted on dealing with CID, and made a formal complaint to a Detective Inspector. He took it seriously – by which I mean that he didn't just write it off as Colin's imagination – but he was honest with me too. He took a look at the original report, then he told me straight out that unless the janitor turns out to have been lying about being on his break, they've got bugger all to go on.

'There are no witnesses, none of the other visitors reported anything, and they've lost contact with them now; no one thought to take their names and addresses. The guy promised me that he'd put out appeals on Radio Tay, Kingdom Radio, and in the local papers for anyone who was in the Castle at the time and who might have seen something, but he didn't hold out any hope.'

'Okay,' said my Dad. 'Don't you worry about it any more. You get off to Glasgow; I'll keep on top of the police. The Head of CID's a patient of mine and he's coming in on Thursday. I'll make bloody sure he pulls out all the stops.'

He turned as Prim came into the room carrying a tray laden with four mugs and a plate of biscuits. 'Hello lass,' he boomed, 'and how are you? Bloody silly question though. I can see damn well how you are; you're looking great.

'How are the wedding plans coming along?'

She grinned. 'They're taking shape. Oz has a quiet week ahead, before he goes to London to finish his part in the movie, so I'm trusting him to go up to Gleneagles and make the final arrangements – taking my mother with him, of course.'

I looked at my father. 'Did you know that "Mother in law" is an anagram of "Woman Hitler"?' I asked him.

'No, I did not; but I'll grant you that it's an interesting concept. A bit like, "Ascend in Paris" being an anagram of "Princess Diana". Coincidence can be remarkable sometimes. Look at you, for example; everywhere you've gone lately, disaster seems to dog your footsteps.

'Anyway, what about the date of this union of yours? Christ, here you are planning it, and I don't even know whether Mary and I'll be free or not.'

'We'll give you a clue,' Primavera laughed. 'It'll be within the next two months and it'll be on a Saturday.'

'That's fine,' said Mary, coming into the room after tidying up in the kitchen. 'I'll keep them all free. Give us enough notice so that I can shop for a new outfit. Gleneagles demands it, I think. Don't you agree, Mac?'

If my Dad had been wearing glasses he'd have peered over them at her. 'Frankly, my dear,' he answered, disdainfully, 'I doubt if Gleneagles gives a stuff. But if I've learned one thing in this life, it's never to get in the way of a woman when she's set course for a frock shop – not unless, as sure as twelve plus one is an anagram of eleven plus two – you want to end up with footprints on your chest.'

30

We were back in Glasgow for six o'clock, having been invited to dinner by Everett and Diane Davis, in their big, comfortable villa in Cleveden Drive, in Glasgow's West End. The house could have been custom-built for them; it dates from a time when high ceilings and wide doors were a standard feature of domestic architecture. In most modern houses, Everett would have difficulty standing up straight.

Liam Matthews was there when we arrived, with his steady girlfriend, Erin Doyle, an Aer Lingus hostess who tried to fit her schedule round his. In its early days, the relationship between Liam and the Boss had been difficult – even I had had trouble with the Irishman then – and it was only his exceptional talent that had kept him in a job. But since Erin had come on the scene the mercurial Mick had straightened out his attitude, and had become one of the most popular members of the troupe.

'How has your quiet weekend gone, you guys?' Diane asked, as she handed us a drink. The Princess, as they call her on the show, is an absolute stunner. Her own relationship with Everett had known its problems too; there had been one huge crisis, but somehow it had served to bring them closer together, and to strengthen them as a team.

'Not so quietly, I'm afraid,' Prim answered. 'Oz's nephew managed to get himself dropped into a hole in the ground, up in the Castle in St Andrews. We've spent a good chunk of the last two days in and out of hospital.'

'Is that one of the little lads you've had at some of the shows?' Liam asked.

'That's right.'

'Careless of him, then.'

'Careless of me, maybe, to let it happen,' I told him. 'But it wasn't Colin's fault. The poor wee chap had help; he was dazed after it, but he's dead certain that someone shoved him in.'

'Oh no,' said Erin. 'Who would do that?'

'That's the big question. The police are investigating, but there are no definite leads yet. We did have a call from them though, just before we came out tonight. They've found a local resident who says she saw a couple of kids horsing about in the area at the time. St Andrews isn't all that big a place, so they have a fair chance of tracing them; that is if they're locals, and not tourists.'

Liam whistled. 'The curse of Oz strikes again,' he proclaimed. 'First, those two guys down in London try to beat you up, and wind up in hospital. Now it's your nephew ends up in an ambulance. Are you safe to be around, I asks myself?'

I frowned at him. 'You're the second person today to make a crack like that. I've got to tell you, chum; my sense of humour's wearing thin.'

31

Outside, Glasgow moved slowly through the night, gearing itself up for the start of a new week. Our apartment sits high above the city, looking south towards and beyond the River Clyde. No one can see in, and the view from the big windows, which reach down to floor level, is too interesting and too beautiful for us to think of closing the curtains.

Sat up in bed with my back against the high wooden headboard, I could see the traffic as it made its way across the Kingston Bridge. The main Clyde crossing is never quiet, not even in the middle of the night. A steady stream of cars, vans and heavier vehicles flowed in either direction on business legitimate, and no doubt in a few cases, slightly dodgy.

Prim stirred beside me; she sort of snuffled in her sleep, then mumbled, 'G'roff . . .' I couldn't help smiling at her as she lay there. It's the only time she ever looks vulnerable, like a kid. Awake, she's always in control, always in charge of herself; at times, I confess, I look at her with a sort of private awe.

I love her for all of it, though, and I respect her. Most of all I like her. I'm a lucky man, blessed with a host of interesting, intelligent and amusing friends, but above them all is Primavera Phillips. When she came into my life the effect was explosive; at first I was overwhelmed by it but when the shock waves died away the landscape of my life was different, and I could see things more clearly than ever before.

She took me from Jan, yet she led me to her also; a lesser woman would have been embittered by the unwitting cruelty I showed her then, yet when that was over and I needed a crutch to keep moving, there she was propping me up. She didn't push herself back into my life; indeed she wouldn't have come if I hadn't asked her. Yet I hadn't hesitated. There's a Paul Simon song, 'Something so Right'; if I'm ever on *Desert Island Discs*, or anything like it, I'll have them play that for Prim.

Right then, looking down at her, I saw the lids of her left eye unstick themselves. 'S'up?' she mumbled. 'Heartburn? Y' know you shouldn't eat garlic.'

'What's up with you?' I chuckled. 'You sounded as if you were giving someone the message there. What did I do?'

'Not you,' she said, awake now, and rolling over on to her side. 'My Mum. I was having a dream about our wedding; I was in this fluffy white dress and she was fussing all over me.'

'Fluffy white dress? You never told me that.'

'Of course not. That's women's work.'

'Fine, but you? In a big flouncy dress?'

She smiled. 'It's okay, it won't be a Royal Wedding job. It'll be tight-fitting and simple, like I usually dress when we go formal. I'm even going to have it re-modelled afterwards so I can wear it again.'

'Very economical. But what if I hadn't overheard this dream of yours and I'd turned up in jeans, alongside you in the white dress?'

She snorted. 'As long as you turn up, I don't care if you're in your M and S boxers. But don't worry about that; Susie's helping me with the dress, and it's Mike's job to make sure that you turn up appropriately clad. The white tux that you wear on the telly sometimes, that'll be fine.'

'Sod that. You're wearing new – I'm wearing new.'

'That'll be good news for Slater's,' Prim murmured. Then she yawned. 'But come on. You still haven't answered my first question. What's keeping you awake?'

'My brain.' I told her. 'My over-active brain. I've been thinking about my Dad's throwaway line today, and about what Liam said tonight. They're right, both of them. Just lately, everywhere I've gone, mayhem's dogged my fucking footsteps.

'Susie comes to see us, and someone cremates her car right on our doorstep. I meet Noosh in Aberdeen and some gangster takes a shot at her. I go down to London with the GWA and two guys turn up looking to break my arms. I take the boys out for the day and someone shoves wee Colin into a bloody great hole.

'On the basis of all that, my love – and I'm not even going to think of some of the other things that have happened over the last couple of years – am I, or am I not, an unlucky guy to be around?'

Prim laid her left hand flat on my stomach. 'On the basis of most things that have happened to me since I met you – and I'm not just talking about the silly money that seems to flow in our direction all the time – I'd say you've brought me more luck than anyone I've ever met.

'Don't get paranoid over a couple of silly remarks, Oz, please. Luck had nothing to do with any of those things, anyway, and none of them save one had anything to do with you. Someone – Stephen Donn, from the looks of it – had made a very specific threat to Susie before her car blew up. Noosh What'shername seems to have brought some heavy baggage back from Russia. As for Colin, we had that report of youngsters being seen in the vicinity, and shoving the wee chap into that Dungeon was so reckless and stupid that it only makes sense as a kids' prank.'

She paused, stifling another yawn. 'The only thing that concerns you directly, is the London incident. We don't know for sure who sent those men to do you. Maybe it was Stephen Donn giving you a warning not to get too close, maybe it was your rejected admirer or her husband, maybe it was someone completely different.

'Whoever was behind it was in deadly earnest. Luck didn't come into that, either.'

'That's a comforting thought.'

'You haven't had any trouble since, have you?'

'Not personally, no.'

'Right, forget it.' Her arm slipped round my waist and pulled me gently down until I was lying beside her, my face close to hers on the pillow. 'Now, since you woke me at this unsocial hour, the least you can do is . . .'

Clearly, my luck had taken a turn for the better.

32

For all that I indulge in them every now and again, the truth is that I've never really understood mother-in-law jokes. The best humour, as I see it, has to be based on reality and the concept of the Wife's Old Dear as a descendant of the velocirapter runs counter to my experience.

I've always found that it's the daughters who have the really sharp teeth, and the really ripping claws.

Granted, my first experience of the species was somewhat unusual, given that Mary was both my mother-in-law and my stepmother, for in either role she's as kind and gentle a woman as you'll meet in a day's march. Nevertheless, I didn't anticipate any problems with her successor, whom I'd liked from the day we met.

No, the prospect of going with Elanore Phillips to Gleneagles Hotel to make the wedding arrangements did not, of itself, make me particularly nervous. What did worry me were the strictures laid down by Prim before I set off for Auchterarder. 'You know what Mum's like,' I had been warned. 'She loves a big production, and she'll try to push you into it.

'I want a very informal do. You can sign up for the poshest fork buffet they have and for the top of the range wines, but I do not want a sit-down lunch and formal speeches. Dad will propose a toast to us, we will each of us say a few words in reply, and that's it. Given our history, I will not put you through the ordeal of making a full-scale speech and having people hanging on your every word looking for possible references to Jan.

'Nor will I put myself through the ordeal of having to listen to it.'

She paused for breath. 'But Mum would, you see. You've heard her; all she can think of is the fact that when Dawn got married quietly in the States, she was somehow cheated out of something. She doesn't see anything but that. She'll use every weapon in her arsenal to try to cajole or bully you into agreeing to a formal job . . . but don't you dare. She isn't even seeing the guest list: I'm damned if I'll have her stuffing it with her Old Biddy pals from the church.'

After that, heading up to Perthshire I felt like an ancient Greek warrior, given his shield and told to return bearing it in victory or borne dead upon it in defeat.

She wasn't wrong either. I had never visited Semple House on my own before – on every occasion I had been there, Prim had too – but when I arrived I was greeted as if I'd ridden up on a donkey along a road strewn with palm-leaves. Remembering how that story carries on, I didn't feel too comfortable.

I had planned to take Elanore and David to lunch at Gleneagles before she and I met the functions people, but the table was set when I arrived. One of the things I like about Prim's mum is that there's no subtlety about her – the tactic was clear: soften up the boy with her awesome kitchen skills, then go for the finisher. She opened her campaign over the soup. 'Before I forget, Oz,' she said, gauchely. She reached into a cavernous handbag and produced a white envelope. 'Give this to Primavera for me, won't you. It's a list of my

Auchterarder friends whom I'd like you to invite.'

I took it from her without comment, then sneaked a quick glance at David. I was impressed by the depth of his concentration on the Cullen Skink.

The bell for Round Two sounded over the steak and kidney pudding. 'You know, Oz,' she began, confiding in me as a member of the family, 'I love my older daughter dearly, as does David, and as do you, but we all have to admit, don't we, that she can be very wilful.' As she spoke, her husband forked up a particularly large morsel of dumpling, cleverly taking himself out of the discussion.

'She knows her own mind, does Primavera,' I conceded. I was about to add, 'And mine too,' but I stopped myself just in time.

'Yes, my dear, but what she has to realise is that this isn't just her day, it's yours too.' Her big punch almost landed, but just in time, I followed David's example and dived behind a smokescreen of steak and kidney.

Prim's father has a remarkable metabolism. If I ate lunches like that on a regular basis, I'd have trouble fitting into Everett's living room, yet he manages to stay slim and straight-backed. I have come to suspect that he has developed a method of burning off calories by pure concentration; this might explain why he's such a quiet, unworldly bloke.

I made it through the treacle pudding and coffee without giving any ground, but I knew that what had happened up to that point came under the heading of mere skirmishing. The real battle would be fought at Gleneagles.

Our appointment there was set for two-thirty p.m.; I thought of asking whether David would like to join us, but that would have been unkind of me and potentially dangerous for him. So Elanore and I set off together in the Freelander – she's a big woman, not built for a Z3.

We were greeted in the foyer of the majestic, baronial hotel by the functions manager and her young male assistant. 'Mr Blackstone,' the middle-aged lady exclaimed, hand outstretched, 'welcome to our hotel. And welcome also . . .' I introduced Elanore.

'Ah, the mother of the bride. How nice that your daughter can rely on you at this time.'

I decided that I'd better take a grip of this meeting from the start. 'I take it that you've had a chance to consider my fiancée's e-mail setting out our requirements.'

'Yes, we have. We have some thoughts on them. Let's start with the date.' She led us through to a small office behind reception. 'This is fairly short notice, you understand,' she said, showing us to seats round a small conference table. 'We're heavily booked, as always, but we can offer you a function suite on the first Saturday in November, if you can be ready in time. Beyond that there's nothing until February.'

'That will be fine,' I said.

'Excellent. I had you pencilled in for that, so I'll confirm it this afternoon. Now, there's one thing I want to raise with you. Ms Phillips' e-mail said that you want a buffet reception. That's quite unusual for a wedding.'

'Indeed,' Elanore concurred, by my side. 'Perhaps you could offer suggestions for a formal meal.'

The manager nodded. 'We anticipated that, Madam.' She nodded to her assistant, who delved into a big, leather-bound folder and produced several sheets. 'We have some sample menus here.' The young man handed them straight to Elanore.

'And the buffet menus, please,' I said, with a smile, holding out my hand.

'Certainly, sir.' He produced several more sheets and handed them over.

'As to the wedding ceremony itself,' his boss continued, speaking more to Prim's mum than to me, 'we'll have theatre-style seating for that in your suite, then give you a small break-out area for drinks while we set up for the meal.'

'That's fine,' I said grabbing the baton once again, 'and for a buffet set-up you can serve drinks straightaway and simply move the seats around the walls.'

'Yes,' said the woman. I forced her to look at me. 'The thing is, you see,' I continued, 'my fiancée, as her mother would be the second person to tell you, is a very determined person. And the thing is, also, so am I. We want all of our guests to be comfortable and relaxed.

'There are two guys coming to our wedding who weigh a third of a ton between them. Either one of them could eat your chef, tall hat and all, if he felt peckish. We don't want that to happen, so what we need is the best hot and cold buffet you can provide. There will be forty guests, so if you cater for fifty, that will allow for our large friends.'

There was a chilly silence beside me, but we were in the last round, and I knew I had to go for a clean knock-out. This wasn't a GWA wrestling match, this was serious stuff.

'We want you to serve Krug after the ceremony, then Premier Cru Chablis and a good Fleurie with the buffet. When we reach the coffee stage, there should be a fully stocked bar available.'

'On a cash basis, sir?' The young assistant asked, looking up from his notes.

'Don't be silly. These are our friends, and our guests.'

'Dancing, sir,' the manager interrupted. 'What about dancing?'

'No dancing, thank you. The thought of Jerry Gradi doing the Twist just beggars belief. If he side-swiped someone with his arse, it would be a hospital case. We know our friends, we know ourselves, and we want everyone to be relaxed.' I paused, and looked at Elanore.

'Most of all, I want . . . I want Primavera to have the day of her life, and I *will* see that she does.'

I turned back to the manager. 'Are you clear on all of that?'

She smiled. 'Yes, Mr Blackstone, we'll meet all of your wishes.'

'Good. Send us a cost projection as soon as you can.' I took out my cheque-book. 'In the meantime, let me leave you a deposit. Two grand be enough?'

'Quite enough. We'll look forward to seeing you on the day.'

'You'll be seeing me the night before,' I said. 'I want you to reserve a suite for me, and another for my best man, Mr Dylan and his partner, Ms Gantry. I will yield to one tradition, that I shouldn't see the bride just before the wedding.'

33

'I could say that my daughter has you well trained, Oz,' said Elanore, back in the kitchen at Semple House. The drive back from Gleneagles had been silent, and I had felt guilty for every moment of it about having to sock it to her in the way I had.

'I could say that,' she continued, 'but I won't, because it wouldn't be true. You're your own man and you understand Primavera better than anyone she's ever known.' She smiled. 'You handled me beautifully too. When Prim told me that you were coming up to make the arrangements I thought I had a chance. I should have known better.'

She held out a hand. 'Here; you'd better give me back that guest list. She'd just tear it up anyway.'

I gave a relieved laugh and handed back the envelope which she had forced on me earlier. As I did so, David came into the room. He looked at us, from one to the other as if checking for bloodstains. 'Business done?' he asked. 'Arrangements made?'

'Yes,' Elanore answered. 'I'm even looking forward to it.'

'Thank God for that,' he exclaimed. It was the most emphatic thing I'd ever heard him say.

He turned to me. 'Oz, I could do with a walk. I expect you could too, after that lunch. Care to join me before you head back to Glasgow?'

'Sure.' I agreed at once; I had never been in the company of

Prim's Dad outside his own home. Just as I'm very fond of Elanore, so I've liked David Phillips, retired furniture maker turned wood-carver, from the moment I met him, but I found him a hard man to get to know. He's the antithesis of my own father, who wears everything on the outside.

I'd discussed him with Miles, and I knew that he was no closer to him than I. So, although I had planned to head straight back to Glasgow, I jumped at the chance of a wander around Auchterarder with him.

It was a pleasant afternoon as we stepped out of the gate of Semple House, into the street. The Perthshire town has two claims to fame; one is Gleneagles, which is truly one of the world's finest hotels, while the other centres around its assertion that it has the longest Main Street in Scotland. That's why they call it the 'Lang Toun'.

Semple House is right on the edge of Auchterarder; it turned out that David's plan was to walk the length of the legendary street and back again – a fair hike, but we both had the fuel for it.

We walked in silence for a while, until I began to think that conversation wasn't on the agenda at all. So when David did speak, it took me by surprise for a second. 'I've always found that there are two ways to handle Elanore when she has her mind set on something,' he burst out, with no preamble. 'One is to have a screaming row, and the other is to capitulate.

'I've never been one for screaming,' he murmured, wistfully.

'Now when the girls lived at home, we had some ructions then. Dawn's the quiet one, like me, but Primavera . . .' He smiled. 'As you've learned for yourself, she won't back down from anyone, never would. I must admit that when I heard

Prim's plans for the wedding, then listened to Elanore, I thought we were in for warfare. Then, when I heard that you were coming up to make the arrangements, not her, well to be frank Oz, I thought you were being lined up as a human sacrifice.

'Yet here you are, having had your own way, and still with the regulation number of arms and legs, and still able to hear. How the hell did you manage it?'

'I haven't had my own way, David,' I corrected him. 'I've had ours. Prim and I have a simple rule; if we don't agree on something, we don't do it. When we have decided on something together, nothing will shift us. As far as our wedding's concerned, the way it's going to be is the way we both want it. Essentially, that's what I told Elanore. I hope I didn't upset her.'

'Upset her? You impressed her, my lad. I must say, I like that principle of yours; do only what both of you want.' He scratched his chin, 'Too late for me, though. Too old to change.'

I looked sideways at him as we walked. 'You don't fool me for a second, you know,' I told him. 'Whatever accommodation you and Elanore have, you're as happy as Larry with it. I've never heard her propose anything that you didn't give the nod to. But have you ever thought that she only suggests things she knows you'll approve of? When was the last time you let her do something you really didn't fancy?

'The pair of you are just like Prim and me in effect. You just go about it in a different way, that's all.'

David gave a gruff chuckle, then lapsed back into thoughtful mode. We walked on through the centre of the town, until we reached the outskirts on the other side, and turned to retrace our steps. Auchterarder is on a main tourist drag, so there was plenty of bustle around its centre, people moving from shop to shop, buying everything from scarves to shortbread.

'You know there is one thing I'd like to be able to do more, Oz,' my future father-in-law said as he side-stepped a massive, cashmere-wrapped American matron.

'What's that?'

'I have a secret passion,' he said. Whatever it was, I thought, it was a well-kept secret. 'For draught Guinness.' Yes, very well-kept indeed.

'The trouble is,' he went on, 'I can't indulge very often. We're Churchy folk, Elanore and I, and if I was seen plodding down to the local every night tongues would wag. Anyway, I don't like going into pubs on my own; never have.'

I took the hint. 'Fancy a pint,' I asked.

'Thought you'd never ask, my boy.'

We crossed the street to a stone-built hotel with a public bar, and stepped inside. The place was surprisingly busy for the time of day, so I had to ease myself into the small counter. The barman looked up, but not at me. 'Yes, gents.'

'This bloke's first,' said a voice behind me.

I thanked him, without turning round. 'Pint of Guinness and a pint of lager,' I ordered.

The man poured the Guinness first and left it on the crowded bar to settle. As he was pouring the lager, I turned and called to David, who had found a small table. 'Crisps, nuts?'

'God no,' he answered. 'We'll be expected to eat when we get back.'

I paid for the drinks and carried them across. 'Cheers,' said Prim's Dad, eyeing Ireland's national drink with anticipation. He picked it up and took a gulp. 'Mmm, bitter. But the first one usually is. The next three or four are usually fine.'

'Hold on there. I've got to drive home tonight.'

'Don't worry. I'm not much of a soak. One more after this and we're off; the walk back and a couple of Elanore's scones should see you all right to drive.'

'I'll maybe wait for an hour after that,' I said.

'Whatever.' He drained his glass. I had only shifted a couple of inches of mine. He stood up. 'Same again.'

'Make mine a half-pint, please, David. I'm not in your class.'

He smiled. 'Sorry. I've been looking forward to this since we left the house, that's all.'

'I can see that, all right.'

We polished off the second round at a more reasonable pace, and left it at that. As we walked back, David was silent at first but as we drew closer to Semple House, he broke out into a fit of coughing. 'Fuck!' he said, as he struggled to suppress it. I'd never heard him swear before, so I looked at him in surprise.

'You and Miles,' he said suddenly, as we turned into his driveway. 'You think I'm a dry old stick, don't you. Old David, as dull as the wood he carves. That's it, isn't it.'

His outburst took me well aback. 'No,' I protested. 'That's not true at all. We respect you, both of us, and as for your work, your carving, you've got the rare gift of taking dead wood and giving it a richer, more colourful life than it ever had before. There's nothing dull about that, mate. I wish I was as creative as you.'

'Don't fucking patronise me, son,' he growled. 'I know what you think.'

He had me annoyed now. 'No one's being fucking patronising here, expect you, maybe. You're a talented guy and you know it.'

He shook his head. 'No, dull old David, that's me. David, never Dave, always David. Do you know?' he shouted, suddenly. 'No one's ever called me Dave in my whole fucking life! I've always wanted to be a Dave!'

There were tears in his eyes as he fumbled for his Yale key. Out of the blue, he looked stooped, old and sad.

As he groped in the pocket of his jacket the big door swung open. 'What's all the noise about, David?' boomed Elanore. 'I could hear you in the kitchen.'

'Dave!' he shouted. 'That's fucking Dave to you!'

She frowned at me like a good-sized thunderstorm. 'Is he drunk?'

'No I'm fucking not,' he bellowed. 'This is the new Dave. I'm goin' to be like these lads – an intellectual. You know what I mean; shaggin' actresses and all that stuff!'

She took him by the elbow and drew him into the house. He struggled, but he seemed to have no strength to resist her as she frogmarched him into the sitting room and pushed him down into his armchair.

'Oz, coffee!' she ordered.

'Listen, Elanore, he's only had a couple of pints.'

'I can smell them!'

'I've got it,' David shouted. His voice sounded triumphant. 'I'm going to carve myself. No more toy soldiers, no more fucking chess men. From now on everything I do's going to be Dave: Super Dave, Action Dave. How about that, Oz?'

'And fuckin' dragons. S'all right dear, not you; I mean real fucking dragons. Well not real, but lifelike. Got to be money in fucking dragons.'

'It'd be a terrific circus act,' I retorted, trying somehow, to humour him. 'But how will you get them to stay still while you fuck them?' Beside me, Elanore snorted.

'Wrestlers!' he bellowed, I could carve your . . .' In mid-sentence he started to cough again, until it turned into a choking fit. 'Water,' he gasped suddenly. 'Throat's dry.' I grabbed his shoulders and looked at him, his eyes were wide, the pupils dilated and fixed.

'Elanore,' I said quietly, glancing over my shoulder. I could have shouted, like David; he was in a world of his own. 'He isn't drunk. He's ill. I don't know what it is, a stroke, possibly. Whatever it is, you'd better call a doctor, quick.'

34

'One of us has got to say it, so it might as well be me.' I looked grimly at Prim. 'We've got to stop meeting like this.'

She shuddered. 'Don't I know it; two hospitals in as many days. How's Dad?'

'Talking to the fairies, last time I saw him. He's not going to die, don't fear that, but the doctor is still trying to work out what's wrong with him.'

'What did happen?' she demanded. I had phoned her as soon as the family GP, Dr Cusman, had called for an ambulance to take David to Perth Royal Infirmary, but all I had told her was that her father had been taken ill. I don't know what the Glasgow to Perth speed record is, but I was willing to bet that the Z3's engine was sighing with relief out there in the car park, now that the journey was over.

'It was the weirdest thing,' I said. 'Your Dad and I were out for a walk, and we stopped off for a drink. He had a couple of pints of Guinness. On the way home he started getting argumentative; by the time we got there he was raving, effing and blinding and everything. Elanore thought he was pished, of course; so did I, until I had a look at his eyes.

'I tell you, my love. I've never been more pleased that my father made Ellie and me learn first aid.'

Prim nodded, emphatically. 'Me too.'

I couldn't hold back a grin. 'I'll tell you something else

too. For the rest of his life, your Old Man's going to be called Dave, like he wants. Oh, Christ, but he was funny. "That's fucking Dave to you", he shouts at Elanore. Oh, but you should have seen her face!'

I couldn't help it; inappropriate or not, I was seized with sudden laughter, so hard that I hugged myself in a vain attempt to contain it, until there was nothing for it but to sit down on one of the hard chairs which lined the ward corridor and wait for it to subside. It was infectious; when Elanore appeared, back from the ladies', the first thing she saw was the two of us, convulsed with laughter.

'Sorry Mum,' Prim gasped. 'Oz was just telling me what happened to poor Dave.' She corpsed again.

Even her mother smiled, faintly. 'It was astonishing,' she said. 'I have never heard words like those from your father's mouth.'

'How much did he have to drink?' Prim asked me, her self-control regained.

'Two pints of Guinness.'

'He wasn't drunk then.'

'How do you know?' Elanore asked her.

'I've been chumming Dad to the pub for years,' she replied. 'So has Dawn. When we were single, every time either of us came home, he always asked us to go for a walk with him, and it was always the same performance. Up the Main Street and into the pub on the way back. The way he can shift Guinness, you'd think it was about to be made illegal. If he was raving after two pints, he's ill.'

Her mother stared at her, astonished. 'The secret life of David Phillips,' she gasped. 'Sorry, Dave.'

'What did Dr Cusman say?' Prim asked, serious once more.

'He wasn't sure,' I said, 'but he couldn't rule out some sort of cerebral attack, so he whistled up the ambulance pronto. The admitting doctor here ruled that out right away, but like I said she hasn't committed herself to a diagnosis yet. All she said was that he was going to be all right.'

'I wish she'd hurry,' Elanore exclaimed. She had been tearful as we followed the ambulance to Perth Royal Infirmary, but she had calmed down once the doctor had assured her that David was not having a stroke. Still, the waiting was getting to her.

'It's better that they do it right than that they do it quickly, Mum. This is Sister Phillips talking to you now.' There are times when I forget that Prim is a nurse by profession. 'Oz, describe the symptoms again,' she said.

'It started with a coughing fit.' I told her. 'Then he got aggressive; not physically, but loud and hectoring. He started swearing like a trooper too. By the time we got him into the house he was more or less delirious. Then he started choking, and asking for water. That was when I looked at his eyes and saw that the pupils were dilated. And that was when your Mum called Dr Cusman.'

She frowned. 'Mmm.'

'Does that tell you something?'

'Doesn't it suggest anything to you, with your first aid training?'

'Cerebral shock, that's all. Have you got any other ideas?'

'Yes, but I don't want to second-guess the doctors. Let's just wait. Where's the coffee machine? I'm gasping.'

We spent another twenty minutes in the stuffy corridor

before the admitting doctor reappeared. She hadn't given her name before, but I saw from a plastic tag pinned to her uniform that she was Dr Shula Sharma. Instead of launching into a bulletin on David's condition, she asked us to follow her. We all thought that she was taking us to see him, so we were surprised when she showed us into a small glass-walled cubicle, where a man waited.

'Mrs Phillips?' he began, addressing Elanore. 'My name is Drew Law; I'm the consultant in charge of this unit.'

'What's wrong?' said Elanore, clutching her blouse in a gesture of sudden fear. 'What's wrong with my husband?'

'Your husband is fine, Mrs Phillips. He's recovering well. It's what brought him here that I need to discuss with you.'

There was something about the man's tone that I didn't like; I couldn't put my finger on it, but somehow he seemed just a touch menacing. I don't like doctors who think they can bully people. 'The ambulance was fine,' I said, 'and the crew were very professional. Now come to the point, please.'

'Okay,' he replied, not backing down at all. 'We've treated Mr Phillips for poisoning; we've pumped his stomach and flushed his system out generally. I'm waiting for a lab analysis to confirm the substance involved, but I'm pretty certain that it's atropine. If that's the case I'm going to report this incident to the police.

'The patient isn't coherent yet, so maybe you can tell me how he came to consume it? I didn't find any traces of deadly nightshade in the stomach contents, by the way, so we can rule out the possibility that he's been chewing the plants at the foot of the garden. That's the only means I can think of by which one could ingest that chemical by accident.'

'David and I had a drink,' I told him, 'just before he was taken ill. All that I can suppose is that it was contaminated.'

'What about food?'

'We all ate the same lunch.'

'That doesn't rule out the possibility that Mr Phillips' portion might have been spiked.'

The colour left Elanore's face. 'There is no such possibility,' Prim snapped at the man. 'This conversation is over. Where is my father? We insist on seeing him, now.'

'Yes indeed,' I added, taking out my cellphone. 'By the way, you needn't bother reporting this to the police. I intend to do that myself, right now.'

35

'Are you going to give me any argument about it now?' I asked her. 'Maybe you're right; maybe I'm paranoid. But that doesn't mean that they ain't out to get me.'

Prim shook her head. 'No,' she acknowledged. 'I give in. It is crazy, but you've got a stalker all right, Oz. Someone either knows your movements or is following you around; someone with a very sick mind too, to be targeting your friends and family.'

'But not me,' I pointed out. 'Not me. Why?'

'What about the London incident? That was aimed at you.'

'The London incident doesn't fit the pattern. That was a direct attack on me, with nothing subtle about it. Those guys were paid to ambush me and kick my fucking head in.'

I looked at her, as she sat there, slumped in her Dad's armchair, back at Semple House It was almost midnight; Elanore was upstairs, having been given a very large brandy as a sedative, after finally cracking up completely at David's bedside. By the time they finally let us see him, he was much calmer, but he was still dazed and confused, still rambling incoherent nonsense.

'How's it going, Dave?' I had said as I sat beside him. He had gazed back at me solemnly, and replied, 'Rosebud,' pronouncing the word with great care, so gravely that I wouldn't have been surprised if a snow-scene had fallen from his limp fingers.

As I had promised the aggressive consultant, I had indeed called the police. Two detective constables had come to the infirmary and had taken a statement from me. They had tried to interview Dave too.

'Can you tell us what happened, Mr Phillips?' the older DC had asked.

'The cows are in the broccoli patch,' the victim had replied.

'Are they now. Maybe we'd better wait till tomorrow, and talk to you then.'

'No, no!' Dave had shouted. 'They'll have eaten all the fucking broccoli by then.'

In spite of the seriousness of the situation, I couldn't help smiling at the memory as I looked at Prim. 'If there's a good side to this it's that nobody's been killed,' I told her.

'So far,' she retorted. 'But that's more by accident than design. Colin could have broken his neck, Dad could have died, Mike and Susie almost did, and Noosh Turkel almost caught a bullet in the head. We've got to warn everyone close to us, Oz. They're all in danger.'

I shook my head. 'I don't think so; not unless I'm actually there with them. That's been the pattern.'

'Except in London. There you were the target.'

'Yes, and I have to find out why.' I frowned at her. 'I have to do it on my own, too. I want you to stay here with your mother. Look after her, and after old David when he gets home. You'll be safer here too; well away from me.'

'But what about the business?'

'You've been saying you reckon Lulu could run it on her

own. I guess it's time to find out if you're right.'

Prim sat in silent thought for a minute or two. Finally, she nodded. 'All right. Mum and Dad could use me here, that's true. But what are you going to do?'

'Well, tomorrow, I'm going back to Glasgow and I'm going to have a talk with Mike. After that I'm going to find those two guys in London.'

She looked at me doubtfully. 'And how exactly are you going to do that?' she asked.

At that moment, I didn't have an answer for that one, so all I could do was smile at her. 'Maybe I'll hire a private detective,' I said.

She didn't see the funny side. 'Maybe you should do just that. Maybe you should even do the same as Susie and hire a bodyguard.'

'Honey, the way things have been happening I'm the only person who doesn't need one. But maybe I should hire the whole bloody SAS and place them with all my family and friends.'

Prim screwed up her face, as she has a way of doing when something is really getting to her. 'Oz,' she said. 'Think about this. Who hates you so much that they would do all those things? What man, or woman, has it in for you that badly?'

'Forget women,' I told her. 'Assuming that Elanore doesn't use deadly nightshade as a herb in her steak and kidney pudding, someone doctored your Dad's drink in that bar – and there were no women in there, none at all.

'Who could my enemy be? It's a funny old world out there, love; the GWA programming pulls a big television audience. There are bound to be a few nutters among them. It could be that someone out there has taken a deep and pathological dislike to me.'

'Hardly,' she protested. 'You're only the bloody announcer, for Christ's sake. This has to be someone with a more personal grudge.'

'But who? I lived a very uneventful life until I met you. I didn't upset people, and they didn't upset me; I was just an ordinary twenty-something, enjoying himself. Since then, out of all the things that you and I have done together in the last three years, I can think of three people who might have reason to hate me . . . and you know who I mean.

'Of them, two are dead and the other one has to feed himself with a rubber spoon, when he isn't whistling, "When I rule the world", or just plain howling at the moon.'

'Yes, my dear,' Primavera countered, 'I know who you mean. But there's a man you've forgotten, isn't there? Someone that you did think, once, was trying to get you – to get both of us, in fact. If you think about it, he has a far better reason to do you now than he had then.'

It had been a hard day; I had faced down my future mother-in-law and lived to tell the tale, then rushed her poisoned husband to hospital. After all that it was little wonder that my normally razor-sharp powers of deduction weren't quite at their sharpest. Otherwise how could I have forgotten Ricky Ross? Once a high-flying detective with his eye on a Chief Constable's uniform, knighthood and all the rest, his career had ended in disgrace, a turn of events for which he was inclined to blame Osbert Blackstone, Esquire, and no one else.

Still . . .

'Naw,' I exclaimed. 'I know he's a nasty bastard, but he wouldn't . . .'

'Not so long ago you were prepared to accept that he would. You and I travelled a thousand miles believing all the way that he was on our trail. He wasn't then, but maybe he is now. Revenge is a dish best served cold, like they say.'

'Naw,' I repeated; but I knew she had a point. My known enemies currently at liberty made up a very short list: a list of one, in fact, and it was him.

36

I was still pondering upon the possibility of the persecuting policeman next morning, when my whole view of the situation was stood on its head. I had just showered, and was changing into the clothes which Prim had brought with her on her headlong rush from Glasgow, when Elanore knocked on the bedroom door.

'Oz,' she called out. 'There are two constables downstairs. They say they've come for you.'

'Fine, thanks. Tell them I'll be ready to talk to them in a minute. D'you want to give them a coffee while they're waiting?'

There was a pause. 'No, Oz,' she said, sounding a shade alarmed, even through the thick door, 'you don't understand. They've come to take you away.'

'They what?' I finished dressing in seconds. As I trotted downstairs I saw two large policemen, with flat hats and low foreheads, waiting in the hall. I recognised their type at once, having been a probationer constable myself when I was younger and sillier. Looking at them, I had the fleeting impression that their dark uniforms and awkward-looking equipment belts were somehow sucking the light out of the place.

'Mr Blackstone?' said the older of the two, who looked about five years younger than me.

I nodded.

'Yuvtae come wi' us.' I looked at his big lumpen face, into his dull eyes, and saw nothing at all. The guy was expressionless.

I hadn't come downstairs with the intention of being unco-operative, but he had pushed the wrong button. 'Would you repeat that for me, please,' I asked him. 'Slowly and in English.'

'Yuvtae come wi' us,' he said again, deliberately, ignoring my request for a translation. 'We've been telt tae pick yis up and take yis tae Perth.'

'And who told you?'

'The CID wants yis.' Having pushed my unco-operative button, he had now tripped my downright bolshie switch.

'In that case they can come and get me,' I replied. A faint look of uncertainty came into his eyes – the first sign that anything was actually working behind there. His younger colleague seemed to grow a couple of inches and made as if to move towards me.

'Listen,' I snapped, to forestall him. 'I wasn't a copper for very long, but even I know that you cannot walk into someone's house and take him away without any sort of warrant or even explanation. Now, did the CID tell you why they want me?'

'Naw,' the older bloke replied.

'And you didn't think to ask them?'

'Listen, Mr Blackstone. When the CID tells us tae dae something we just does it. We disnae ask them whit fur.' As I stared at his stolid impassivity I realised that the best I would get out of this situation was a few quid in compensation from the Police Authority for wrongful arrest, assault, and maybe irreversible brain damage caused by a restraining blow from a side-handled baton. I decided that I didn't need any of that. I gave in.

'Okay,' I said, then turned to Elanore. 'When Prim comes out of the bathroom, tell her what's happened. I've got no idea what this is about, but I'll get it sorted as fast as I can.'

They hadn't even sent a decent car for me. All the way to the police headquarters in Perth, I sat crammed into the back seat of a Metro, looking at the massive backs of the two trolls. When we reached our destination the younger PC levered me out and seized the sleeve of my jacket as he marched me into the building. I really didn't like that, but I knew that if I had protested they would have ignored me.

They led me up to a duty sergeant at the front desk. 'Prisoner Blackstone for CID,' said the older one.

That was too much. I looked hard at the three-striper, in the hope that he had a brain. 'I want you to remember this,' I told him. 'I haven't been cautioned, or formally arrested, or given any reason why I should be here. I've come voluntarily, and if this gorilla doesn't let my sleeve go right now, my solicitor will send a formal complaint to the Chief Constable before the day is out. If that happens, since you seem to be in charge of these people, much of the shit, when it flies, will land on you.'

The sergeant didn't say a word. However he shot a quick glance at the younger constable, who gave me my arm back. And then the two of them just disappeared. Without a word, they turned and walked back outside to their car, to spend another fulfilling day in the public service.

When I looked round, the sergeant was gone too. He came

back soon, though, with two men in suits. One of them was the older of the detective constables who had taken my statement at the Infirmary; this time he was clearly a bit player.

'Mr Blackstone,' said the senior suit, a bulky man in his late forties. 'I'm Detective Inspector Bell. I'm so glad you agreed to join us.' I checked his tone for sarcasm and found plenty.

I checked my watch. It was five past nine. 'You've got till nine-thirty,' I replied, looking at him deadpan.

That ended the niceties. 'I've got as long as I fucking like, son. Come with us.' Bell and the DC whose name, I recalled, was Slattery led me up a flight of stairs and into a small interview room. The DI switched on a black tape recorder and told it who we all were. And then he gave me an official police caution; read me my rights, as they say on *NYPD Blue*.

Up to that point, I had only been annoyed. Now I could feel a big black cloud above my head, making ready to rain, hard.

'I've been looking at the statement you gave yesterday evening, Mr Blackstone,' he said, getting down to business, 'about the poisoning of Mr David Phillips, of Semple House, Auchterarder. Would you run through the gist of it again for me, and for the tape.'

'Sure, David and I went for a walk late yesterday afternoon; on the way back we stopped for a couple of pints. By the time we got home, he was behaving erratically. This turned to delirium, and the doctor was called.'

'Fine. Now let's concentrate on what happened in the bar. Who bought the first round?'

'I did. A pint of Guinness for David, and lager for me.'

'Who else was there?'

'The bar was quite crowded at that point; I think a bus-load of tourists had come in. I remember there was a bloke behind me; the barman was going to serve him first, but he said no, that it was my turn.'

'So what happened then?'

'The guy poured the drinks . . . Guinness first, because it takes longer to settle.'

'Okay,' said Bell, as if he was building up to something. 'So he pours the Guinness and puts it down in front of you, then goes back to the lager tap. Right?'

'Right.'

'Was that when you put the atropine into the Guinness?' he asked. 'When the barman wasn't looking?'

I gasped in real amazement. 'I didn't put anything into that glass!' I protested.

'So you say. I take it that Mr Phillips got the second round.'

'Yes.'

'And was the bar crowded then?'

'Not the serving area, no.'

'So no one else could have spiked the second one?'

'The barman could have,' I pointed out.

'Forget the barman. He's worked there for twenty-three years, and his brother owns the place. No, Blackstone, as I see it the only person who could have poisoned that drink was you. I'm looking at attempted murder here.'

I was incredulous, but in spite of that, I felt myself go cold with fear. 'Don't be daft,' I protested. 'David Phillips will be my father-in-law in a few weeks. What possible motive would I have for trying to kill him?'

Detective Inspector Bell leaned back in his chair and laughed. 'Listen, son, you shouldn't believe everything you read in crime novels. I don't give a stuff about motives; I don't care what goes on in criminals' minds. I just look for opportunity, that's all. Mr Phillips was poisoned by atropine added to his drink, and only you had the opportunity to do it.'

'No!'

'Who else then? You watched that drink being poured, you picked it up and you carried it over to him.'

I looked back at him, replaying that scene at the same time. 'No,' I said again. 'I did take my eye off it at one point. I turned round and asked David whether he wanted crisps or nuts. The stuff must have been added then.'

'By whom?'

'What about the guy behind me at the bar?'

'What about him? The barman says he doesn't remember him. And why should he? He serves hundreds of punters in a day. Naw, I don't buy your mystery man . . .' Bell paused and a wicked smile spread over his face.

'Unless,' he said, slowly, dragging the word out, 'unless it was the same mystery man who shoved your wee nephew into the Bottle Dungeon on Saturday.'

I felt my jaw drop. 'Surprised you, eh,' the detective continued. 'You never thought we'd link the two incidents, did you. But I've been talking to a lot of people since last night, son. We've never heard of you before on this force, so I decided to try your name on the other Scottish police.

'And guess what? I discover that at the weekend you reported an assault on your nephew in St Andrews Castle. You claimed that he was attacked by an unknown man. Then I find out that a few weeks ago you were involved in an incident in Union Street during a film shoot. You knocked a lady to the ground, then told the investigating officers that someone was about to shoot her from a motorcycle. Yet when they looked at the film that was shot, they couldn't see any gun, or hear anything above the traffic noise. They haven't recovered a bullet either, and they've swept every inch of the area.

'The way they see it now, it was just as likely that you dived at her and tried to shove her in front of that motorbike. They also said that they suspected there was a link between you and the woman, and that you were reluctant to confirm it, although eventually you did. They hadn't any evidence against you, but now that I've told them about this thing . . .'

He paused, leaning forward across the desk. He was an ugly man close up, with more of a snout than a nose. 'On top of that,' he grunted. 'I discover from the Strathclyde that their computer coughed up your name as having called them about a fire at your house a few weeks ago, in which a car was completely destroyed. It was written up as an accident, but when I spoke to the senior fire officer who attended the incident, his attitude struck me as more than a wee bit odd. He told me to fuck off, in fact, when I pressed him.'

'Why don't you then?'

'Aye, you'd like me to do that, wouldn't you,' Bell muttered. 'I won't though; I've got you, son, by the short and curlies. So why don't you just admit it all, eh?'

I glanced at the tape, to make sure it was still running. 'There is nothing to admit,' I told him, as steadily and clearly as I could. 'All of those incidents happened, sure; and I now believe that they were the work of one person, but not me, not me. Someone has a grudge against me and he's taking it out on my friends and family. Investigate that, why don't you, if you can see beyond the end of your piggy nose.'

He scowled at me, but didn't rise to my bait. 'Why should I look further when the obvious truth is right under my not unattractive nose? Like I said I don't need to find a motive, Blackstone, and you don't need to have one either, to have done all these things. You just have to be a bad bastard, that's all.'

Bell rose to his feet. 'This interview is terminated . . .' he glanced at his watch '. . . at nine-forty a.m..' Slattery switched off the tape.

'You can phone a lawyer, Blackstone. I'm arresting you, and you'll be detained while I make further enquiries. After that I intend to consult the procurator fiscal, and I expect that he'll authorise me to charge you with the attempted murder of Mr Phillips. Once you're on remand, we can look at all the other charges.'

He leaned over towards me and tapped the side of his head. 'By the way, when the shrinks have a talk to you, you'd be well advised not to tell them that somebody's got it in for you. You'll be better off going to jail for ten years than to the state mental hospital for ever.'

37

They used to hang people in Perth Prison. I've heard that for many of them, it was the preferred option to being locked up there for life. For most of that day I was afraid that I was headed there myself, without even the opportunity to be topped.

I called Greg McPhillips, my solicitor in Glasgow, but by that time he was already on his way to Perth under instructions from Primavera.

They put me in a cell, down in the bowels of the building, and left me there for hours. They took all my possessions: my wallet, my watch, my pen, my cellphone, even my belt and shoe laces.

Greg was there within the hour. When he arrived we were allowed a brief meeting in my hotel suite, and I told him exactly what had happened. 'What does Prim's Dad say?' he asked, sat alongside me on the hard bench, with its rudimentary rubber mattress.

'Last time I heard him he was worried about his vegetable patch. I don't know if they'll get any sense out of him, but even if they do, I don't think he'll be able to help. I doubt if he could see what was happening at the bar from where he was sitting.'

'Mmm,' he muttered. 'That doesn't leave me much to work with, then.' Greg's bedside manner did nothing to encourage me.

'What will help, then?' I asked him.

'John MacPhee, the fiscal here, did his training period with our firm. He's still a good friend of my father, and I knew him when he was depute in Glasgow. I'll try to get to see him before this man Bell does.'

He left, and I was back on my own in that hot stuffy cell. They didn't even let Prim in to see me. The longer the day wore on, the more convinced I was that I would be spending the night in the slammer. I couldn't remember whether they'd have to charge me first, but the lack of communication made me feel more and more that that was inevitable anyway.

At mid-day, a young constable brought me a sandwich, a mug of tea, and a copy of the *Courier*. At three o'clock, he brought me more tea and a copy of the *Daily Record*. When I asked if I could have the *Financial Times* with my evening meal, he looked at me blankly.

Then, at twenty-one minutes past five, the door opened again, and the custody sergeant appeared. He handed me my belt and laces. 'CID want you again,' he told me. I felt like a possession as I relaced my shoes, relooped my belt, and followed him upstairs, back to the same dull interview room in which I'd been grilled in the morning.

Bell and Slattery were there, but this time, Greg McPhillips was with them. When he slipped me a quick wink I knew it was going to be all right.

'Hello, Mr Blackstone,' the DI began. The courtesy of the title confirmed the meaning of Greg's wink. 'Have they looked after you all right downstairs?'

I nodded. 'It was okay. Mind you, the sandwich was a bit curly round the edges. Next time, I'll have a pizza.'

'I'll make a careful note of that, sir.' He shot me a look which told me quite clearly that he was enjoying this meeting a lot less than our last.

'It's been decided that we should release you, Mr Blackstone,' he said, slowly and, to my ear at least, with reluctance. 'The fiscal doesn't want me to charge you at this stage, so you're free to go, pending further enquiries.' I knew that the last part was a pure face-saver.

'Aren't you going to tell me not to leave town?' I asked.

'We know where to find you, sir.' Bell stood up and glanced at Slattery. 'See to Mr Blackstone's release, Tony.' He gave my solicitor a brief nod and strode from the room.

On the way back to Auchterarder, Greg filled me in on what had happened during the day. He had spoken to his dad's friend the fiscal, as promised, and had given me a glowing character reference.

Mike Dylan had been a big help too. Prim had told him what had happened, and he had phoned Bell, making it clear that there was no way I could have sabotaged Susie's car, since I hadn't been out of the room for more than a minute during all the time they'd been with us. I found out later that evening, when I phoned the man himself to arrange to see him next morning, that he had also told Bell that by arresting me he was compromising a Special Branch operation, and that he'd better let me go before he compromised his own pension . . . a lie, he admitted, but it was one that I appreciated.

However the lion's share of credit for my release went to my nephew Jonathan. He had been interviewed, in his mother's presence, by Bell and Slattery; they had tried hard to trip him up, but he had been adamant that I had never left his side in the Castle, that Colin had run off on his own, and that there was no way I had pushed him into the dungeon.

'The police case was always founded on the closeness of those two incidents, and your involvement in them both,' said Greg. 'When that collapsed there was no way John MacPhee would have gone to court on the Auchterarder business alone, not without really strong evidence against you.'

'Far less without any evidence against me,' I added. I must have sounded a bit sour, for he glanced at me.

'Don't hold it against John,' he protested. 'In the real world the police will always go for the easy option, you know that.'

'Sure I do. That's not what's pissing me off: today's history as far as I'm concerned. No, the trouble is that now I'm back where I started this morning. If I'm not the mad bastard behind all these things that have been happening around me, then someone else is. But given Bell's reaction when I put that to him, the police will never take me seriously.

'No, I'm on my own. I tell you, pal, you don't know the chance you're taking just being in this car with me.'

38

Any visitor to Glasgow who wants to judge the priority given to police-community relations on the public policy agenda need only look at the headquarters of the Strathclyde force. The red-brick monstrosity in Pitt Street isn't just the ugliest building in the city, it's the most forbidding.

I'd have felt mildly uncomfortable stepping through its dark doorway under any circumstances, but after my experience in Perth the day before, it took an effort of will to step up to the desk and ask for Detective Inspector Dylan. Mike seemed to realise this right away, as soon as he met me there. It was as if he was trying to cheer me up; he was beaming and whistling . . . very badly, as usual . . . an old tune from *South Pacific*.

He walked me, not to his office, but to the canteen. I was pleased to see that we were the only people there. 'What's up, Oz?' he asked, as he brought two coffees and two rolls, stuffed with square, sliced Lorne sausage, across to our table. I'd told him when I called that it was his turn to lay on breakfast. 'I thought this would be the last place you'd want to come today. I like the Horseshoe, too.'

'It's safer here,' I told him. 'Nobody's going to lace the brown sauce with powdered glass.'

'That's true. I wouldn't trust the probationers not to piss in the coffee urn, though. I'll give you a tip. If you ever eat in a jail make sure it's with the prisoners, not the staff.'

I treated him to the Blackstone scowl. Until recently it had been a rare sight; now I was afraid that I was becoming too good at it. 'I'd have been eating in one today, if your Perth colleague Bell had had his way. Thanks, by the way, for your help in getting me out of that.'

'No problem. I'm looking forward to your wedding, remember. I fancy a night at Gleneagles, on you.' He paused. 'Keep that to yourself, though, Oz. My boss would not be chuffed if he knew I used my SB position to lean on another force, especially since I was telling the guy porkies.'

'My lips to God's ear alone,' I promised.

'I sort of pity the poor bastard,' Dylan murmured, with a half smile. 'I'll bet he thought he'd got a serial nutter on his hands. He sounded like the sort of polis who keeps the press cuttings on his investigations. If the case against you had held up he'd have filled a whole bloody jotter with them.'

'I'm sorry I ruined his day,' I answered. 'But he didn't do a hell of a lot for mine.'

'I suppose not,' Mike mumbled through a mouthful of peppery sausage. 'What do you want to talk to me about, then? You were mysterious on the phone last night.'

While he ate, I filled him in on my conspiracy theory. By the time I had finished, so had he.

'Are you trying to tell me that when Susie's car blew up that was meant for you?' he asked, wiping his mouth. 'Do you think the wrong car was booby-trapped?'

'No. This guy's been watching me like a hawk. He knows what Prim and I drive. I'm saying he's after my close friends and family, but always when they're with me. I'm guessing that he may have been after making me suffer long-term, like being banged up for life.'

'But why send those letters to Susie?'

It was my turn to attack the rolls, so he had to wait for an answer. 'To start us off on a false trail?' I suggested.

'Think about it. Susie gets the letters, then you and she are cremated in her motor. Tragic, but no one links it to me. Then Noosh Turkel gets shot right alongside me up in Aberdeen. A big coincidence, sure, but it's different forces who investigate, so they won't make the connection.

'Then my wee nephew's shoved down a twelve-foot drop; potentially fatal, and I'm there. I report it, and I kick up hell's delight with the police, so they remember my name.

'Next day, someone poisons my future father-in-law and I'm the obvious and only suspect. And as soon as the first copper feeds my name into a computer, all that stuff pops out.

'And, apart from the fatalities, that's exactly what happened.'

It was Mike's turn to watch me eat. When I had finished, it was his turn to quiz me. 'Are you telling me that I've had a Special Branch operation, phone taps the lot, watching the wrong man?'

'Yes, I suppose I am. Stephen Donn doesn't know me from Adam, far less have a grudge against me.'

'Jesus! So who do you reckon could hate you this much?'

'What about Ricky Ross?'

Dylan gasped, audibly. 'Ricky?' His old boss in Edinburgh; disgraced and kicked off the force for reasons not unconnected with Prim and me. He seemed to do me the courtesy of thinking about it. 'Ricky?' he said again. 'He hates your guts, that's for sure, and he's tough. If someone in a balaclava hauled you up close and kicked your head in, he's just about the first guy I'd look for. But I worked for him; I know him, I think, reasonably well.

'If he was really minded to, and he thought he could get away with it, he might just be capable of coming straight for you and killing you. But he wouldn't touch anyone else. He wouldn't kill me just to set you up, or your wee nephew, or anyone else.'

He frowned. 'But there's something you've missed, isn't there?'

'That's right,' I agreed. 'London. That connects to me too, and I need to find out how.'

'Maybe I can help you. Wait here.' He stood and walked out of the canteen, leaving me alone for more than five minutes. When he came back he was carrying a folder.

'Remember I said I was going to have someone check the hospitals in London? Well I did, and they came up with something. I wasn't going to do anything about it, since I thought that incident was closed, but . . . Do you see anyone in here you recognise?'

He handed me the folder. I opened it and a face looked out at me; it was the sort of portrait they take full face and profile, with a number hung round your neck. The last time I'd seen the subject he'd been in more than a bit of pain. There was another photograph below it; the man with the sore throat.

'I see you recognise them. In that case . . .' He took a piece of paper, torn from a notebook, from his pocket, and handed it across to me. 'Those are their names, and that's the pub where they drink, and where they were probably paid by the man who sent them to do you.

'They're a couple of small-timers, with small-time form. They work as collectors for a loan shark, mainly.' He looked at me. 'Listen Oz, I can't get involved any more than I have down there. You could always make a belated complaint to the local police, I suppose, but you'd need to be careful. You might have trouble explaining the guy's broken arm.'

'That's all right,' I assured him. 'I know how I'm going to handle it.'

'Be careful, then. These are rough people; you might not be so lucky next time.'

'Don't worry, luck won't come into it.' I picked up my coffee, but the mug was cold so I decided I didn't fancy it any more. 'What about the other incidents? When I tried to sell my theory to Bell, he thought I was daft.'

'He would. You probably are. But I'll grant you, the idea that different people would make unprovoked attacks on your nephew and Prim's Dad within three days stretches credibility a bit. There are open investigations on these incidents as it is, and thanks to Bell – you have to give him credit for something – the CID in Fife and Tayside, and in Aberdeen for that matter, will be comparing notes from now on. That's as much as the police can do. From your point of view, you're right to keep to yourself as much as you can. I can put a discreet watch on you, just in case, and I will.'

Mike smiled. As I looked at him, it struck me that maybe he wasn't quite as bad a detective as I'd always thought. 'There's one part of your theory I don't buy, though,' he said. 'Stephen Donn. He did have a reason to threaten Susie, and he's been behaving oddly, no mistake. Those photos didn't vanish on their own.

'He's up to something, and the Amsterdam connection makes me think it might be drugs. That's part of our remit now, so it gives me an excuse to keep looking for him.'

I shrugged my shoulders. 'Just you do that, pal,' I told him. 'But I'll be looking for someone else – starting in London.'

39

Liam was all for a trip to London, when I asked him, especially when I said that I would pick up the tab. I only found out when we landed at Heathrow in mid-afternoon, and she met us, that Erin had a between-flight lay-over in the capital that night.

We settled into the Rubens, not far from Buckingham Palace; I went for a look at the Queen's Art Gallery, leaving Ireland's couple of the year to amuse themselves until it was time for my minder and me to do our business.

'So,' Liam asked as the taxi headed for the East End, 'who were those masked men, then?'

'There names are Ronnie and Vic Neames,' I told him. 'They're brothers.'

'How do we know they're going to be at this pub?'

'According to Mike's contacts on the Met, we'd find them there every night of their lives. It's not just their local; if they have an office, that's it.'

'And they work for a tallyman, you said. I think I'm going to enjoy this. I hate those bastards; when I was a kid in Belfast I saw the misery they can cause.'

The pub was called the Duck and Diver, just off Barking Road, not far from the West Ham United football ground. The taxi driver seemed just a touch nervous as I paid him, as if he was anxious to get on his way. The bar was quiet as we stepped inside, but it was still short of seven, so that didn't strike us as odd. We fitted ourselves up with a couple of pints of lager and sat in a corner booth, spinning them out and watching television. We had been there for just over half an hour when *EastEnders* came on. I had the feeling that I was part of the cast, back on set.

We made the beer last as long as we could, until we started drawing odd looks from the barman. I was just about to go across to order two more when the door beside us swung open and three men walked in off the street. They were all big, and one had a cast on his right arm.

Liam put a hand on my shoulder and stood up. 'Hello there, lads,' he called out. 'I thought you'd never get here.'

They swung round at once, all three of them. Ronnie Neames was the one with the broken arm. His eyes widened in surprise as he recognised Liam, then me: and a wicked smile crossed his face. 'I've dreamed abaht seeing you two again . . . on our turf.

'Vic, Mickey,' he said to the other two. 'I owe these bahstards some broken bones.' As he spoke, I saw the barman make himself scarce. The two heavies started off in the opposite direction, towards us.

Liam Matthews is big, but not huge. However, he is very, very fast, and he has an impressively high Dan black belt in karate. Poor old Mickey never knew what hit him; in fact, it was Liam's right foot, just under the jaw. He rose a couple of inches into the air, then hit the ground with a thud that shook two empty glasses off the nearest table. Vic stopped in his tracks.

'Wise fella,' drawled the Irishman. 'We didn't come here to

beat you up again, boys . . . although personally, I wouldn't mind a bit. My pal here wants to talk to you, that's all. So come and sit down; it would be bad for your business if the punters saw me drop another of yis, wouldn't it.'

Leaving their fallen pal where he lay, the Brothers Neames came over to our table, pulled up two stools and sat down. 'Good of you,' I said. 'Like Liam says we're not here for bother. We just want to talk to you about the guy who paid you to do me over.'

'We don't know nuffin',' croaked Vic, hoarsely. I guessed that my stunner move was still having an effect.

I opened my jacket just wide enough to let Ronnie see the bundle of notes in my inside pocket. 'I'm not so sure about that,' I murmured. 'Have you seen the guy since?'

The big thug shook his head, and rested his plaster cast on the table. 'No. Didn't expect to. You guys showed up un-damaged on the telly, din'cha.'

'Describe him for me again.'

'In 'is twenties, fair 'air, wearin' jeans and them sunglasses I told you abaht before.' Ronnie looked at his brother. 'What would you say, Vic?'

'That's 'im, Ron.'

'What about his accent?' I asked.

'He didn't have one,' Ron replied. 'He spoke proper, but not posh. Nuffin' you could pin down.'

'Okay. Now, I want to know exactly what he said about me. Why did he want me done over, and how did you know to come for me?'

The big thug looked at the table. To my surprise, he seemed embarrassed, and not a little nervous. 'Well,' he began, 'the fing is . . . It was really this geezer 'ere we was supposed to do.'

'You what?' said Liam, starting from his chair. I grabbed his arm and pulled him back down.

'That's right, mate. The bloke said 'e wanted you done.'

'But why, for Christ's sake?'

'He never said, and we never arsked.' He paused. 'Sometimes in this life, you can know too many things,' he added. I'd never have taken him for a philosopher; just goes to show, doesn't it.

'Did he say anything at all about me?'

'Nuffink,' Ronnie declared, 'only that 'e wanted your 'ead rearranged.'

'Tell us exactly what happened,' I said.

'The geezer turned up 'ere looking for us; told us 'e'd been sent by the man we work for. He showed us a picture, see,' the Cockney went on, 'of the two of you together. He said he wanted your mate done, beat up bad, like. We was supposed to follow 'im back to 'is hotel, then once everyone 'ad gone down for the night, Vic was to jemmy the bedroom door – that's one of 'is specialities . . .' said his proud brother, 'and I was to cave 'is bleedin' head in wiff a baseball bat.'

'You mean kill me?' Liam demanded.

'Well put it this way, mate; we wasn't told not to. But we never meant to go that far, 'onest.'

'But you said you would, for four hundred?'

Ron shook his head. 'No. He gave us five 'undred down. The deal was another grand each once you was done. But even that ain't enough for killin' a geezer.' He turned back to me, avoiding Liam's glare.

'Like I said we was never really up for killin' 'im. We thought let's just give him a kickin', five 'undred quid's worth like.

'So we went to the show, to see if there was a chance of doin' 'im there, afterwards. But once we'd seen 'im in action, we didn't fancy it at all, did we. So we thought, why not go for you instead, give you the kickin', then tell the geezer that 'e'd pointed to the wrong bloke in the picture. That way, maybe we'd get to keep the money, no fuss.

'You mean you'd just have given it back if he'd asked?'

'Mister, anyone who'd pay us to kill your mate could pay someone else to do us. Besides, there was something about this geezer. We didn't fancy 'im, like.'

'If I were you then, lads,' I said. 'I'd watch your backs. The guy's been a bit busy since then, but you're right. If he ever does get round to asking for his money back, you could be in trouble.'

'This guy,' Liam muttered. 'Could he have been Irish?'

'On 'is grandmother's side, maybe, but that's all. Didn't sound it.'

'What about the baseball bat?' I asked. 'Why did he specify that?'

'Dunno. We were told to leave it there though. I thought that was funny at the time.' I didn't; I got the point right away.

'What about the photograph? Was it posed like a GWA publicity shot?'

Big Ron shook his mis-shapen head. 'Nah. Wasn't like that. It was an ordinary photo, and yet it wasn't. You didn't know it was being taken; it was like the coppers 'ad been watching you and takin' yer picture.'

'I see,' I said – and I did. I picked up a beer mat, ripped off the facing, and wrote my cellphone number on the white surface beneath. 'If you ever do hear from him again, get in touch with me.

'Come on, Liam, let's leave the lads to take care of their wounded.' Mickey was still on the floor; he was conscious and moaning softly as the barman held a wet towel against his jaw. As I stood Ronnie nodded his head in the general direction of my jacket.

'But what about . . .?'

'What about what?'

'Abaht the money, mate? You said . . .'

I smiled at him. 'I said not a bleedin' word . . . mate. So long.'

40

'It all fits now, Mike.' We were at a corner table in one of my favourite restaurants, one of Glasgow's oldest and finest Asian eateries, not far from the university. Liam and I had caught the ten-fifteen shuttle from Heathrow, allowing me time to make a few calls and to arrange to meet my policeman pal for lunch.

'Ronnie and Vic were shown a snatched photo of Liam and me. This guy has been keeping very careful tabs on me and my friends, then setting them up. The jigsaw's complete: the London incident wasn't an odd piece; it fits exactly.

'It's just as well that the Neames brothers take a cautious approach to their business. If they had jemmied Liam's door open and he'd woken up in time, they might have left in body bags – but if not, he might.'

I paused. 'Christ, Mike, but I had some job calming him down last night. I had to tell him what's been happening, but it took me a while to convince him that I wasn't crazy. He wouldn't have it at first; reckoned that it was someone out of his past, not mine. He had two theories, either that he had knocked off the wrong man's woman at some point – before he met Erin, Liam would have shagged anything that moved – or that something from his youth in Belfast might have come back to haunt him.'

'Did he say what?'

'No. And I didn't ask him. Eventually he accepted what I was telling him, that the attack was linked to me rather than him.'

'Wait a minute, though.' Dylan paused to munch on a pakora. 'If someone had broken into your man's bedroom and caved his head in, why should that have been linked to you?'

'Because a couple of years ago Liam and I had a very public falling out, in Newcastle. It was my first weekend with the GWA. He came on way too strong to Jan, I got the red mist and banjoed him.'

Dylan stared at me. 'You thumped Matthews?' he gasped.

'Like I said, I didn't think about it at the time. Fortunately Everett was there, and he stepped in. We're all fine with each other now, but it was the talk of the town at the time.'

'Sure, but that was two years ago.'

'Which tells me that my evil-wisher knows a hell of a lot about me; maybe he's been watching me for all that time. And what about the baseball bat?' I added.

'What about it?'

'They were told to leave it there.'

'So?'

'So the police could put me in the frame for the job, eventually. If Liam had been done, they'd have been bound to search the hotel for a weapon. No way could they have proved I'd smuggled it out of the hotel in the middle of the night, especially if I hadn't. But if they'd found it in Liam's room . . .

'Later on, in the context of a string of charges against the mad serial killer Blackstone, the very fact that the bat and I were in the same hotel might have been enough.'

'Not for the Crown Prosecution Service, surely.'

'Oh no? Given my history with Liam? Ladies and gentlemen of the jury, we submit that Mr Blackstone, with a long memory for an old insult, had opportunity, access, and oh look, there's the weapon. You tell me they wouldn't have run with that.'

'Maybe,' Mike conceded. 'They'd have given you some trouble over it, that's for sure.' He spooned some Lamb Madras on to his boiled rice. 'So what's the next move, maestro?' he asked.

'That's the trouble, I don't have one. This guy's paralysed my life, man – or he's trying to. I could make myself safe, I suppose, by hiring a bodyguard and hiding in my flat, but if I do that I might as well be in Perth nick.

'There's only one positive thing I can do: get back out there and try to smoke the bastard out. I'm off to Cardiff tonight with the GWA: I spoke to Everett before I came here and put him in the picture. I offered to pull out of the show, but you know the Big Man. He told me that chances are I'm imagining the whole thing, but that even if I'm not, there's no way he'll back off from any maternal fornicator. So it's business as usual, but he's going to treble security at the arena and in the hotel, just in case.

'Then on Monday, I'm due in London to complete my stint on Miles' movie. I called him as well, although Prim had already been in touch with Dawn. They have on-site security too, so there should be no risk there.'

Dylan nodded. 'There's not much else you can do. I'll make sure that your folks, Ellen, Prim and her parents are all under police observation. How's Mr Phillips, by the way?'

'SuperDave? He's recovering well. His brain was pretty

fried by the atropine, but they don't reckon there'll be any lasting damage; they're letting him home this afternoon. Prim's staying up there for the weekend.'

'Best place for her. When she gets back to Glasgow, tell her to travel everywhere by taxi. That car park of yours is vulnerable, as we all know too well.

'Mind you, Oz,' he continued, 'my guess is that the man may have played himself out. If he's watching you as closely as you think, he'll know that you spent Tuesday with the police and that you were released. He'll know as well that you've been to London with Matthews, and even if he didn't follow you there, he'll have guessed why.

'So chances are, he'll have worked out by now that you've rumbled his strategy.'

I liked his reasoning. 'That's good news, then.'

'For your nearest and dearest, maybe; for you maybe not. This guy's been prepared to kill or maim your relatives and friends just to make you suffer. He may not be inclined to walk away, simply because he can't do that easily any more. He may decide instead to finish it all with a direct attack on you.

'So I would watch it, Oz. I'd be very careful. In fact, it might not be a bad idea to hire that bodyguard.'

Having cheered me up for a second, he'd dropped me right back in it. I waited until he was chewing on his next mouthful of our shared Madras, before I said, 'Don't you think I should hire a food taster as well?'

41

I really did think about hiring that minder; but eventually I decided that since the most vulnerable part of my weekend was going to be the time I spent standing in the middle of a Welsh wrestling ring in front of thousands of spectators, he wouldn't have been much good to me when it really mattered.

So partly for that reason, partly out of pride, and partly because, despite the lottery cash and all the other money in which I was wallowing, I was at heart still a parsimonious Fifer, I decided that I would do without close personal protection.

I met the GWA crowd as usual that afternoon, having first called my Dad to explain to him what I believed had been happening, and having phoned Noosh Turkel, to tell her – without going into too much detail – that the chances were that the Russian Mafia did not, in fact, have a price on her head.

Understandably, Liam was still slightly worked up by our discovery that he had been the original target of the bungling brothers. To reassure him, I called Dylan and persuaded him to check to confirm that there was no Irish intelligence to suggest that he was on anyone's hit list.

I can't deny that I was nervous as the lights went up for our live Saturday show in the Cardiff National Arena. There I was, in a red tuxedo no less, standing in mid-ring booming out my usual welcome to *GWA Battleground*, to a crowd which for all I knew might have included a crack shot with a sniper's rifle. I was out of there as fast as I could; I hoped that the punters wouldn't notice, but Everett did.

As I settled back into my ringside seat, I heard his voice in my earpiece, from his position up in the production tower. 'Buddy,' he said. 'I told you I didn't mind if you did your announcements from ringside rather than up there in full view. But if you're gonna do it like usual, you do it like usual; you don't bolt out of there like the Roadrunner with Wiley E Coyote on his ass.'

I glanced up into the gloom, in his general direction, and nodded.

As it turned out, no one shot me, or blew me up or anything else. After the show, Liam walked me out to the bus and, back at the hotel, he insisted on sharing a room with me. All through the weekend I kept in touch with Prim, Ellie and my Dad, but I was reassured. None of them had seen anything unusual. Back at Auchterarder, David was recovering well from his poisoning. He was quiet, and not a little embarrassed. 'I offered to take him for a pint,' Prim told me. 'You should have seen the look on his face.'

'Ask him if he's started on his new range of models yet.'

I didn't fly back to Glasgow with the team on Sunday. Instead I caught a train to London where I was met by Miles' and Dawn's assistant, Geraldine Baker. It's no myth; movie stars, when they're working, really do have people to do everything but think for them – although, in the case of one or two who come to mind, thinking is virtually the only thing they're not capable of handling personally.

She wasn't alone; waiting with her on the platform as I jumped out of the train was a slim dark-haired bloke, a newcomer to the team. 'Hello Oz,' she greeted me. 'This is Mark Kravitz, he's just joined the production team. Come on, the car's just outside.'

The studio scenes of our movie were being shot on a massive sound stage just south of London, in Surrey. For the duration, Miles and Dawn had rented another mansion, this time near Farnham. It wasn't quite as big as the one on Deeside, but it was pretty tasty nonetheless. It was big enough to accommodate them plus, from the cast, Scott Steele, Nelson Reed, who played the bad guy, and me, plus Frank Gilet, the director of photography, Weir Dobbs, the assistant director, Kiki Eldon, the PR lady and Geraldine. Some of the grafters on the production crew were accommodated in hotels close to the studio, but most, I gathered, could commute from London.

We got there just in time for dinner. Dawn had hired a chef from a London agency, a big black guy who appeared in the drawing room while we were sipping sherry, to run through the menu for us. Once he had finished, my future sister-in-law took my arm and pulled me into a corner. 'Miles and I flew up to see Dad yesterday,' she said, quietly. 'He's okay, thank God, but he's had a bit of a shake. Oz, it scares me just to think about it.

'We're taking no chances with this character. For as long as you're with us, Mark will be going everywhere with you. We've hired him from a firm of security consultants.'

I'd have appreciated being consulted myself about that, but I wasn't of a mind to protest. I didn't want to leave any more casualties lying in my wake. So I simply nodded and said,

'Fair enough. I'll pick up his tab though; this is my problem, after all.'

'Oh no,' Dawn insisted. 'We're all involved. Mark's fee is part of the production costs; we've even done a deal with his firm. They get billing in the end titles.'

I had to laugh. 'I can see it now: bodyguard to Mr Blackstone, Mark Kravitz.'

'Not quite. Personal assistant to Mr Blackstone, actually.'

'Bugger me,' I gasped. 'I'll be getting a star on my door next.'

She gave me a funny wee smile. 'You never know . . .' she whispered, turning and walking over to the bar on the sideboard.

'How you doin', son?' Scott Steele bore down on me, hand outstretched. 'Good to see you again.' I noted that he was not one of nature's sherry-sippers. The old boy was straight into the straight malt.

'Not bad, actually. Glad to be back with the team.'

'Aye, I heard you had a difficult time last week.'

Jesus, I wondered, *how much does he know?*

He answered my silent question at once. 'Dawn says her father's on the mend, though,' he said. 'I was glad to hear it. Food poisoning can be a real leveller, especially for us older guys.'

As well as a chef, Miles had hired a butler. He brought our conversation to an abrupt halt with a call from the doorway, 'Ladies and gentlemen, dinner is served.'

Prim and I don't regard ourselves as super-rich, only ordinary rich. So it would be pretentious for us even to think about hiring a private chef. But if we ever did, I wouldn't look past the guy who cooked for us in that Surrey mansion. His menu was at first sight robust, lobster, followed by a mango sorbet freshener, then medallions of beef in a rich port-enhanced sauce, but he had the touch and sensitivity of a true artist. By the time the crème brûlée arrived, all the movie talk had subsided, and we were discussing nothing but our chef and his talents. He chose the wines too, a nice white Rioja and a rare but very interesting light German red.

We were well into the coffee and Sambucca before I remembered why we were there. 'So what's the schedule for the week, Miles? I asked, across the table.

'Easy for you tomorrow, mate,' he replied. 'You're in the sound studio beginning your narration sequences. That's where you'll be all this week, in fact. Next week though, you're on set.'

I frowned at him, my curiosity stirred; I hadn't been expecting that. At once, he answered the question which was written on my face. 'We've been playing around with the ending, Oz. One of my few virtues as a movie-maker is my flexibility. If I think something will work, I'll go with it. I've never been completely sold on the way the script finished, neither has Dawn. So when she suggested an extra twist, I had the screen-writer work it up. It involves you.'

'Hey,' I said, doubtfully. 'I'm stretched to my limit as it is.'

'No you're not, Oz. You're still finding your limit. We've all been watching you work, Dawn and I, and Weir; you're never going to play Hamlet, old son, but you can do this.' He reached under the table, picked up a sheaf of paper, and tossed it across to me.

'That's the revise; read it, learn it and get ready to rehearse it. We shoot it next week.'

I picked it up and began to read, as conversations continued around me. There wasn't a lot of it, but I studied every line slowly and carefully. The deeper into it I got, the further removed I seemed to become from everyone in the room. As the implications of the changes dawned on me, the only sound I could hear was my own heavy breathing. As I finished and looked up, I realised that was because everyone was watching me.

'What the hell's this?' I asked. 'I'm the villain?'

Miles nodded. 'That's right. You and Dawn are the bad guys.' He laughed. 'Shit man, anyone can make a rich-girl-snatched-for-ransom-rescued-from-the-jaws-of-death-by-heroic-boyfriend type of movie. But I like my endings to have zing. So in the end, you and I land on the deserted rig carrying the access documents to the Lugano bank where Scott, your father, has lodged the ten million pounds ransom money. We expect to find Dawn, your sister in the movie, and the bad guy we've been tracing all through. Only we don't. There's no one there but her.

'I realise that she's planned the whole thing, but what I don't twig at first is that you're in on it too. The twist is that Scott has remarried and has changed his will to leave everything to your new step-mother; you and Dawn don't like it. You know also that he has an illness which will kill him inside two years, so you dream up this kidnap scam to claim your inheritance, sort of in advance.

'Like you can see from the script, it works.'

I stared at him. 'But I'm not qualified for this,' I protested.

'Sure you are. You're a natural, Oz. I suspect that you've been a bit of a play-actor all your life.'

I thought about that. It's certainly true that when I was a kid I had so many imaginary friends that I wasn't sure at times what I was doing and with whom. Christ, thinking back, I almost had to keep a diary. In those times too, Jan and I used to plan adventures and act them out. But still . . .

'Isn't it a risk, though? Okay, you're happy with what I've done so far, but every step forward is into unknown territory.'

'Where's the risk?' Dawn countered, in her LA-modified Perthshire accent. 'You take a look at Miles' record as a film-maker, not just from the critics' viewpoint, but in financial terms too. He's always made money on his projects, often very big money, yet he's always flown by the seat of his pants. If this doesn't work we'll go back to the original ending, and the cost of the extra shoot will be all that we've lost. Even then, we've had good luck with the weather, so that won't put us over budget.'

Weir Dobbs leaned over and looked up the table at me. 'Don't get carried away here, Oz,' said the chubby wee New Yorker. 'We've given you a few extra scenes, that's all. Everyone agrees that this is a better ending, but it's your character that makes it work, not you. Read the script carefully and you'll see that it's Miles and Dawn who have to do the serious acting, not you.'

I treated him to a mock scowl. 'That's you friggin' movie people all over, isn't it,' I told him. 'First you build a guy up, then you slap him right back down.'

'You better believe it, son,' Scott Steele chuckled.

'What d'you say then, Oz?' Miles asked.

I looked him dead in the eye. 'Same as I always say. You better talk to my agent.'

'Jeez,' he said, turning pure Aussie. 'You are learning this business.'

42

Voicing over isn't all that difficult, honest. Ever since I've been involved in it, I've been amazed at the silliness of the money in relation to the skills required for the work. Maybe I'm down-playing it, but when I was in her class at primary school in Anstruther, Mary taught me not just to read, but to do it with feeling, with expression and with an understanding of the meaning of the words.

That's all I've ever done whenever I've stood in front of a mike with a script in my hand, or stood up in a wrestling ring with a prepared text and a list of circus names in my head. If anyone wants to call it performing, that's fine by me, but I know what it is; it's just like being back in Mary's class, reading or reciting in front of the other kids.

If the money is silly for television ads, then for movies – especially American projects – it's positively insane. Late in my first day in studio, most of which I had spent wearing headphones and rehearsing my narration lines, getting them, without too much difficulty, just as Weir Dobbs wanted them, Mark Kravitz called me to the phone.

It was Sly Burr. 'Hi kid,' he oiled down the line. 'How's it going in Hollywoodland?'

'It just feels like Surrey to me,' I told him. 'You know what I mean. They still have Tory MPs, every dustbin has its own fox, and all the kids belong to the pony club. A bit like

Neverneverland; the PR girl here even looks like Tinkerbell.'

'Is that right?' said Sly, almost blankly. Like many show-biz people, unless he is haggling over money – or maybe especially when he's haggling over money – Sly has no ear for anyone's voice but his own. 'To business, kid, to business,' he went on. 'I had a call from Miles this morning, about the new scenes he wants you to shoot.'

'Bloody Hell!' I exclaimed. 'I was joking when I told him to speak to you.'

'What for? I know you're going to be brothers-in-law and such, but this is business, serious business – and not just for you. I get a piece as well, remember. Okay, so he calls me and he tells me what he plans to do with you, so I tell him, "Wait a minute there, Miles, this changes the whole deal. You hire my boy as narrator, now you want to give him a key part. It can't be for the same money."

'Then he tells me I'm a chiselling bastard and I tell him "Sure, I am; that's why guys in your business hire guys like me". Then he laughs and we get down to the nut-cutting. At the end of the day, I've got you feature billing below the titles, and you're in for half-a-point.'

'Fine, Sly,' I said. 'Now tell me what that means.'

'It means that in the movie credits, on the posters and in all the promo material, you'll have separate billing. You'll come after Miles, Dawn and the guy Steele, and you'll be billed separately. "Introducing Oz Blackstone", that's how it'll read.'

'Didn't you think about consulting me on that?'

'Shit no, kid; you do your business and I'll do mine.' The old gormer's good at his business, I have to admit.

'So what's this half-a-point thing then?' I asked. 'Type-size on the posters?'

'You kidding me? You're a Scotsman and you're asking me that? Scots and Jews, we're brothers in the pocket-book. I've negotiated us half a percentage point of the gross, on top of the deal we agreed earlier.'

'And what does that mean?'

'It means that of every ten dollars that goes across the box-office, you get fifty cents.'

'Fifty cents for every ten dollars?' I gasped.

'Ahh, sorry kid,' Sly chuckled. 'My Jewishness again; I meant every hundred.'

'And what's *Snatch* liable to make?'

When I heard Sly sucking his teeth at the other end of the line, I knew we were still talking big bucks. 'We can't be certain,' he said, 'but none of Miles Grayson's movies ever gross less than a hundred.'

I knew, but I asked the question anyway, just to hear the pride in Sly's voice. 'A hundred what?'

'Million, kid, million. I'd say those extra scenes are going to net you at least half a million dollars . . . less my cut, of course.'

43

I was useless for the rest of the day after that. We did a few more runs through of the narration script, but Sly's interruption had broken my concentration. Eventually Weir called it off.

'I don't know what that agent said to you, kid,' he told me, 'but from now on, if he wants to talk, he calls you back at the house, not here. In studio you focus on the job, not the dough.'

This annoyed me, just a bit, since I had never been in it for the money, not at all – well, not much, anyway – but I recognised that the assistant director had his own pressures, and that every hour in that sound studio cost seriously large bucks, so I bit my tongue.

By the next morning, with some help from another master-work by the chef, I had forgotten all about it. You may think it strange, but over the last few years I've discovered that I don't actually care about money. Sure I seem to be a human magnet for the stuff, and I like having it, yet it doesn't dominate my life. Of course winning the lottery was an amazing moment, but there was something surreal about the whole thing, and afterwards, I left it to Prim to decide what we were going to do with it. The thing is, I've had a few surprises in my short life; some have been pleasant, but others – and one in particular – have been very, very bad. Since then, I've been pretty blasé about good news. I remember hearing, years ago, some pompous political prick declaring grandly on television that all the darkness in the world cannot extinguish the light of one small candle. From where I stand, there are some things so bad and so black that not even the brightest sunshine can ever blind you to them, or make you forget.

So as I walked into the studio for my first full day of recording, there was nothing on my mind but my lines and the way I would deliver them. I had been driven by Mark Kravitz, and so I had arrived ahead of Weir. The only two people in the sound suite were Pep Newton, the engineer and Stu Queen, our sparks.

'Ready to do it for real?' asked Pep, a dark stocky man whose looks hinted at Spanish ancestry.

'Ready and able.'

'That's good,' said Stu, a bit foreign-looking himself, but taller and fairer. 'Let's hope Dobbs is ready too. He was getting a bit precious at the end, yesterday.'

'Weir'll be fine,' I assured him. 'He had a couple of relaxers after dinner last night and declared himself happy with the way things went.'

As it turned out, he may have had one or two more that I didn't know about; when he arrived he grunted his good mornings like a small, ill-tempered, grizzly bear. I haven't had many hangovers in my life, but I know the signs when I see them. When we got to work, it was as if everything we had done the day before counted for nothing. The little swine took me back to square one; what had been right was now wrong, what had been virtue was now vice, where I had been doing fine I was now worse than useless. I began to wonder if Weir had been told about my half point, and didn't like it.

I took it for just over two hours; until, after the eleventh abortive take, the seventh consecutive burst of abuse came through my headphones. 'Blackstone!' the assistant director screamed. 'You're so fucking dense, I'll bet that light bends round you. When will you ever get this right?'

A strange feeling swept over me. The Oz temper is usually kept pretty well under control. In fact I can only remember losing it three times in my whole life. The first time was at secondary school in Anstruther, when some pompous little twat of a French teacher accused me of pronouncing the word 'soldier' without the letter L.

'You're betraying some Glaswegian ancestry there, boy,' he smirked.

'No, sir,' I replied, straight-faced, because he was wrong; I knew it and the whole class knew it. But he had decided that he was going to have a laugh at my expense.

'Oh, yes,' he insisted.

I was never a sensitive kid; I never minded when one of my peers took the pee out of me, so to speak. But this guy hadn't earned that privilege. As I glared at him, I felt a sudden uncontrollable wave of outrage erupt within me. Looking back now, I suspect it was perhaps the first truly adult emotion I ever experienced.

I left my desk and walked to the front of the classroom, to where Mr Clark, the teacher stood. I was sixteen; by then I had almost reached my full height, and my weekend labouring on farms for pocket-money had made me stronger than I looked. I stopped in front of the now uncertain Modern

Linguist, seized him by the lapels and lifted him off his feet until his eyes were level with and locked on to mine.

'No, sir,' I repeated, loud enough for the whole class to hear. Then, with satisfaction flushing the anger away already, I put him down and walked back to my desk.

That was all I could think of as I took off my cans and walked out of the soundproof studio, round and into the production booth. It had been a long time since I had forked up a bale of hay, but when you work out with wrestlers a couple of times a week, it keeps your muscles in trim. Mind you, Weir's a bit heavier that Mr Clark, the wee French teacher, so when I picked him up I slammed him against the nearest wall.

'I'm told that movie people are supposed to be temperamental,' I growled at him. 'Will this do?'

His eyes stood out in his pudgy wee face. 'What have you got against me, pal?' I demanded. 'What have you got against me?' As I blurted the words out, I had a sudden vision of Weir Dobbs skulking in my car park, of Weir Dobbs on a motorcycle, of Weir Dobbs creeping up behind my nephew . . .

I suppose that I knew all the time that it couldn't have been him who was stalking me. He had been with the unit all the time, he came nowhere near matching the physical description of the man who had hired the Neames brothers, and if he had been in that bar in Auchterarder I'd have spotted him straight away. But right at that moment I wasn't thinking straight. All of it, the close shaves, that scary day in the cell in Perth, it all caught up with me as I glared at the little New Yorker; it was his bad luck to be in my sights at the time.

'What's your problem, eh?' I shouted, slamming him against the wall, hard, once, twice, three times more.

'Nothing, Oz, nothing,' he squeaked, but I wasn't listening.

Happily, just at that moment two exceptionally strong hands gripped my arms and pulled me off him. 'Easy, man,' said Mark Kravitz. 'That's supposed to be my job. Let's take a coffee break, eh.'

Dobbs, mouth hanging open, nodded vigorously. 'Yes, yes,' he agreed. 'Thirty minutes,' he shouted then rushed from the room.

'Good idea,' Pep Newton drawled. 'I need to load more tape anyway.' I had forgotten about him and about Stu Queen. When I turned to look at them, they both avoided my gaze.

'Sorry about that, lads. I lost it there, I'm afraid.'

Pep flashed me a smile which suggested that his views on assistant directors might not be all that different from mine. 'Ah, that was nothing, boss,' he said. 'I worked on a movie once where one of the actors took a shot at the AD when he started acting like that. Sure, there were only blanks in the gun, but that didn't stop the guy from pissing his pants.

'There was another project, too, where the AD wound up a girl so bad they had to take her off set and sedate her. The trouble with these guys, you see, is that deep down they all think they should be the Director, yet most of them never will; not on big projects anyway. Sometimes – like when they've got a hangover – they take it all out on the supporting cast, like Weir tried today. There's a lot worse than him though; he's not like that usually.'

I sighed. 'Ah, shit. I'd better apologise to him.'

'No!' Pep retorted. 'Never apologise to an AD for any-thing. Ain't that right, Stu?' Queen nodded, emphatically. 'No, when you go back into studio, you look at him through the glass like you'd like to do it again. Come on, let's get us a coffee; maybe you can give him the evil eye across the canteen.'

As it turned out, he wasn't there. I bought the coffees, and three Wagon Wheels, and took them to a small table in the corner.

'Thanks, Slugger,' said Stu, with a light laugh, as I set a coffee before him. 'Here was me thinking that all that wrestling stuff was fake, too.'

'It is,' I told him. 'But the guys, now they're for real. Wrestling's a very controlled business; what they do looks like mayhem, but if they ever lost their tempers in there, you'd really see some stuff. I broke ring rule number one back there; I let the red mist come down.'

'Ah, we all 'ave our red mist moments,' said Pep. 'I'm an Arsenal supporter, so mine are usually about Spurs – or Spurs fans. ''Ow about you, Stu?' he asked.

The spark stirred sugar into his coffee. 'I don't know if I have any,' he began, then paused. 'Yes,' he said at last. 'Someone hurt my sister once. That made me very angry.' He looked across the table in a way that made me glad I'd never met his sister.

When we resumed work I didn't follow Pep's advice about the evil eye to the letter. Instead, I simply ignored the guy, and read my lines as I had rehearsed. For the rest of the day, just as that French teacher had been after the event, Weir was as good as gold, and nothing required any more than two takes. When we finally broke, he even apologised, and, since Pep and Stu were in earshot, I let him.

By Thursday afternoon, all the narration recording was in the can, a day ahead of schedule. When we were finished, and Pep and Stu had left, Miles came to the studio and reviewed the tapes scene by scene, against the rough film edit. He looked at them solemnly and in silence, with Dobbs, Mark and me standing behind him, waiting. He ran them through twice then swung round on his chair and grinned at the assistant director.

'Fine job, Weir,' he said, jerking a thumb towards me as he spoke. 'You sure got the best out of this guy. Well done.'

'Thank you, Miles,' the New Yorker replied, without a flicker of a smile. 'I won't pretend that it was easy, working with a beginner, but I seem to have managed.' I'll swear I could hear Mark Kravitz flex his biceps beside me.

I felt myself getting hot under the collar again, until Miles turned to me. 'All credit to you though, buddy,' he told me. 'It's always a damn sight easier in the production booth than it is when you're stood up there doing it. As a bonus you've got us an extra day to rehearse those end scenes. That's what we'll do tomorrow.'

And that's what we did, all bloody day. The final scenes began with Miles and me, in a light motor cruiser, approaching the North Sea oil platform on which the kidnapped Dawn was being held, mooring it alongside, and climbing a long steel ladder up one of its legs, to the accommodation module. Most of the authentic location footage had already been shot, using stand-ins, but a section of the ladder had been duplicated in the studio so that we could be seen in close-up during the climb, exchanging a couple of lines of dialogue.

We rehearsed those scenes in the morning, then after lunch we moved on to the outdoor set which replicated the platform deck and the accommodation below. It was a massive, cross-sectional structure, open on one side for the cameras, and big enough for a Jet Ranger chopper to be parked on the helipad, just like the real thing. According to the storyline, Miles and I were expecting to find Dawn held prisoner by Nelson Reed, but when we got there, Dawn wasn't anyone's prisoner. In the scene, Nelson sat in a swivel chair in the rig's command cabin, with a silly smile on his face, only he was dead, and she was standing behind him holding a gun.

'Thank God you're safe,' was Miles' last line in the movie, for as he dropped the case which contained the details of the account in which the ransom money was waiting and moved towards her, arms outstretched in relief, she raised the pistol and shot him twice in the chest, then once in the head for luck; without as much as a 'Goodbye, sucker'.

Even without the blood capsules which would be used in the takes, Miles's astonishment as the first two bullets hit him almost had me convinced. I was supposed to be anyway; the script called for me to have a look of shock on my face . . . but only for a few seconds, before it turned into a conspiratorial grin. That was the hardest part for me, getting that change of expression right. We rehearsed it again and again, videoing and playing back over and over, the camera close up on my face, until eventually, it began to come good.

'You see Oz,' said Dawn, 'you really can be an evil bastard when you set your mind to it.'

44

I found it hard to concentrate that weekend. I was really pumped up by the time I left the mansion to join the GWA team – fortunately, we were in Glasgow that weekend – and switching into my ring announcer character was almost more than I could handle.

I wasn't helped by having Mark Kravitz around; I had wanted to leave him behind in Surrey, but Miles had insisted that he should be with me full-time, at least until the movie was finished. Not that I had anything against Mark, mind you; it was simply that not having seen Primavera for a few days, I wasn't overjoyed by the prospect of having a bodyguard in our spare room.

Nevertheless, I managed to come to terms with it all, in time to put on a reasonable performance for the Saturday show. It was as well, for Everett sprang a surprise on me; for the first time in the history of the GWA, the announcer was announced himself. As the title music faded, and the special effect whizzbangs died away, the voice of big Daze himself boomed around the hall; 'Welcome to *Battleground*, fresh from his starring role in *Snatch*, Miles Grayson's sensational new movie, our very own Oz Blackstone!'

I knew nothing about that – Everett had kept quiet at rehearsal – and I almost proved it by fluffing my first introduction.

Naturally, Mark spent the whole day with me at the SECC. I tried to persuade him that I couldn't be anywhere safer than in that arena, in the midst of all those guys, but like most people who don't know them, he had a jaundiced view of professional wrestlers. By the end of the afternoon that had changed, as he watched the full run-through of the programme of matches, and saw the force of the hits which the guys took.

'I have to tell you, Oz,' he whispered, a suggestion of awe in his eyes as he watched the enormous Daze despatch three opponents in the wind-up 'contest', 'I've always thought most of these guys were big fat Nellies, but that big fella, he's something else. And your Irish pal, I can tell just from looking at him that he can handle himself.'

That was no small compliment, coming from Mark. He struck me as a quiet, circumspect man, and it was rare for him to offer a comment.

After the show, Prim and I teamed up with Susie and Mike for a meal at the Malmaison. When I called him to make the date, I suggested to Dylan that they bring their minder along to compare notes with Mark, but he told me that he had been stood down at the end of that week. 'Oh yes,' I said. 'Coming round to my way of thinking about that car-bomb, are you?'

'It sticks in my craw to admit it, but that's the likeliest explanation.'

'What about Stephen Donn? Have you given up on him?'

'Yes. I couldn't justify it any longer. The boy seems to have disappeared off the face of the earth – as far as his mother's concerned anyway. She's had no phone calls, no e-mails, no nothing, so I've lifted the wire tap.'

'So,' I asked him later, in the restaurant, 'if young Mr

Donn's off the menu as far as your lot are concerned, what about me? Is anyone really trying to find my bloody stalker?'

Mike frowned. 'I have to confess, Oz, there's a certain lack of co-ordination among the various investigations. Mind you, it's more difficult when you've got no information to share. Your pal DI Bell has got absolutely nowhere with the Auchterarder incident, and it's the same story in Aberdeen and Fife. The boys up in Grampian haven't even found that bullet yet. I hate to say it, but I can only see one chance of catching the bloke.'

I caught his meaning at once. 'Sure. If he has another go.'

Prim glanced at our minder. 'But with Mark looking after you, surely he's not going to.'

'No, but with all due respect to Mark, I'm not going to live my life with a baby-sitter. Once I'm finished with the movie I go back to normal and we'll see what happens.'

'Doesn't that scare you?' Susie blurted out.

'Too right it does,' I told her, 'but like Mike says, if this person is after me, it may be the only way to flush the bugger out.'

'What do you think, Mark?' Dylan asked.

Kravitz took a sip of his mineral water. 'It's an unpleasant prospect,' he answered. 'But that's how it has to be if the situation is to be resolved. Before I do go, I can train Oz in basic anti-terrorist procedures. They wouldn't be any good against a sniper's bullet, but if this guy was going to shoot anyone, he'd have done it already.

'Since I've been on the case, I haven't seen a trace of anything suspicious. Maybe the guy has run his course, but if he has, you'll still have an uncertain time until that becomes clear.' He glanced at Prim. 'Maybe it would be a good idea if you two lived apart for a while.'

She stared at him. 'What? We're being married in a few weeks.'

'I know,' said Kravitz. 'But I've been asked for a security assessment. Where I was trained, we began by minimising the risks.'

'And then eliminating the threat,' I added. 'Usually with a round in the middle of the forehead.'

'Sure, boss, but I don't think we can do that here. Only guys like DI Dylan are allowed to go around tooled up these days. So guys like me, other than on very special occasions, have to adopt a more cautious approach than we might have in the past. That's why I'm suggesting that it would be safer if you isolated yourself as far as possible.'

'Maybe,' said Primavera, quietly. 'But we're a partnership in every sense of the word. If I'm in danger through being around Oz, then so be it. It won't be the first time, anyway. We're not as soft as you may think we look, Mark. If anyone does have a pop at us, God help him.'

We did our best to put thoughts of our uncertain future out of our minds for the rest of the weekend. I had thought of going up to Perthshire to visit SuperDave, but Prim felt that if we turned up there complete with bodyguard, it could only worry her mother. Instead Mark and I decided that we would catch the last Sunday shuttle back to Heathrow rather than leave at sparrow-fart next morning.

I was heading for the door when the phone rang. 'You take that, love,' I said to Prim. I waited, just a touch impatiently, while she dealt with the caller.

When she rejoined me in the hall, she wore a surprised look. 'You'll never guess who that was.'

'Saddam Hussein?'

'Susie might say so,' she retorted. 'It was Joe Donn. He wants to see me tomorrow; says he's got something for me that might be important. So I said that I'd go out to Motherwell for ten o'clock tomorrow.'

'Just you be careful,' I warned her, jokingly. 'That old sod fancies you.'

45

Aside from the fact that I didn't like being apart from Primavera, I enjoyed being back in my Surrey cocoon. It offered an escape from my problems in the real world, and of course there was the work.

Miles began with a refresher on the new scenes which we had rehearsed the previous Friday. Then, once he was satisfied that we were all together and ready to shoot, he moved us on to the movie's final dramatic scenes.

These belonged entirely to Dawn and me; apart from the inert presences of Miles himself, and Nelson Reed, both by now playing the parts of stiffs. The storyline gave us ten minutes to get clear of the platform on the Jet Ranger, before an assault force of Royal Marines came in low over the sea on troop-carrying choppers, and abseiled down on to the deck, ready to mop up if necessary. Oh yes, I forgot; according to the script, I could fly a helicopter.

The plan was that I was to carry the two 'bodies' up to the deck, weight them down with chains and toss them over the side, then Dawn and I would make our escape. Then came the final twist; I was to take the money and jump into the Jet Ranger alone, leaving Dawn on the deck. 'You can't trust anyone these days, can you sister? So long.' Not a difficult line, you'll agree. All I had to master was that sardonic grin again, and I was getting good at them.

Game set and match to Oz? Not quite. As the chopper rose into the air, Dawn would spot an emergency pack on the deck, complete with loaded flare gun. Her one wild shot would get lucky and smash into the cabin. Goodbye me, in a huge fireball, courtesy of the special effects team.

Given recent events, I might have been forgiven if the ending had given me the creeps, but within my bubble of unreality, the vision of Susie's blazing car didn't enter my head, not once.

We rehearsed those sequences all day, not that I really had to take off in the Jet Ranger; the second unit had shot that a few days earlier on the real rig, using the stunt team. No, the hardest part for me was carrying the two guys up two flights of stairs. I could have had a stand-in if I had insisted, but Miles was keen that I should do it myself if possible, so that I could be seen in close-up.

I managed okay, thanks to Mark Kravitz; he showed me the best way to pick up a dead weight, and how to balance while I was carrying it. I didn't ask him where he learned the techniques; I had a feeling that I'd rather not know.

Fortunately neither of the two 'bodies' were giants. Miles is well built, but a bit smaller than me; as for Nelson Reed. If you've ever seen any of his movies you wouldn't believe how small he is; he's Alan Ladd-sized, honest. It's amazing what a good cameraman can do to disguise vertical deprivation.

I must have lugged those guys up those stairs at least half a dozen times before we moved on to the scenes in the studio deck. That wasn't too easy either, because those chains weren't the pretend sort, like the chairs they use in the GWA to bash each other over the head. They were the real thing, and heavy enough to weigh down a couple of bodies for burial at sea.

For most of the day Dawn's role was largely inactive, so when her big moment came, she was determined to get it right. She fired three or four dummy flares before she declared herself satisfied.

'Okay,' said Miles, finally, having returned from the dead. 'That's it. Tomorrow we shoot for real, and after all this rehearsal, I'll be looking for first-take wraps, every time.' He turned to his wife. 'Honey, you and Geraldine take Nelson back to the mansion. I've got plans for Oz and Mark.'

'Such as?' I asked. After all that heavy lifting, I fancied nothing more than a long, hot bath.

'I fancy a game of squash, mate. I've been sat on my arse all day, and I need to loosen off.'

'You're not serious.'

'Too right. I've booked a court in Farnham, and Gerrie's been out to buy us gear, so no excuses.'

I'm no great shakes as a squash player, but on my worst day, I can still beat Miles Grayson. He's ten years older than me, and although he's pretty fit for his age, his hand-eye co-ordination is lousy. I believe him when he says that as a cricketer, he couldn't bat for toffee. I suspect that the guys he plays with in LA let him win most of the time. However, Mac the Dentist only taught me to play one way.

The big problem Miles has is that he doesn't know that he's crap. He's Aussie-born, and he was raised playing games where the basic requirement is a willingness to run through walls. Fortunately for his acting career, a dislocated shoulder finished him for rugby when he was only seventeen, otherwise he wouldn't have grown up nearly so good-looking. Sadly for his squash game, he brings his field sports tactics on to court, where there really are walls and they don't give.

He's keen though; he never gives up. If his persistence wore his opponents down it wouldn't be so bad, but it doesn't. It's always him who ends up as an oil slick on the floor after an hour or so; and that's how it finished that evening in Farnham. Mark Kravitz watched us through the glass back wall. Miles offered him a game too, but he refused, insisting that he had to keep his mind on the job. I was quite pleased by that; he did look as if he could handle a racquet.

On the way home, Miles insisted on stopping at a roadside pub to top up his fluid level, so it was past eight o'clock when we made it back to the mansion. We headed straight for the drawing room for the ritual of pre-dinner drinks. Scott, Weir, Nelson and Gerrie were waiting for us, three Tio Pepes and one Lagavulin in hand.

'Well?' Reed asked. 'Who won the battle?'

'Youth had its day,' Miles drawled. 'Where's Dawn?'

'She hasn't come down yet,' Geraldine told him. 'Want me to go and fetch her?'

He grinned and shook his head. 'Nah. She'll be playing with her hair. I'll go get her when dinner's served.'

'That could be a while yet,' Gerrie warned. 'The chef held everything back until he was sure that you three had arrived back.'

'No matter. If Dawn's passing up on a gin and tonic, she must have a good reason.' He reached for two Budweisers from an ice-bucket on the sideboard, uncapped them and handed one to me.

We had killed two more when Mr Jones, the butler, arrived

257

to call us through to the dining room; still there was no sign of Dawn. 'I guess I'd better fetch her,' said Miles, at last.

'That's all right,' said his assistant. 'I'll go.'

We followed the butler through for dinner, and took our usual places. The starters – calçots; which I recognised as a Catalan delicacy – were set out for us, but no one made a move to begin before Geraldine and Dawn joined us.

Yet when Gerrie did come into the dining room, she was alone. 'Miles,' she began, hesitantly, 'did Dawn say anything to you about going out tonight?'

'No,' he replied, frowning. 'Ain't she there?'

'No, there's not a sign of her in your room.'

'She's probably gone for a walk. It's a nice evening.'

I felt a cold hand gripping the pit of my stomach. 'Still,' I said, pushing my chair back and rising from the table. I walked out of the room in search of the butler.

I found him in the kitchen. 'Mr Jones,' I called to him. 'Did you see Mrs Grayson leave the house?'

'No sir,' he replied. He turned to the chef and the under-waiter, with an enquiring look, but they shook their heads.

'Did she say anything about going out? For a walk, maybe?'

'No, sir.'

I almost asked him if he was sure, but stopped myself. Mr Jones looked the type who was always sure. Instead, I marched back towards the dining room.

Mark Kravitz was waiting for me in the hall. 'Something up, boss?' he asked quietly.

'Could be. Come on.' As we took the stairs two at a time, I was vaguely aware that Miles was following us. As Geraldine had said, the master bedroom was empty. We looked around;

there were no discarded clothes or shoes to be seen, but Dawn's handbag lay on the bed. Mark walked across, picked it up, and took a look inside.

'Her purse is still here,' he announced, 'and her cellphone.'

'Fuck it!' My anxiety was now shared by Miles. He stepped into the bathroom. 'She's had a shower,' he called out to us. 'And all the clothes she was wearing today are in the laundry basket.'

'What's missing?' Mark asked.

Miles looked around the room. He pointed to the dressing table. 'Her make-up case is still there.' As he spoke he walked to the wardrobes which ran along one wall, threw them open and looked inside. 'I reckon there's a pair of denims gone, and a cream sweater. And a new pair of shoes: I don't see them either.'

'What type of shoes?'

'Clark's. Trainers, sort of.'

Kravitz crossed to the window and checked their catches. 'These are all secure. Come on.' We followed him out of the room. Naturally, he knew the layout of the house like the back of his hand; he led us along a corridor then turned left, until we stood before a half-glazed double door that I had never seen before.

'This is a fire escape . . .' he said. Reaching out, he took hold of the crash bar which stretched across it, and pushed lightly. The door swung open. '. . . and very recently, some-one's used it, then closed it after them as best they could – you can't close these things properly from the outside.'

'Why the hell would Dawn leave by the fire escape?' Miles asked, sounding rattled and bewildered.

'She wouldn't, unless she didn't want anyone to see her . . . or unless someone else didn't.'

There was a long, deadly silence, as Miles faced up to the truth which had come to me downstairs. 'This could be your man, Oz, couldn't it?' he whispered.

'I'm afraid so,' I acknowledged. 'He's just picked a softer target this time. I'm sorry, man.'

'It's not your fault.'

'No,' said Mark, grimly. 'If it's anyone's, it's mine. I should have put someone on Dawn as well. But hold on; before we jump to conclusions let's search the grounds. We'll look like right Charlies if we push the panic button then find her asleep in a garden seat. Let's search out there before we do anything else. Come on, down this fire escape.'

We followed him down the steel staircase; it was almost dark outside, but as we stepped into the garden, movement sensors triggered a series of bright halogen lamps set along the back wall of the mansion. The grounds, two acres in all were set most in lawn, with four benches dotted around in various places. They were all empty.

'Wait a minute,' Kravitz exclaimed, then walked briskly across to the far corner of the property, where a path led through the shrubs to a gate in the back wall. It swung on its hinges. 'Fuck!' he swore quietly. 'This was secure when I rechecked it this morning. It's been jemmied.' He stepped through the open doorway and took a quick look outside. 'There's a narrow road out there,' he said as he rejoined us. 'And there are fresh tyre marks on the verge. From the size of them I'd say they could have been made by a van.

'I'm sorry, Miles. I'd say for sure that someone's taken her.'

I've seen Miles Grayson happy, serious, drunk, sober, you name it; until then I'd never seen him frightened.

'How the hell could they have got in?' he protested.

'Probably the same way they got out,' Mark guessed.

'But you can't open those doors from the outside either.'

'Sure you can, if you know what you're doing.'

'What can we do?'

'Call the police, for starters,' said the bodyguard. 'But first; let's have another look at the bedroom.' As we made our way back to the house, I saw Gerrie, Scott, and the others staring at us through the dining room window. I ignored them and ran back up the fire escape, on Mark's heels.

'What are we looking for?' I asked as we stepped back into the bedroom.

'Something that wasn't here before,' he answered. 'Miles, does Dawn have any jewellery with her?'

'Yeah. There's a safe behind the mirror in the bathroom.'

'Open it, please.'

We watched as the actor did as he was told, spinning the dial, clockwise, clockwise again, then anti-clockwise, before pulling the small door open and peering inside. 'The stuff's still there,' he growled. 'But . . .' He reached into the safe and drew out a long brown envelope. 'What the fuck's this?'

Okay, I know that there are millions of brown envelopes in use in Britain, some offering junk mail bargains, some containing bills, some in politicians' pockets. But when I saw the one which Miles held in his hand, I was back in the Horseshoe Bar, watching Mike Dylan reach into the pocket of his Hugo Boss jacket.

'I'll bet you that what's inside is unsigned, was written on a word processor, then run off on an ink-jet printer, and that it's virtually untraceable.'

Miles and Mark looked at me. 'You'd better handle it carefully,' I said, 'just in case, but there'll be no prints on it, other than yours.'

It wasn't sealed. Miles slid two fingers inside and drew out a single sheet of white A4, folded twice. 'No police,' he read aloud, 'or your wife is dead. Neither the locals, nor Mr Dylan in Glasgow. Involve them, and I'll know. You will be contacted again and given instructions on how to secure the return of Mrs Grayson. This is not a movie, this is for real; do as you're told or you'll be looking for a new co-star.'

He held it up for us to see. It looked just like Susie Gantry's love-letters; I shuddered as I thought of her car, exploding in flames.

'What d'you think?' Miles growled. His eyes were narrowed and his mouth was set in a tight line. The fear had gone; suddenly he looked very dangerous.

'I think you should take it very seriously,' I said.

'Oh I will, Oz, I will. Finding this bastard and getting Dawn back is my life's work for now; and when I do that, I'm going to kill him.'

'Like he says, Miles,' Kravitz interrupted, quietly, 'this is not a movie. You have to control your anger in these situations; you can't allow yourself to focus on side issues like getting even. Recovering Dawn, that's the only objective.'

'If you say so,' Miles snapped, sounding as if he meant not a word. 'Where do we start?'

'With the police, I'd say.'

'No fucking way! You heard what he said.'

'Every kidnapper says that; almost invariably it's a bluff.'

'I don't like "almost". I will not take the slightest risk with Dawn's life.' He looked at me. 'Oz, this is the same guy? You certain?'

'Absolutely. The letter is identical to the ones Susie received. Plus, he knows about Dylan.'

'So how do we play this?'

'We'll need to keep it close for a start, among ourselves. Dawn's a celebrity; if she doesn't show up for work tomorrow, it'll be public knowledge damn soon. So we shouldn't even tell the people downstairs the truth about what's happened.'

Miles nodded. 'I'll deal with that. Afterwards?'

'We do some serious thinking . . . while we're waiting for the next contact from the guy.'

'What does he want, d'you think?'

'One of two things,' Mark answered. 'He wants money, or he wants Oz . . . or maybe he wants both. This is the end of the game, that's for sure.'

'It is for him,' Miles snarled. The anger seemed to crackle from him in sparks. He held up a hand. 'Okay, okay, okay,' he went on. 'I'll try to keep a lid on it, I promise. It's just so fucking difficult. You got any thoughts about this so far?'

'I'm a minder, Miles, not a detective. But I know this. We're dealing with someone close.'

'Close to what?'

'Close to Oz, close to everything. With luck we should be able to put a name to him.'

'Miles . . .' Gerrie Baker's voice floated through from somewhere outside the bedroom.

'Let's get this started,' the Australian muttered. 'Okay,

Geraldine,' he called out. 'We're coming; we'll see you back in the dining room in a minute.'

He turned to us. 'I know how we're going to play this, to begin with at least. When we get down there, you guys follow my lead. Whatever I say, you back it up. Come on.'

He led the way down the wide staircase and back to the dining room, where the rest of the party were waiting for us. The chef was there too, looking more than a bit pissed off. 'Go get Mr Jones and the waiter,' Miles ordered. 'I want them to hear this too.'

When the full household, minus one, was assembled Miles looked solemnly round the room. 'What I'm going to tell you doesn't leave here,' he said, making eye contact with the three domestics, one by one. 'Understood?' All three nodded.

'Those of you who've worked with me before will know that Dawn and I can get a bit edgy when we get close to the end of a project. This time it's been worse than usual; she's got herself really uptight. We found a note upstairs, saying that she's gone away for a few days.

'I trust my wife to do what's best for me and for our project, so I'm going along with that. At the same time, I don't want any crap in the press. You know what the showbiz writers are like; you show up alone in a McDonald's and next thing you read, your marriage is on the rocks. So the official line is that Dawn's got a virus, and that shooting has been suspended for a week.

'Weir, Gerrie, right now I want you to get hold of everyone we hired for the rest of the week and tell them to take a holiday until next Monday. Tell them not to worry, they're still on salary; but we don't need them for the rest of the week, that's all.

'If anyone asks why, just tell them that Dawn's sick.'

Kiki Eldon, intervened, tentatively. 'The press might speculate that she's pregnant, Miles,'

Miles looked the PR lady directly in the eye. 'As a matter of fact, she is.'

I don't think that anyone else noticed, but when he said that, my head spun. In that instant, I wasn't in that plush Surrey dining room, at that time. Instead I was in a restaurant in Barcelona two years earlier, listening to Mike Dylan, but not believing him, as he told me that my world had fallen apart.

For a few minutes I was ignored as Weir and Gerrie went off to make their phone calls, and as the chef went off to do what he could to rescue dinner. When Miles was free of distractions I buttonholed him.

'I've got to tell Prim what's happening,' I told him.

'No, no, no,' he protested. 'Don't involve her.'

'Listen man, I need her. And if I keep her in the dark, it won't be you she kills when she finds out.'

He gave in, and I went off to my room to call my fiancée on my mobile phone. She was at home, in front of the television when I rang her. She had been expecting to hear from me earlier, as she was quick to tell me.

'I'm sorry love. We've had a crisis down here. It's your kid sister, I'm afraid.'

'Oh dear. What's the silly girl done now?'

I told her.

There was silence when I had finished, but no gasps of

disbelief. Prim knows I don't play that sort of trick.

'I'm coming down there,' she declared. I didn't even consider trying to dissuade her.

Instead I simply said, 'Okay. Mark and I'll pick you up at the airport tomorrow morning. Call me with your flight number.'

'Sod that. I'm coming now. I'd rather drive through the night than lie sleepless here. Tell me how to find your mansion and I'll be with you for breakfast.'

46

She came in the Freelander rather than the low-flying missile that was our Z3, but even then she beat breakfast by over two hours. She phoned me, mobile to mobile, from Farnham, not long after four a.m., to warn me that she was close by.

Mark met her at the end of the driveway and brought her into the house, where Miles and I sat waiting. Like Prim, neither of us had been able to sleep.

I was comforted by her arrival, and I believe that Miles was too. There's something very capable about her, something completely unflappable, even – no, especially – in the most difficult situations.

You may remember the old joke about the bygone Prime Minister visiting a remote part of a last vestige of the Empire in Africa. As she stepped from her transport, the assembled natives cried out together, 'Magumba! Magumba!'

'What are they saying?' the PM asked the High Commissioner.

'It's a traditional greeting, Madam,' he rumbled.

'Magumba! Magumba!'

They walked on a few yards until the High Commissioner cried suddenly, 'Careful, Madam. Mind your feet. Don't step in the magumba!'

I sometimes recall that story when I think of Prim. Not because she's worked in one of the deepest parts of Africa, but because when the magumba hits the fan, there is no one I would rather have next to me than Primavera Phillips.

I've seen her in a crisis – like the time she saved our skins in Geneva, or the night she saved Jerry Gradi's life in Barcelona – and on each occasion there was a calmness and an inner certainty about her that made me know that everything was going to be all right. That morning, as she settled herself beside me into the big soft couch in the mansion's sitting room, clutching a mug of coffee, I had the same feeling.

'Right boys,' she began. 'What have you done so far?'

'We've talked all night,' said Miles. 'About Dawn, and about who might have taken her; but other than that we've done nothing.' I showed her the note which Miles had found in the safe.

'No police or he'll know!' she snorted. 'Arrogant bastard! How will he know, exactly? He must think he's the only person who ever kidnapped anyone. Doesn't he realise that there are specialist teams set up to handle this sort of situation? You have called them, I take it?'

Miles shook his head. 'I'm not taking that risk, Prim.'

'The risk is in not calling them, man,' she protested.

'Look, this man tried to kill Oz's nephew, your father, Susie and Mike. Now he's got Dawn. Yet we still don't know anything about him. For all we know this guy could be a cop himself.'

'Miles, that's paranoid.'

I put a hand on her thigh. 'Maybe so, love, but it's my enemy who's induced it. He's shown us how dangerous he is. Maybe that's what all these attacks have been about; to establish that he is very serious, and to make us all very afraid of him.

'Mark's reading is right. This person has been very close to us all along. He chose the ideal moment to abduct Dawn, when Miles and I were away playing squash with Mark minding us. He had sussed the place out and knew how to do it. Up the fire escape, take Dawn quickly and quietly, leave the note, then out the same way, van at the back gate, and off. We reckon that he's had at least two hours' start on us, before we even knew Dawn was missing. He could have been in the Channel Tunnel within that time.'

'But wasn't it still a big risk for him to take? Weren't there other people in the house?'

'Only the staff, and none of them saw or heard her leave. One of the hired cars brought her home first. Nelson Reed and the rest of them waited and squeezed into Geraldine Baker's car.'

'What about the driver?'

'From a car hire firm in Guildford. Miles called them to cancel tomorrow's pick-up and in the process he found out that the car and the driver reported back in on time. So no way was it him. No, it's someone who was watching the studio and took his chance.'

'Or someone who was in the studio all along. What do you know about the production crew?'

'They're all pros,' Miles answered. 'Most of them, apart from the key people, who're full-time, are specialists hired on a daily or weekly basis. They've all got industry track records, or they come from reputable agencies.'

'Will they all be at the studio tomorrow?'

'No. I've stood them down for the rest of the week.'

Prim glowered at him. 'That's a damn shame,' she said.

'Why?'

'If you hadn't, we could have seen who turned up . . . and who didn't.'

Her coffee was untouched, the mug cooling in her hands. 'Call the police, Miles.'

'I can't, Prim . . . not yet, anyway. Not until the guy's made contact and told us what he wants.'

'Why don't you just read your script?' she murmured.

'What d' you mean?'

'You guys are making a movie about a kidnapping, aren't you?'

Both of us looked at her, our sleep-deprived eyes suddenly wide. 'So?' I heard myself croak.

'So in the script, the leading lady, my sister, is snatched from a country house. That's a coincidence, is it not?'

She was right; it was such a bloody obvious coincidence that we had been staring obliviously past it all night.

'So what does the script say that the kidnapper wants?' she asked.

'Ten million pounds lodged in a private bank in Lugano, accessible by code and transferable anywhere in the world.'

'What does that mean?'

'It means that the kidnapper is given the code and can make a call at once, moving the funds to another bank of his own choice, anywhere in the world. After that he's free and clear.'

'Okay,' Prim said, 'let's wait for his call. Don't tell the police yet, if you really feel that's the way to play this. But if

I were you I'd start getting ten million together right now.'

She swung her feet off the couch and stood up. 'If that's what's going to happen, I'm going to grab a couple of hours' sleep. You should, too. Where's our room, Oz?'

She was right. There was no longer any sense in staying awake; our chains were being pulled hard enough as it was. We said good night – or good morning – to Miles, picked up Prim's bag from the hall and went upstairs.

I was in bed, watching my fiancée undress, when a memory came back to me from the weekend. 'Hey,' I asked her, 'what did Joe Donn want?'

She gasped, then grinned. 'I'd forgotten all about that. He had something to tell me. I'm too tired, it's not relevant and it's too heavy to go into. But what he really, really wanted was to show off.

'He's been doing a bit of detective work – something that you should have thought of, actually. Remember that girl Myrtle, who had a fling with his nephew while her boyfriend was in the slammer?'

'Sure, I remember her.'

'Well, old Joe went to see her. She used to work for him, after all. He reminded her of an office outing, one they had all gone to during the brief time when Stephen was at Gantry's, and he asked her if he was right in thinking that she had a camera with her.

'Clever old guy.' She chuckled. She shrugged her bra on to the floor, stepped out of her knickers, then reached into her bag and took out a stiffened envelope. As she slipped into bed she handed it to me. 'She did, and when she dug out the photos she had taken, there was one of the boy Stephen. Joe had it blown up and gave it to me.

'It doesn't mean a thing now, but I decided to bring it down anyway. The original's there too.'

I took it from her and shook out the two photos. One was a group shot, typical office party stuff; I barely glanced at that before picking up the enlargement and gazing at it sleepily . . . then I woke up, abruptly.

I knew the guy. Oh, sure I knew him. But not as Stephen Donn, occasional book-keeper. I knew him as Stu Queen the spark, our movie electrician.

I was halfway down the corridor to Miles' room when Geraldine Baker opened her bedroom door, and I remembered that I didn't have a stitch on.

47

'Look, love, I know you're Dawn's sister, but he's her husband; that puts him in the driving seat as far as I'm concerned. So if Miles says no police, I'm not going over his head.'

She frowned at me in the mirror as she ran a brush through her hair. 'Maybe you're not, but I don't like sitting on my bum with Dawn's life in danger. It's not just Miles who cares about her, and you and me. There's Mum and Dad, and thousands, maybe millions, of other people who've seen her on the screen and feel part of her.

'Those of us who are here don't just have a duty to Dawn to get this right; we owe it to all of them too.'

I pulled my belt tight, fastening it in the sixth hole; two years earlier, before I started working out with the wrestlers, I could only manage the fourth. 'Fuck all them,' I said, bluntly. 'It's Dawn I care about. If I thought you were right, then sure, I'd force Miles to call the Old Bill. But Mark Kravitz is our hired gun; he's the security expert, and he has a personal and professional reputation to protect. I don't hear him demanding that we bring in the coppers.'

She put down the hairbrush and looked at me, evenly. 'To borrow your expression, fuck Mark Kravitz.'

'Don't do that, please. Not so close to our wedding.'

Not even a trace of a smile crossed her face. 'Don't give me reassurance, Oz. I want action; we have to do something.'

I know when to give in to Primavera. It's one of the secrets of our sucess as a couple. 'Okay,' I told her. 'Let's talk to Miles.'

We found him alone in the dining room, looking at breakfast with little or no interest. 'Where is everyone?' Prim asked.

'I've sent everyone home, or in Kiki Eldon's case, back to her office. I don't want any of them around; just you two.'

'What about Mark?'

'He's gone too. We don't need protection any more; it's happened already. We know who Oz's stalker is now, but there's not a Goddamned thing we can do about it. It's like a chess game, and he's captured our Queen.'

I didn't like his mood; he seemed to be beaten, and all of a sudden I was on Prim's side of the argument, one hundred per cent.

'Look,' I told him. 'To quote a famous ex-boxer, we may be just prawns in the game of life, but we're not quite helpless. Even prawns can topple over-confident kings if there are enough of them. We've got a rogue knight on our team too. I'm going to call Mike Dylan; he's been in on this from the start anyway . . . come to think of it, it was him who started it.'

'No,' Miles protested, weakly. 'Queen, or Donn, if that's his real name, said he'd know if we called the cops.'

'Mike isn't the cops. He's Special Branch; he can do things without the rest of the force knowing about it. He has done already. It was him who put me on to the brothers Neames, remember. Stephen Donn was a mystery to us. He was a night person; no one knew anything about him. But now we have an alias, someone else in the same skin. Maybe Dylan can find out something about Stu Queen – like where he lives, for a start.'

'How? I've already called the agency who hired him out to us. They don't have an address, only a mobile phone number.' He took a slip of paper from his shirt pocket and pushed it across the table.

'Okay, that's a start,' I said. 'Let's give it to Dylan and see what he can come up with. Look behind most mobile phone numbers and you'll find a direct debit drawn on a bank account. This isn't the Pope we're after, Miles. This bastard's fallible just like the rest of us. Maybe this number will lead us right to his front door.

'Then there's the van. We know already that there's no vehicle registered with the DVLA in Stephen Donn's name; not this Stephen Donn, anyway. But what about Stu Queen? Maybe he owns a Transit, or a Movano, or something similar, and maybe Mike can trace him through the log book.'

The movie star looked up at me; only a man now; a weak, vulnerable bloke like the rest of us. No way could he have got away with playing a thirty-something that morning. 'And if we can, what does he do when Dylan's stormtroopers batter down his door?'

'Oz, Prim. I'll give this man whatever he wants just to get Dawn back, and our baby.'

Primavera gasped beside me, and out of the corner of my eye, I saw her hand go to her mouth. I hadn't told her that Dawn was pregnant; that truth held a special sort of pain for me, and I couldn't bring myself to talk about it, not even to her. Miles didn't know that, but Prim did; she squeezed my arm in a way that said everything.

'I know you will, Miles,' she said, gently. 'I wouldn't put Dawn in danger any more than you would. But she's in danger already; the more we know about the person who's holding her, the better we'll be able to deal with him when the time comes . . . however we go about it. Now; do you agree that we call Mike?'

Eventually, he nodded, wearily. 'Do it. But on a mobile phone; if there's even the slightest chance that Donn has a tap on the line here, you'd better not use it.'

I agreed with that. As always, I had my cellphone hooked on to my belt. I took it out and keyed in Dylan's direct line number in Pitt Street. He was there.

'Mike, it's Oz,' I began. 'Listen; is this line secure?'

'Of course it's fucking secure, you bammer. This is Special Branch.'

I complimented him on his ever-improving grasp of Glaswegian; and then I told him what had happened. About Dawn's kidnapping, about the letter, about Stu Queen who was really Stephen Donn, and about his uncle's part in identifying him.

'I've always said,' he said, when I was finished, 'that the secret of good detection is luck. Doesn't matter whether you're a seasoned professional like me, or an inept, stumbling amateur, like you or like old Donn.'

'Luck, mate,' I told him grimly, unimpressed by his flippancy, 'will be getting Dawn back alive.'

'Sure, I know. Sorry.'

'Can you help us in this, discreetly? Whatever ransom the guy wants, Miles will pay it, but in the meantime, will you find out anything you can about him?' I read him the mobile number. 'We think he has a van too. Medium sized.'

'Big enough to build a hidden compartment inside it? That's a favourite dodge with kidnappers. There was once a guy who was stopped by the police with a victim inside his Transit. They opened the thing, looked inside, and still they didn't know.'

'Big enough for that, I guess.'

'Mmm, right.'

'Mike, can you look into this without telling anyone else?'

'Of course I can. I keep having to tell you. I'm Special Branch; I can do what I fucking like. Leave it to Uncle Michael.' I could almost see his reassuring smile. 'What are you lot going to do in the meantime?' he asked.

'Miles is going to call his accountant and start liquidating assets.'

'How much can he raise?'

'Ten if he has to.'

'Ten what?'

'Don't be gauche, Dylan.'

'Ten mil, eh,' he whistled. 'It makes my scrotum tighten just to think about it.'

'Think yourself lucky. Young Stephen Donn may not have one of those after Miles and I get hold of him.'

'Let's hope Miles has a couple of interesting new paperweights in due course, then. How about you and Springtime – I assume that Prim's there – what are you going to do?'

'Wait for the guy to send us another note, telling us what to do next.'

'Aye, if he writes.'

'Or for a phone call . . .'

'Aye, if he phones.'

'Whatever. You just get on with your end as fast as you can. Okay?'

'Okay. I'll call you back when I have something.'

'Call my mobile, okay? Don't use the land-line, for—'

I heard Dylan sigh '—for security reasons. Just don't insult me by saying it. Honest tae fuck, do you think I sailed up the Clyde on a water biscuit?'

He really has been in Glasgow too long, I thought, as I pushed the red button to end the call.

48

We spent a hellish day, Prim and I, waiting for the doorbell or the telephone to ring, and watching Miles struggle to keep himself under control. At one point in the early afternoon, I really did think that the world's fourth most famous person was going to come apart before my eyes.

I took him for a walk around the garden. 'We're all different animals,' I told him, 'and we all feel different things. But maybe this will help you. When I had my big crisis, two years ago, I got through it by finding something to focus on. I was angry, just like you are now, and in despair, but I built a mental shell out of my rage, and I used it to keep me on track, while I did the things I had to do.

'So if I were you, I'd do my best to concentrate on Stephen Donn. Don't think about anything else; most of all, don't think about Dawn. What's happened to her has happened. We don't know what the outcome will be, but we're doing everything we can to ensure that it works out okay. Pretty soon we'll be told what to do, and when we are we'll have some decisions to make.

'When we do make them, we'll have two objectives in mind. First and foremost, getting Dawn back safe, and, eventually if not at the same time, getting our hands on Stephen Donn.'

Miles stared at the ground in front of him as we walked. 'I

don't know if I want to get my hands on Stephen Donn, Oz. I wouldn't trust myself not to kill him.'

'Well I'm going to catch up with him, sunshine. That's the only picture I have in my mind at the moment. The bastard has chosen me as the focal point of all this mayhem, and I'm going to find out why. At the very least, I owe him a real doing for a wee hurt boy up in Fife, and he's going to get it. You can hold my jacket if you like.'

'Hey,' my future in-law looked at me with a strange, sad grin on his lined face. 'What happened to the harmless, amiable clown I met up in Oban those years back?'

'The amiable clown's still there, I hope. But he isn't harmless any more. When Fate stamps on your toes there's usually nothing to do save learning to live with the pain. But when it's people who do it to you, then if it's in your power, you hunt them down and do it right back.'

'What about turning the other cheek?'

'Do that, and you get your arse well kicked.'

In spite of himself, Miles laughed. 'I promise you this,' I told him. 'I don't know why but I'm certain of it. This time next week, we're going to be finishing that movie. And think of the publicity it's going to get when the telly and the tabloids get hold of the story.'

'In that case we'd better catch Donn,' he said, grim once more. 'Otherwise before long folks'll be saying I set the whole thing up myself.'

He punched me lightly on the shoulder. 'Thanks pal. I know I was wobbling back there; I'm back on track now. I'm even thinking positive. You remember that guy Pep Newton?'

'The sound man? Sure.'

'He seemed to me to be buddies with Stu Queen. How would you and Prim like to go talk to him? I'll stay here to man the phones.'

'If he calls.'

'Or wait for the mailman.'

'If he writes.'

'Ah, what the hell. If Donn has read the script, he'll think it takes a couple of days to get serious money together.'

I nodded. 'Okay. We'll go and see Pep if you want. How should we play it, though?'

'Tell him there's some sound-editing needs doing and we have to find him?'

'Do feature players usually go looking for staff?' I asked, innocently.

'They do if Miles Grayson sends them. Tell him that Geraldine's gone off for a few days too. I'll call her now and get Pep's address.'

49

Movie work may not be the most secure way to earn a living, but the top people are paid well and hired pretty well full-time; Pep Newton was one of the best. He was so good in fact that he had picked up, at an hour's notice, an extra four days' work on a music video, as we discovered when his fresh-faced blonde wife answered the door of their distinguished-looking apartment in Dolphin Square, not far from the Palace of Westminster.

Rather than get into a pointless discussion with her on the doorstep, I told her that it was nothing important, but that we'd come back in a couple of hours, at around seven. We killed the time in the Red Lion pub in Whitehall, playing Spot the Politician and listening to the *sotto voce* sounds of medicinal spin.

Pep was at home when we went back to the Square. He was surprised to see me, but pleased nonetheless, and he made just the right amount of fuss of Prim.

'Come eat with us, Oz,' he insisted. 'Jenny's done a pasta sauce and there's always plenty. It's just ready. Hey Jen,' he called through to the kitchen. 'Two more plates, okay, and stick some extra linguini in the pot; we got honoured guests. This is the guy I told you about; the actor who spread that fat bleedin' Yank all over the control room wall.'

Mrs Newton's face appeared round the kitchen door,

smiling. 'You're the wrestling man? I didn't realise that before. I read about you in the *Mail on Sunday* magazine. Didn't you win the lottery as well?'

'No,' I answered, putting a hand on Prim's shoulder. '*We* won the lottery; we picked three numbers each.'

Jenny whistled. 'Life's a bitch and then you're rich, eh.'

'That's how it was for us, right enough.'

We joined them in their small dining room, at a round table. 'Pep,' I said, rolling strands of linguini on to my fork, 'this is a trivial call, really. Gerrie's away for a couple of days or she'd be doing this, but we were handy so Miles sent us. We need your mate, Stu Queen the sparks, back at the studio. He was stood down too quick last night; there's some wiring work needs doing on the big set.

'We've tried the only contact number we have for him, but no joy. D'you know where we can find him?'

The dark Spanish eyes looked at me, a little curiously. 'I haven't a bleedin' clue, mate,' he said. 'The fact is, I hardly know the guy. I've never worked with him before, and I'd never even heard of him, until he turned up on the production team up in Scotland.'

He stirred his pasta around on his plate, mixing the sauce through it. 'What's all this about, Oz?' he asked, quietly.

'Nothing,' I said, with as much wide-eyed innocence as I could manage. 'Like I said, we're just Miles' errand people.'

'No I don't mean this, I mean the whole thing. I saw Dawn on set yesterday afternoon; she looked as fit as a fiddle. Virus my bum. What's up? Have she and Miles had an up-and-downer? I've worked with them before. I was there when they met in fact, on that project up in the Highlands a few years back. She's nice, but she can be a fiery little thing from time to time.'

'She's the quiet one of the family, mate. She's Prim's sister.'

'Of course,' Jenny exclaimed. 'I'd forgotten that. It said that in the *Mail on Sunday*, too.'

'There's nothing wrong with Dawn,' said Primavera. 'Or with her and Miles. She's just found out that she's pregnant. It'll be a first for both of them, and Miles is over the moon. When she told him last night, he insisted that she was taking a week off. The virus thing was a cover story to keep the press at bay. That's what's really behind it all.'

Nice one, girl, I said to myself, as the sound man's face split into a wide grin.

'Ahhh,' he exclaimed, as he swallowed hook, line and sinker, 'I knew it was something big. I know how much a week's delay costs. I'm part of it.'

'Going back to the boy Queen,' I ventured, a little later. 'Do you think he might have picked up some extra work on the fly? We checked with his agency; they haven't placed him anywhere.'

'Like I said, mate,' Pep replied. 'I wouldn't know. The guy never says much about himself. That's unusual, for our world's a bit of a co-operative. We exchange information all the time about projects coming up and stuff, and where there might be work going. He doesn't. It's as if he's only interested in this one job and that's it.'

'Real mystery man, eh.'

'That's right. He's a good enough sparks though. Used to all sorts; high voltage work and everything. He's worked in the Middle East; he did tell me that, and out of Rotterdam, and Singapore.'

'Where's he from?'

'Haven't a clue about that either. You can't tell from listening to him, that's for sure. I thought he might have been Scottish like you, then I thought there might be some European in there.'

'How did he get on the project if he's such an unknown quantity?'

Pep finished off his linguini. 'It was a last minute thing. Originally, it was Zoltan Szabo who was booked in for the job; I know 'cause he told me the week before. I work with Zoltan a lot of the time. But he had to pull out, and Stu was handy so the agency slotted him in.'

'What happened to Zoltan?' Prim asked.

The sound man frowned, his black brows forming a hairy ridge. 'Bad, that was. There he was going home from the pub the very night before we was due to go up north to start work on the project, when . . . *Bang*.' The word sounded round the small room.

'He was hit by a car; broke both his legs. And you know what? Bleedin' driver didn't even stop.'

50

'This much is certain,' Miles Grayson growled. He seemed to have taken my advice; he was doing a damn fine job of focusing his anger. 'I will never use that agency again, and I'll do my best to see that no one else in this business does either.'

I had to agree with him. Zoltan Szabo had been knocked down and almost killed by a hit-and-run driver, and next day a new and previously unknown electrician had shown up out of the blue, ready and willing to take his place on the project.

No one had asked a thing about him, and no one had known a thing about him – other than that he was there and the agency was no longer in a hole.

'Should we go to them tomorrow and ask to see the file they hold on Stu Queen?' I asked.

It was Prim who answered. 'No. They'd be bound to ask why we were so interested in him. We'd have to give them a hell of a strong cover story; they might get nervous and call their lawyers. They might get silly and call the press. The whole thing could blow wide open.'

She was right too.

I looked at Miles across the top of my glass, where an ice cube big enough to have been the centrepiece of another movie was fighting to submerge a slice of lemon. 'So we don't really know any more than we did before we spoke to Pep,' I muttered. 'That Stephen Donn posed as a film sparks to get on set and among us, that he's a real bad bastard and that he has Dawn.'

'We do,' said Prim. 'We know that he's worked in other places as an electrician. Maybe he was Stu Queen there too.'

'Maybe he has a criminal record as Stu Queen,' Miles suggested.

'If he has, Mike will find it,' I countered. 'But if he has so what? We know already that he's a fucking criminal. No, we're back where we were, sat on our hands.'

'And the Goddamned phone hasn't rung all day, other than once when Kiki Eldon called to tell me that the press have bought our story, without question.'

'So maybe tomorrow, we'll have mail,' Prim mused.

I blinked. 'Hold the phone,' I exclaimed. 'Maybe we've got it now. Dawn's got an e-mail address. You and she talk that way all the time.' Miles, who had been slumped, sat upright in his chair. 'Could she access it from here?' I asked him.

'Sure, she has a lap-top.' He was out of that chair in a second, running out of the room and up the big staircase. Less than a minute later he was back, clutching an Apple Mac Powerbook, with a modem cable flying behind it.

He crouched beside the telephone jack point and changed cables; Mr Mac was powering up already.

'You do know her password?' I asked.

'Fuck!'

'No, it's unlikely to be that. But why don't you try P-R-I-M,' Prim suggested. 'They're usually four letters, and my password is D-A-W-N, so you never know.' Miles nodded, moved the cursor to the apple symbol in the top left-hand corner of the colour screen and opened the Internet software.

A box, with a cursor flashing on an empty line, appeared on screen. We watched as he keyed in P-R-I-M.

An on-screen dialogue told us what was happening step by step as the modem dialled the Internet provider. After a few seconds, the connection was made, and a soft – and very well-known – voice told us that Dawn had mail.

'What do I do now?' asked Miles. 'I don't use this stuff.'

'Gimme.' He obeyed at once, and passed the lap-top across to Prim. She pulled down the e-mail section of the menu, gave two quick commands to retrieve the waiting messages, then, when the process was complete, broke the Internet connection.

There were three new messages in the off-line mailbox when Prim opened it. One was from 'DPhil' – SuperDave, I guessed – the second was from someone with an all-numeral Compuserve address, and the third was from 'stuer@hotmail.com'.

'That's him,' said Prim. 'Funny guy. Stu Queen: S-T-U and then E-R, the Queen.'

'You sure?' asked Miles.

'There's a quick way to find out.' She clicked on the small envelope symbol to open the document. The screen cleared then filled with a new window, containing a page of text. 'It's him,' she cried out. 'Look there. He sent it this afternoon.'

She fell silent as Miles and I perched on the couch on either side of her, leaning close so that we could clearly see the message on the flat LCD screen. We read it together.

It began politely:

Hello Mr Grayson,
I hope that you haven't taken too long to work out how

I would contact you. That could be bad for Dawn's health. I assure you that she's safe and sound for the moment. Whether she remains that way depends on your co-operation.

I know enough about the film business to be sure that Snatch will make you another fortune at the box office, especially when the news of this incident breaks – I have no doubt you will ensure that it does. What I propose is that to secure your wife's safe release, you anticipate those profits and send some of them in my direction. Ten million sterling, seems reasonable and achievable in the circumstances.

I appreciate that arrangements like these can't be made on the instant, so I will allow you twenty-four hours from the receipt of this message to transfer the funds to a new account in the Bank Neder, in Lugano, Switzerland. The money should be cleared for immediate transfer by simple coded instruction, to another account of my choosing.

Please send me a one-word reply, 'Yes', immediately, to confirm that you have received this message and that you will comply. Then, within the twenty-four hours specified, I will expect to receive a second message containing the code word which will allow me to make the next transfer.

Forty-eight hours after that, when the money and I are no longer traceable, I will send you a further e-mail telling you where Dawn can be found. Be assured, she will be unharmed and will be fed and watered during that two-day period.

I do not want you to feel, Mr Grayson, that you are simply a random victim. Equally, I hope you will not waste your life in futile pursuit of me when this is over. Think of me as a working man who is taking an opportunity to secure his future. The only person you should blame for what has happened is Oz Blackstone.

I look forward to hearing from you.

Stephen Donn.

It was only when the message finished that I realised I had been reading aloud.

'Cool son-of-a-bitch,' Miles hissed. And then he looked at me. 'Why, Oz?' he asked, with pain in his voice. 'Why is all this happening, and what does it have to do with you?'

I shook my head. 'I have no idea. I promise you, I have never met Stephen Donn in my life, and I have never done anything to upset him.'

'What about his Uncle? You told me about him getting kicked out of Susie's company. Could he be blaming you? Could he have sent his nephew on some sort of crazy revenge mission?'

'Not a chance,' said Prim, evenly. 'Especially since Susie was one of the targets.' Something in her tone made me tense as I looked at her. 'Joseph Donn is Susie's real father,' she continued. 'He told me that when I went to see him. But she doesn't know, and she never will because I promised not to tell her. When Susie's mother left Joe for Jack Gantry, she didn't know at the time, but she was already pregnant.

'Jack told him when he asked him to come into the business. He confessed to him that he was sterile – that fits, for Susie's an only child. Old Joe would kill Stephen himself, for that stunt with the car.'

In my mind, two pennies dropped simultaneously; I couldn't handle both so I let one roll on the floor for a while.

'He's read the script,' I said. Miles stared at me. 'Think about it,' I told him. 'He's asked for ten million sterling. He wants it deposited in a secure bank account for onward transfer. Straight out of the *Snatch* script.'

'Surely he couldn't be that arrogant?' Prim asked.

'What's arrogant about it? He didn't expect to be identified as Stu Queen; not after removing all those happy family snapshots. He didn't reckon on Uncle Joe putting one over on him.'

'Okay, Oz,' said Miles. 'Maybe you're right; maybe this guy is using our own plot against him. But he's got Dawn for real.'

'Can you send the first reply message like he says, Prim?' he asked.

'Sure.'

'Then do it. Give him his "Yes". I'll call my accountant and tell him to make the transfer to the Lugano Bank, code word "Elanore".' He took out a cellphone, punched in a short-code number, and barked those instructions to the person who answered.

When he was finished he nodded to Prim. There was a small box beside the message labelled 'reply'. She clicked it, typed the single word into the new window which appeared, then re-established the connection with the service provider and pressed the 'send' symbol. 'Message sent successfully' appeared on screen a second or two later.

'Done,' she pronounced. 'Now. We've got twenty-four hours to find him.'

'Why?' Miles asked, grimly. 'Because you think he's going to kill Dawn anyway?'

I could tell from the sudden flicker of fright which crossed her face that that possibility hadn't occurred to her. I answered for her. 'No. Why should he do that? Stephen's planning his early retirement on your money. If he kills Dawn, then he will never have a moment's peace anywhere in the world, for he will know for sure that the three of us will hunt him down, literally to the ends of the earth.'

'Oh yeah. How would we do that? Where would we even start?'

'Well for openers, he's got a mother. In those circumstances I'd put the thumbscrews on her myself for any clue to where he might have gone. No, this is his big play. Killing Dawn would be stupid, and stupid this boy ain't.'

'Okay, so where's the clever bastard hiding my wife.'

'Go into the script again,' said Prim. 'What happens in the movie, when Dawn's kidnapped?'

Miles frowned. 'Nelson Reed takes her to an abandoned offshore oil platform. Donn's not going to follow the plot that closely; that really would be stupid.'

'I agree with you that he wouldn't take her to that place. Think of this, though; when you send him the code word, Dawn will be out of his hands for forty-eight hours while he makes his getaway. "Fed and watered", he said. But not able to contact anyone, surely, not able to raise the alarm and set us on his trail before he's got where he's going. He won't leave an accomplice to guard her; that wouldn't make sense. So he must be holding her where he believes she can be left safely alone for that length of time.

'Somewhere the buses don't run. Somewhere the postman doesn't call. An uninhabited island?'

A third penny dropped; this time I picked it up. 'No. A rig after all; but not that one. Prim, Pep Newton hardly told us anything about Donn that we didn't know before, but there was one fact, wasn't there?'

She nodded. 'He worked offshore, the Middle East, out of Singapore, out of Rotterdam.'

I didn't wait for a reply; instead I took out my mobile phone and called Dylan, on Susie's number. He answered the phone, sleepily. 'Mike, it's me.'

''cking Hell, Oz. Do you know what time it is?'

'It's countdown time,' I snapped at him, excited. 'The money's in place, code word Dawn's mum's name, and now we've got twenty-four hours before we give it to him and he scoots. I need you to check something now. I want a list of abandoned gas or oil production platforms in the southern part of the North Sea, including, in particular, the Dutch sector. I need it now.'

'Okay. Keep your phone switched on.' The drowsiness had gone from his voice.

Miles was frowning at me. 'You think . . .?'

'It's not just our best shot, man. It's our only shot.'

'But how the hell would he get her on to a rig? He'd need a chopper, assuming he could fly one, and they don't leave those lying around, do they?'

It was one of those rare moments when two people realise the same truth at exactly the same time. We stood there staring at each other, open-mouthed. Prim must have thought we were idiots, but then she hadn't seen the open-air studio set, or the real Jet Ranger parked on the mock helipad.

51

The night security guard on the studio gate looked at us doubtfully; Prim, Miles and me in the Freelander. 'I don't know, sir,' he said, peering at us from his shelter at the main gate, taking care not to step out into the heavy autumn rain.

'My orders are not to let anyone in once the lot's closed, you see. No one at all.'

Miles wound down the rear window. 'Not even me?' he asked, grinning.

'Gawd,' the man exclaimed. 'I didn't recognise you in this light, Mr Grayson. I suppose it's all right for you to go in.'

'Thanks,' the mega-star replied. He waved his bare left wrist at the man. 'It's a bad sign when you start leaving fifty grand Rolexes in your dressing room.'

'Want me to get it for you, sir?' the second guard called from within the hut.

'That's okay. You stay here in the dry. I need to pick up some papers as well.'

'Very good, Mr Grayson.' The first guard raised the barrier and Prim drove through the gateway. I glanced into the back seat and saw Miles slip his watch back on to his wrist. The studio was the size of a large village, and laid out as such, with pavement walkways and street lighting. The rain slashed through the car's headlight beams as I gave Prim directions to the big outdoor set. She drove slowly and carefully, and so it was over two minutes before we turned the last corner and saw the outline of the massive, mocked up oil platform.

Huge tarpaulins were lashed across its open side, giving some protection from the driving rain, but we had no interest in the substructure of the thing. All that we could do was stare up at the deck, and at the empty helipad.

'Shit!' Miles whispered. 'The son-of-a-bitch is a pilot.'

'Or he has a pilot with him,' Prim suggested.

I pointed to the side of the set, where the road ran closest to it. A dark shape was parked, there, squat and chunky. 'Drive us over there, love.'

She pulled up behind the vehicle, a medium-sized LDV truck with plain panelled sides. I jumped out into the rain and tried the back doors; they swung open, and I stepped up and into the space, crouching as I went. The beams of the Freelander lit up the compartment. At first, I thought it was empty, until I saw the line which ran down its back wall. Keeping my shadow out of the way, I touched the blue painted structure and felt it move beneath my fingers. It was a sliding door; I moved it out of the way, to reveal a second cabin, tiny, but big enough to take a passenger . . . as it had. The floor was padded with carpeting, folded over three times to give some cushioning against the hard floor; there was a ring, welded to the back wall, and from it there hung a chain with, on the end, a studded leather dog collar.

'Bastard!' I hissed, picturing Dawn tethered inside the truck. I felt my teeth clenched tightly together as I looked at the floor of the truck again. Half of the secret cubicle was in darkness and so I groped around in it, wishing I had had the brains to bring a torch. My hands bumped against something rough. I picked it up; a length of rope, knotted tightly, but cut through cleanly with a blade. I fitted the severed ends together, and judged that the loop which it formed would have secured a small person's ankles. I pressed myself back into the dark side of the compartment, allowing in as much of the bright halogen light as possible, looking for other, more ominous signs – like blood – but, to my relief, finding none.

I jumped out of the van and back into the Freelander. I was still holding the rope; I passed it into the back seat. 'No doubt about it,' I said. 'Dawn was there. It's an abduction vehicle, purpose-built.'

Miles rubbed the hemp against the stubble of his chin, with real anguish on his face. Then his eyes hardened again, 'Prim. Take us to the production office. There's some stuff there I want to check.' He snapped out directions. 'First right, second left, then look for a two-storey half-timbered house with a small garden in front.

'I wasn't thinking earlier, Oz, when you called Mike. We don't need him to pinpoint disused North Sea platforms. I researched that when I was planning this project; the report's in my files.'

Prim drove a bit more quickly this time; she found the office which looked like a house in under a minute. Miles fumbled with a bunch of keys as we ran up the short drive. He unlocked the door then threw the light switch and ran upstairs, with us on his heels.

He led us straight into one of the upper rooms, which was furnished with a desk, a bar, a few chairs, and a wooden filing cabinet. He slid the top drawer open and flicked through folders, quickly. 'Gotcha, you beaut,' he hissed, lapsing unconsciously into broad Aussie, as he pulled one out.

He scanned the document which was stitched inside, then handed it to me. I was going to read it, until he spoke.

'Like I thought, the advance team came up with three possibilities: the one we chose in the end, one in the Norwegian sector, and a third, known as Beta platform, in Dutch waters. Logistically that was by far the best option; it was the easiest to reach and service, and the weather was guaranteed better. But technically, it wasn't what we were looking for. We did a recce and decided that it just didn't look the part, so we opted for the location off Aberdeen.'

'Does it have a helipad?'

'Of course.'

'Could we fly over it and see if there's a chopper there now?'

'No, that wouldn't tell us for sure. The platform has a hangar; it could have been rolled in there.'

He looked at us, from one to the other. 'What do you think?'

'It's all we've got,' Prim replied, voicing my thoughts word for word. 'But we have to bring in the police, especially since the platform's in Dutch coastal waters. If we're going to rescue Dawn unharmed, we're going to need a specialist assault team.'

'We've got one,' Miles growled. His eyes were slits; at that moment he didn't look a bit like any face I'd ever seen on a movie poster. 'I never told you guys, but when I was a youngster, before I got into this business, I was in the Australian Marines; special forces. I don't use it in my publicity; I don't even talk about it, because some of the things we did wouldn't stand looking into.

'I know how to get on to that rig, and I know what to do when I get there.'

'Miles,' Prim protested. 'That's crazy. You can't stage a frontal assault on the thing, on your own.'

'I sure can. But maybe I won't have to. You're a diver, aren't you, Oz.'

I nodded. 'You know I am. I dived a lot when I was in my teens and early twenties. And I still go down now and again when we're in Spain.'

'Ever done any wreck diving?'

'Of course I have. The Firth of Forth's full of the bloody things.' I knew what was coming. 'Hold on a minute though. Prim's right. You and I can't run a private rescue mission, in foreign territory, or anywhere else for that matter.' I glanced at my watch. 'We've still got twenty-two hours to play with, before you have to e-mail the code word. If we go to the police now, with what we have, they can stage the rescue.'

Miles shook his head, firmly. 'What do you know about the Dutch special forces? Nothing. What do you know about the British? Only that when they go in they go in shooting. That's if they didn't spend all the time we have arguing about jurisdiction. There's a better than even chance they'd botch it.

'Tell me this straight. What do you think this guy would do if he was cornered?'

He had me there. 'I think there's a pretty fair chance he'd kill Dawn.'

'And if we do nothing, if we let him take the money and run, can you give me a cast-iron guarantee that he won't kill her anyway?'

'You know I can't.'

'Then will you help me?'

'Miles . . .'

There was a long silence, until at last his eyes softened. 'Listen,' he said, softly, 'your Prime Minister is a buddy of mine . . . or he likes to think he is. If I call him, and get his personal okay on what we plan to do, with the proviso that if anything does go wrong, they take the bastard out as soon as he lifts off in that chopper . . . if I do that, will you come with me?'

I couldn't say no, could I? Well, maybe I could have, but when it comes right down to it, I'm as crazy as him. 'Okay,' I agreed. Prim said nothing; she just glared at the two of us.

'That's what we do then. I'll make the call right now; it could take a while to get through to him, so in the meantime, why don't you guys go back and talk to the two stooges on the gate. Get them to tell you how come they let Stephen Donn in last night, but didn't log him out.'

'Right. And I'll get them to confirm that there was only him in the driver's cab.'

'Could there have been a helicopter pilot hidden in the back, with Dawn?'

'No way. You couldn't have got Danny de Vito in there with her.'

I was in the doorway, and Miles had his hand on the phone, when I remembered that penny, the other one that had dropped earlier, only I'd neglected to pick it up. 'Hey,' I asked. 'Do you have the shooting schedule here for the whole project? A file that shows who's due where on what days?'

'Sure.' He rose from the chair behind the desk and went back to the filing cabinet, found another folder and handed it to me. I read it silently, put it back, then headed off with Prim to question the security guards. As I did, I was beginning to think a very bad thought.

As it turned out, only one guard had been in the hut at the main gate when Stu Queen had talked his way in, with his security pass, to retrieve a piece of equipment he had left. And, as it turned out further, that guard had gone for an extended comfort pause when his mate had returned, and had assumed that the guy in the van must have checked out while he was enthroned.

Miles was waiting for us at the door of the disguised office when we returned from our interrogation. I had got tough with the guys at the finish, warning them that their continued employment was in my hands, so they had better keep their mouths tight shut not just about that incident, but about our visit . . . at least, I thought but didn't say, until the leasing company which owned the Jet Ranger found out that it was missing.

'Well,' I asked. 'You got the PM on-side?' I don't think I had really believed him earlier.

He looked at me, just a little crestfallen. 'Yes, 'he answered, 'but only up to a point. I told him the whole story. He was appalled; he's got a crush on Dawn, I think. I tried to persuade him that you and I should go in alone, and eventually, he had his staff make a call to Australia. They faxed him my service record; once he'd read that he said I could go on the operation . . . but it has to be led by the Special Boat Service.

'He's gone off to speak to the Home Secretary and the Chief of the Defence staff, to get the support teams lined up, and to square the whole operation with the Dutch Prime

Minister. He doesn't think that will be a problem.'

'What about me?' I was actually beginning to feel disappointed; looking back on it, I must have been crazy.

Miles grinned. 'He took some persuading, but you're included. I told him that there are a lot of people on my movie crews, and one or two of them – like Donn – never become familiar faces to me. I finally convinced him that, since the one photograph we have is blurred, you are the only person who can identify Stephen Donn straight away, if we find him on board.'

When I get a bit nervous, usually there's this wee hamster which starts doing revolutions on a wheel in the pit of my stomach. Not this time, though; this time it felt like a big black rat, its claws pounding at the treadmill. It took me more than a few seconds to bring it, and myself, back under control.

From that moment I couldn't think about anything else but what we were going to have to do.

'When do we go in?' I asked.

'Dawn,' he replied; I was secretly pleased that now he looked as nervous as I felt. 'Appropriate, eh.'

52

The sun wasn't up, but the sky was lightening, pink in the east. It was seven-twenty – Central European Time, since we were on the Continent, in theory at least.

In fact we were on a Dutch pilot cutter, having sailed out of Rotterdam about ninety minutes earlier. A Royal Marine detachment had flown us over from Aldershot barracks in one of their two assault helicopters. The squad was on-shore, locked and loaded, ready for back-up action if required, but their commanding officer was at sea with us, ready to lead the raid.

The wet-suit felt strange to me. I hadn't told Miles any porkies about my scuba experience, but it had been a while since I had done anything serious, and longer than that since I had dived in North Sea conditions.

'Right, gentlemen,' barked the Marine Lieutenant, whose name was Ardley; he was the youngest of the four of us in the ship's small wardroom, no more than twenty-five, I guessed. 'If you'll look here . . .' He unrolled a chart on the table, then held the corners in place using mugs as paperweights. The thought of Stephen Donn's nuts came viciously to me as I looked at them.

He pointed at the map. 'At this moment, we are here, in this navigation channel, sailing north-eastwards. Our closest point to the platform will come in eleven minutes and we will be half a mile away from it. At that point we will slow for a few seconds and you two, Sergeant Roper, and I will go into the water, from the port side of the vessel, to avoid any tiny chance of our being seen by anyone on board the rig.'

I felt a fresh wave of panic sweep over me, but I fought it off. 'We will submerge to a depth of a few feet, and approach the platform underwater, maintaining a south-south-westerly course which will take you straight to it. When we see the legs we will dive a bit deeper, to ensure that our approach cannot be seen from above.'

He rolled up the chart and produced a plan, which he spread out on the table. 'This is the lay-out of Beta platform. It has four strong metal legs, as you can see. The access ladder is attached to this one, on the north west corner. When we climb it, we will reach a walkway. We'll leave our tanks and other unnecessary equipment there, and make ready to enter the platform.'

'That's going to be the difficult part, isn't it?' Miles murmured.

'Easier than you think. When this platform was operational, there was an emergency escape pod, right at its base. It's not there any more, but the ladder and latch which led into it, they are. They're accessed through a door in a store-room, but also from the walkway. That's where we head for; we find it, climb the ladder and we're inside.'

We nodded, as the lieutenant continued. 'As you can see from the plan, all the working parts of this installation are in the lower levels, with accommodation above, just below the helideck and hangar. Operationally, the place was run by three people. So we won't have much to search. There are three cabins, a mess, the shower room and heads, and a galley – that's it.

'The stairway which leads up to the living module comes out here, next to the heads. We'll be in a corridor, without windows, which may or may not be lit. Better for us if it isn't. We'll carry torches, but even on the lower level, we'll use these night-glasses.' He reached under the table and produced two headsets, which looked like strap-on spectacles for a very, very short-sighted man. I recognised them as night-glasses from a Territorial Army ad on which I'd done the voice-over.

'How do we carry those?' I asked him.

'We won't have weights on this dive. We'll carry these and our other equipment in watertight bags, strapped to our chests.'

'What other equipment?'

Ardley reached under the table again, and produced a black metal automatic pistol, fitted with a silencer. I gulped. It must have been pretty theatrical, for the other three grinned at me. Until then, Sergeant Roper had been impassive. He was only a wee man, around the same age as me, but his lined face looked as if it had been carved out of stone.

'Don't worry, Mr Blackstone,' said the officer. 'This is for Mr Grayson. He's firearms qualified; you're not. No offence, but no way would I have you following behind me on an op with a loaded weapon.'

'I'll have live rounds, then,' said Miles. 'I thought it might have been just for show.'

'Nothing's for show in this one,' Ardley murmured. 'Which brings me to the real business. Our political commanders have accepted military advice that this is to be treated as a counter-terrorist operation. That means that if we find Mrs Grayson's abductor on board the platform, we are authorised to kill him, there and then. No warnings, no "hands up" – we may shoot the bastard where he stands.

'Don't worry about the aftermath. There won't be any; we'll have a back-up team to clean up the mess.'

He looked hard at me, killer-hard, and then at Miles. 'You gentlemen volunteered for this mission. Do either of you have a problem with what I'm telling you?'

I had a big problem; I hadn't bargained for this at all. I suppose I'd imagined that when we caught up with Stephen Donn, it would be a bit like a movie. He'd either chuck it, or he and Miles would have a punch-up which would end with him on the floor. I almost backed out of it then. I knew that if I had, none of the guys would have said a word about it. But then I thought of Dawn, and of Colin, and for some reason, inexplicable at the time, I thought of Jan; in that moment I found, for the first time in my life, the real dark side of Oz Blackstone.

I shook my head. As for Miles, he didn't even bother to acknowledge the Marine's question.

Lieutenant Ardley looked at us both, and then his face changed. 'Look guys,' he said. 'I have to tell you that I think you're crazy to come along on this. I know about your record of counter-terrorist special ops service in the South Pacific Basin, Mr Grayson, how you were decorated twice and everything else, but that's a long time in the past.

'I'm sure you know that you're only coming because of your personal connections, and as you can guess, that it's against our advice. We could run this mission just as well without either of you along. Until we go over the side, it's still not too late to let us.'

'I can do this, son,' Miles replied, quietly.

'But what if something goes wrong?'

'Then I'll blame myself for the rest of my life. But you sure as hell wouldn't want me blaming you.' He checked his compass and his dive computer, then picked up one of the watertight bags from beneath the table and began to pack it, fitting gun and night-glasses in beside a two-way radio. 'Come on,' he said. 'It's nearly show-time.' He glanced at me. 'This one we do first take, buddy.'

When we were packed, Ardley led us up on deck. We pulled on our tanks, checked our regulators – top quality, befitting special forces – and fitted our face-masks. By the time we had finished, the pilot cutter had slowed almost to a halt, its engines idling noisily.

'Total radio silence until we've secured the platform,' the Marine shouted, 'but once we have, I'll make contact at once, and call in our back-up people. Remember, south south-west.'

We nodded and followed him and Sergeant Roper as they toppled backward into the grey water.

I've always liked diving, as long as I can see where I am, and I have something interesting to look at. Navigating ten feet beneath the surface of the North Sea with nothing to look at but a compass is not a fun thing to do, especially when you're shit-scared of what could happen when you get to your objective, and at the same time, of what could happen if your compass is wonky and you don't. But the diver's first, life-preserving rule is, do not panic; I'm experienced and inherently there was nothing difficult about what we were doing then, so I held myself together. We swam on side by side, not caring about the time, for we had plenty of air in our tanks, aware only of our compasses and of the cold.

At last, Roper touched my shoulder lightly and pointed off to his right. I followed his signal and saw for the first time – and with a mixture of relief and fear – four great dark legs, linked together with cross-members, rising out of the black depths and reaching up towards the surface.

We did as we had been instructed, following Ardley down to about thirty feet with the sergeant bringing up the rear, swimming towards the most distant of the platform's two northerly supports. When we reached it, we ascended, slowly and safely, looking for the first rungs of the ladder, and found them just below the waterline.

I had been mildly worried about climbing to the walkway while still wearing flippers, but unlike our studio version, the ladder had been built with divers in mind. *Dress rehearsal*, I thought, suppressing a slightly insane giggle as I clambered up behind Miles, weighed down now by the tanks and my pack.

We were all breathing heavily, even the marines, by the time we reached the promised walkway. It was narrow, but we were able to sit as we eased ourselves out of our breathing apparatus and ripped off the big flippers. The sea was relatively calm, but the wind whipped and cut into us as we sat there, opening our packs, towelling off our hands and faces, fitting on rope-soled canvas shoes, then finally strapping on the equipment belts which carried the guns, or in my case, only the night glasses and radios.

'Let's go,' Ardley murmured, when we were all ready.

'Careful, this walkway will be slippy.'

He was right, but the shoes gave us a good grip. The platform was about two hundred yards from corner to corner, and the escape hatch was just off centre, not far from us. We could see the four big hooks from which the emergency pod had once hung, its small loading platform, and its ladder. It was light enough in there for us to be able to check for footprints. There were none; the metal floors were showing signs of rust and it looked as if no one had been there for years.

Now Roper led the way up the ladder, and I followed, feeling cocooned inside its safety rings. It wasn't a long climb, only about ten feet, and in seconds, I found myself staring at a big metal door, with an iron lever for a handle. 'This is the first uncertain part,' Roper called down to us. 'Let's hope this bastard isn't rusted shut.'

For a few awkward seconds I thought that it was, as I watched him heave at the handle, trying to force it from vertical to horizontal. It wouldn't budge at first, and I thought we were done, until he braced his broad back against the safety rail of the ladder gave one final, tremendous push. Metal screamed, as the catch came undone, and the door swung inwards. We followed the little sergeant inside and stood stock still for a few seconds, listening for sounds from above, in case the noise of his struggle had carried up there.

There was a little light spilling into the module from the doorway, but suddenly it went out. I pulled on my headset, squeezed my eyes shut, then opened them again to see Ardley, greeny grey and ghostly, closing the door and taking out his gun. Looking around in that odd light, I had another mad moment, imagining that Miles and I were in the X-Files and wondering which one of us was Scully: it had to be Miles; I'm taller and his hair is about the same length as hers.

'Let's do it,' the lieutenant whispered. 'The stairway should be just along here.' He took a pace forward, then stopped, and turned to Miles and Roper. 'Guys: when we find Donn, I'll take him out. You two be ready for anyone else, just in case we're wrong and he's not alone. If you have to shoot anyone don't worry which part of him you hit, just fucking hit him, and keep on doing it until he's no longer a threat.'

'I'll do him.' Miles said it quietly, hoarsely, as if he'd borrowed Clint Eastwood's voice for the occasion.

'Let's not argue about this—' Ardley began.

'You ever killed anyone, son?' Roper and I looked on, as the two of them stared at each other. Eventually, the young Marine shook his head. 'Well I have, in my special forces days; more people than you've got years in the service, I guess. My wife's at risk here; if there's the slightest chance you might turn out to be gun-shy, I'm not taking it.'

'We'll see.'

'No. I'm telling you.'

When the going gets tough, as they say. Ardley looked at him and nodded. 'Let's go then,' he whispered.

We crept along, the four of us, through the platform's great, pipe-filled hall, until the shape of a stairway came into our night vision. It was wide, and rose for about thirty feet and as far as we could tell; no light spilled down from above. Tensing more and more with each step, we climbed the metal treads silently, Miles and Ardley in the lead, scarcely daring to breathe as we reached the top.

As we stepped into the corridor, we flattened ourselves against its walls. It was dark, but through our glasses we could make out the doors of the shower rooms and heads; there were two of each, since the Dutch had many women engineers. Beyond, the corridor stretched out: three cabin doors to the left, and on the right, those of the dayroom and the galley . . . from which came a narrow, searing crack of light, the sound of music, and the unmistakable smell of frying food.

I heard Miles take a deep breath and looked across at him. He was holding his pistol upright in front of him, and nodding towards the door. He beckoned Ardley close with a nod of his head. 'You kick it open,' he said, in the faintest whisper, 'and I'll go in shooting. Back me up fast as you can.'

Ardley nodded; he took off his night glasses and signalled to Miles to do the same. 'The light could blind you, otherwise,' I heard him murmur.

My heart had been pounding since we had reached the top of the stairway; it dropped into third gear and picked up even more revs as I watched them creep along the corridor and take up positions, Miles tensed and faced the door, Ardley slightly to one side. 'Okay,' he mouthed, levelling the gun. The young marine grasped his in both hands, lifted his right foot and slammed it against the heavy door, as fast and as hard as he could.

I couldn't stop myself; I leapt after them as it swung open. I was there to identify Stephen Donn, after all . . .

Alone, unfettered and unharmed, Dawn screamed as she turned to see, framed in the doorway, a black figure from the depths of Hell.

Miles screamed right back at her as, at the final moment,

he swung his pistol up and shot three holes in the galley
cupboard.

53

I don't know how long I spent leaning against the wall of that corridor, hyperventilating, staring at the ghostly green roof through the night glasses which I had neglected to remove, and wondering if I'd pissed myself inside that wet-suit. I've no idea how long Miles spent framed in the doorway, head bowed, shoulders shaking, gun hanging limply from his fingers. I've no idea how long it took Dawn to recover her senses, and stir from her faint.

I only know that if Stephen Donn had come bursting out of the wardroom or one of the cabins with a blazing Uzi, we could all have been goners.

But he didn't. Ardley resumed command, and as Miles and I got a grip on ourselves, he and Roper checked the accommodation module, room by room, in case he had heard us, heard the muffled gunshots, guessed the game plan and was hiding for his life. There was no doubt, though; the five of us were alone on the rig.

I went back to the kitchen; Dawn was sitting on the floor, crying quietly. I noticed for the first time that she was still wearing the clothes which Miles had reported missing from her wardrobe, a day and a half earlier; except that they were green. As, finally, I tore off the night glasses, Miles lifted her gently to her feet. 'It's all right, honey, it's all right,' he soothed her, as her sobs grew louder. 'I'm sorry we gave you such a scare. We were expecting to find Stephen Donn.'

'Who?' she mumbled, bewildered. 'Who's he? Stu Queen, the sparks, kidnapped me from the mansion; he was the only one here.'

'Stu Queen was a phoney,' I told her, as I blinked my eyes to help them readjust to the world of colour. 'Stephen Donn is the guy who's been tracking me all along, making it look as if he was pursuing a vendetta against me, through my family and friends. Stephen Donn snatched you.'

I was beginning to recover my reason. 'Mr Grayson,' said Ardley from the doorway. 'It's time to call the cavalry.' He took the radio from his belt, switched it on and held down the 'transmit' button.

'This is the recovery team,' he called into the mike. 'Beta Platform is secure, Mrs Grayson is safe, we have no casualties. There's no one else here.'

He let the button go I heard a disembodied voice come crackling through a curtain of static. 'Understood, sir; we're on our way. Please check the heli-deck is clear and report back.'

'I'll do that,' I said, anxious, suddenly, to breathe fresh air again. A stairway at the far end of the corridor led to the deck of the platform. I ran up the steps; the door at the top opened easily and silently, and I burst out into a calm, cold, suddenly bright morning, on a steel island, surrounded by grey waters. The deck was clear, okay; it wasn't huge, but big enough to accommodate at least one large helicopter. Opposite the accommodation hatch, by which I stood, there was a wide, open-fronted shelter; the hangar, I guessed. It was empty too. I walked across and looked inside; there were tyre-marks on the oil-streaked floor, and what looked like fuel canisters stacked again the wall. I pick one or two up and shook them; they were empty.

I walked back out of the big garage and across to the doorway. 'The heli-deck's clear,' I called down to Ardley. 'Donn was here, but he's split.'

'Thanks,' the marine replied. 'He must have panicked.' I heard him as he radioed the back-up unit, giving them the all-clear to fly in.

I leaned against the wall of the superstructure for a few seconds, trying to imagine Stephen Donn panicking. I couldn't.

Ardley and Roper came up on deck together to await their squad. I went back below, to find the dayroom light on. Miles and Dawn were sitting at its table, on which were three mugs of coffee, and one plate of well-cooked bacon and a hard fried egg. The food and its smell drew me like a magnet. 'Who's this for?' I asked.

'We don't fancy it, mate,' Miles grunted. 'It's all yours if you want it.'

'TFR.' I sat down. 'So the boy Donn was expecting to be here for breakfast,' I murmured as I picked up the cutlery beside my plate. 'D'you want to tell us what happened, Dawn?'

It would have taken a lot of slap to make up Prim's sister that morning. She was white as a sheet, apart from the patches under her eyes. She smiled at me though. 'I was quietly cooking breakfast,' she replied, 'and this Navy Seal burst in and shot the shit out of my kitchen.' I grinned back at her, relieved that she really was okay. Between us, Miles still seemed to be in a state of shock. 'How did you manage to get in on the act?' she asked.

'Miles has a friend in high places,' I told her, in my matter-of-fact voice. 'He lent us a couple of his boys They'll be here in a few minutes.' I took a mouthful of egg; it tasted okay but had the consistency of a stick-on nylon sole. 'When did he leave?'

'It must have been about three hours ago. He kept me in here, with my wrists held in sort of plastic handcuff things; then all of a sudden, he just got up from his chair and cut them. He told me to sit still, and to wait; that I was a lucky lady – that was the first time he'd spoken to me since we left the mansion – and that someone would be along for me by the end of today.

'I was terrified, all the time; I did what he said; sat here, scared even to step out into the corridor. And then I heard the helicopter take off. Once I was certain he was gone, I took a look around for a radio, or anything that I could use to call for help, but there was nothing. I went into one of the cabins and tried to sleep, but I couldn't, so eventually I got up and looked around again, till I found the food he'd left.'

Miles looked as if he wanted to speak, but had lost the power. So he simply reached out and squeezed her hand.

'What happened back at the house?' I asked her.

'When I got back from the studio, I was up in our room, getting ready to take a shower, and he just came in. I thought I was seeing things at first, then I was going to yell, until he showed me his gun and I knew it was for real. He told me to get dressed and come with him; he took me down the fire escape, and out through a back gate I didn't know was there. He had a van outside.

'He put me inside, tied and gagged me and warned me not

to move or try to make any sort of sound. We travelled for a bit, then he stopped, opened the van and I saw where we were.'

'Before he split, Dawn, can you remember what he was doing?'

She frowned, then nodded. 'Yes. He had one of these super-duper mobile phone things, with a mini-computer inside; a palm-top, I think they're called. Every so often he'd take it out and fiddle with it; I think he was checking e-mail.

'Just before he left, he switched it on, and looked at it.' She hesitated. 'Then, I think, he sent a couple of messages, and maybe received another. It was after that that he got up and left.'

'Can you remember what the time was?'

'No, only that it was hours ago.'

As she spoke, a roaring noise of which we had been aware for some time became too loud to be ignored. A lot of people have gone deaf in later life through flying military helicopters; I understand why. After a couple of minutes, the sound died down. There was a noise above our heads, feet on metal. I got up, went to the dayroom door, and waved Ardley inside as he came downstairs.

'Dawn,' I announced, 'you haven't been introduced. This is Neville Ardley, our CO.'

'Very pleased to see you safe and well, ma'am,' the young man said. 'These guys did well,' he added. 'The ideal search and rescue mission is the one which ends with no shots fired and the captive recovered safely. Ours rarely do, of course. This one was no exception, but no damage done.

'Come on; my men will stay on station here, to wait for the police. Let's get all of you back on shore and into a change of clothes, then we'll fly you back to Surrey. You'd better get all the rest you can, for once the press get hold of this story, we're all going to be busy.'

'No press,' I snapped, so quickly that I surprised myself. 'This thing's not over. Stephen Donn's still out there.'

'Sure,' Miles drawled; he sounded mentally and physically exhausted. 'But where? He could be anywhere. The important thing is that we've got Dawn back and that we've beaten the deadline for sending the access code word.'

'I'm not so sure,' I countered. 'What if he had another means of activating the account? Let's get off this junkyard and find out. A fiver says I'm right; and if I am, I'm not going back to Surrey. I'm staying in Holland for a while.'

54

The marines' chopper landed at the Rotterdam police barracks from which the operation had begun four long hours earlier. As soon as he was reunited with his cellphone, Miles called his accountant and had him check with Lugano.

The return call came in less that five minutes. He stared at me as it came to an end, then stripped a fiver from a roll of cash in his pocket and handed it over. 'The money's been moved,' he said. 'How the hell did you know?'

'I just guessed. Do you know where it's gone?'

'The Swiss won't say; nor will they say how the account was activated. It would take a year and a court order to find out.'

'Don't worry,' I assured him. 'I'll get it back for you.'

'Oz, I'm not worried. I've got Dawn back, and like the soldier boy said earlier, once this story breaks, it'll be worth fifty million in extra box office takings. You know what? I'm going to change the end again, and have you and me go in underwater, like we did today only without the marines. Forget it; let the bastard go.'

I think I looked at him as if he was daft. 'No way, Jo-fucking-se! If this was a bit personal before, it's *really* personal now.'

'Okay,' Miles grunted. 'If you're dead set on taking it further, I'll stay on board.'

'Thanks, but you just concentrate on looking after Dawn. You've got a movie to finish, then other things to look forward to. I'll be there for work on Monday morning, but before then I've got to tie this business off.'

Finally, he was persuaded; he and Dawn went off at once to shower and change into fresh clothes for the flight home; but I dressed quickly and collared Ardley once again.

I found him explaining what had happened to Henke de Witt, the Dutch army captain who had smoothed the way for our operation. At first, I had been surprised that his side had been prepared to allow a British operation in their waters, but I'd realised quickly that if it had gone south, and the fourth most famous person and/or his wife had been killed during the action, they would have been more than happy to let our lot carry the can.

'How good are your relations with your police?' I asked de Witt.

'Excellent,' he replied at once. 'We're a small country; all our services inter-relate. Why?'

'Because I reckon I can nail the kidnapper. To do that, I need some information. Then I need a lift to Schiphol Airport, and someone to open doors for me when I get there.'

'I can do all that.'

'You really think you can find Donn?' Ardley asked.

'If he hasn't shot the craw already – no, even if he has – I'm bloody certain I can find him. You got that news blackout in place?'

He nodded. 'Henke and I have got you another twenty-four hours, here and in the UK; that's the max, though.'

'It's all I'll need.' I reached into my jacket and took out a

photograph, then handed it to the Netherlander. 'That's our
target, Captain, and this is what we need to know...'

55

Captain de Witt had changed into plain clothes; he and I stood at the back of the room, listening as the Dutch customs commander addressed her squad. They nodded as she spoke, each of them glancing occasionally at a copy of the snapshot with which old Joe Donn had put the finger on his nephew.

I hardly understood a word, but I knew what she was telling them. It was mid-afternoon and we had five hours before the flight which we had identified was due to take off; a KLM flight, bound for Jakarta through Singapore.

We would catch him at the gate, of course, but the sooner the better, so the customs team was being instructed to sweep the huge hub airport. The briefing was over, quickly, and the officers dispersed, leaving de Witt and me nothing to do but wait in that small office. I grew more excited, and more tense, by the minute; I'd have loved to have been out there looking myself, but it was too risky. We had one chance at this and if I was spotted first . . .

'Are you always as obsessive as this, Oz?' the soldier asked me, idly. Like many Dutch people, his English was almost perfect. 'You could have left the rest to us, you know, and gone back to England with your friends. I am not saying that this will be dangerous, but you never know.'

'I'm obsessive,' I replied, 'when someone is obsessed with me . . . and when someone thinks they can take the piss out of me and get away with it. As for going home, I have to know all the answers, and I have to hear them for myself.'

We sat there for almost an hour, almost telling each other our life stories. When I had finished mine, de Witt pursed his lips and nodded. 'I understand you better now,' he said. 'I see why you have to be here.'

He had barely finished before the door opened and the commander reappeared. 'We have a sighting,' she said, in English, for my benefit, 'in one of the restaurants on the upper level. Come on.'

We followed the woman out of the room, into the concourse. I know Schiphol Airport well – I travel through it often with the GWA team – so I had a fair idea of where we were headed. The place is so big that even at a brisk pace the walk took us almost ten minutes. Once or twice, air crew buzzed past us on wee motorised scooter things, and I wondered why the customs lady couldn't have ordered up three of those. But we got there, eventually; to the place which I had guessed, a restaurant not far from the Casino, one level above the crowds.

A customs officer was waiting by the doorway; he spoke briefly to his boss. 'Third table from the door,' she told us, quietly, 'in the centre of three ranks.' I knew the layout; I've eaten in the place myself. Henke de Witt nodded and stepped inside, with me at his heels.

We were unnoticed, until we were no more than five yards from the table; then Stephen Donn looked up, directly into my eyes. 'Hello,' I said, treating him to my most self-satisfied smile. 'I'll bet you thought you'd cracked it. Wrong.'

He didn't say a word. Instead he picked up a wicked looking, saw-edged steak knife and grabbed the arm of the

323

woman at the next table. I guessed at the time that he planned to use her as a hostage to make yet another getaway; in fact, that's still my guess, but I'll never know for sure, for de Witt turned out to be quicker on the draw than Billy the Kid.

I know that he snatched it from his shoulder holster, but it happened so fast that it was as if the gun had just materialised in his hand. Before Donn could pull the woman in front of him, a nice round red hole appeared in the middle of his forehead. He stiffened for a second, then toppled backwards, dead as a doornail.

Across the table, closer to us, Mike Dylan pushed himself to his feet, half-turning towards us. Captain de Witt shot him too, through the side of the chest; he gasped and slumped to the ground. I dropped to my knees beside him as he lay, writhing, on the floor. As he looked up at me, I read a mix of shock and terror in his expression; I couldn't do anything to comfort or reassure him, for we both knew that he was dying.

He grabbed my jacket. 'Clever bastard . . . right . . . enough,' he murmured, with a great effort. The words seemed to bubble out of him. Then he stared up, into my eyes. 'Only personal with him, Oz. Just the money with me . . . had to have my own. You understand . . .'

Those were the last words my poor, daft pal Dylan said to me, before he drowned on his own blood.

56

'But why?' Prim asked me; very unusually for her, she was in tears.

'I told you, love, he said that he wanted money of his own. Mike always had fairly expensive tastes; for a Detective Inspector's pay at any rate. He wouldn't live on Susie's wealth, but I guess being that close to it must have been too much for him. Then, I suppose, there was our dumb luck too. Whatever – envy, greed, call it what you like – it destroyed him.'

'That's not what I meant. Why did the Dutchman shoot him?'

I had asked Henke de Witt the same thing myself, rather more forcefully. It took three of the customs people to drag me off him, as Dylan lay dead at our feet. 'Orders, he told me. From our side of the operation; someone, somewhere did not want a Special Branch officer in the dock in a kidnapping and extortion trial.'

I waited for the tears to stop and for her to regain her self-control. It was just after six next morning and we were in our room at the mansion; I had only just been flown back from Amsterdam after a real grilling by secret policemen from Glasgow and Holland, and by a very sinister guy who said he was from the Home Office, but smelled like MI5 to me. We lay on the bed, both fully clothed. Prim had waited up for me all night. As for me, I should have been tired but I wasn't; I didn't feel like sleep at all.

'When did you begin to suspect Mike?' she asked me, eventually.

I leaned back on the bed. 'Not until very late in the day. I knew there was something wrong after a couple of things happened, but I couldn't even let myself think of the possibility that it might be him.

'The first time I should have twigged was when I saw the photo Joe Donn gave you – the original, I mean. It showed Stephen Donn and wee Myrtle at a Gantry office do, but the boy Dylan was in the picture too, right next to them. Yet Mike never said a word about having met him. I wondered about it for a bit, but not for long; everyone in the photo looked a bit pissed, and I decided that probably he had no idea that was Donn, or even any recollection of the thing.

'Then after that, when I looked at the movie schedule, I should have begun to worry about him, but I didn't.'

'Why?'

'Because when Susie's car was torched, Stephen Donn, or Stu Queen, was up in Aberdeen doing location shots on board the rig. He couldn't have done it. So who could? At first I didn't bother about it. I figured that when we found Donn we'd find his partner, whoever it was. As it turned out I was right.

'When I finally did make myself think about it, I realised that Mike had to be the number-one suspect. He probably booby-trapped the car when they arrived: maybe you didn't notice, but he was a minute or two behind Susie coming up the stairs. Later on, as they were leaving, with Susie pissed and rabbiting by the door, he triggered it, leaving himself a few seconds to step back out, ostensibly to fetch her.

'Remember what happened afterwards?' I asked Prim, but answered for her. 'He put the frighteners on the fireman and the Chief Inspector, didn't he. He took control of the investigation himself . . . and then he hushed it up. All along the line, Dylan wasn't hunting Stephen Donn . . . he was protecting him! And the best of it was, all the way along he was taking the piss out of me, winding me up in fun like he always did.

'The only positive thing he ever gave me was the lead to the Neames brothers. So what? They didn't know anything anyway, so giving them to Liam and me didn't do any harm, and helped convince us that our man Michael was really on the case. That was arrogant, but it wasn't risky, not like some of the other things he did.

'Know how I figured where he and Donn were headed?' She gave the briefest shake of her head.

'When I went to see Mike at Pitt Street that time, he came to the front desk to collect me, all bright and breezy, and he's whistling a tune – a tune from South Pacific. *Bali Hai*, it's called. When, finally, the scales fell away and I knew that he had to be Donn's inside man, that scene flashed straight back into my mind.

'Pure bloody Dylan that was; I can see him now counting his money and laughing to himself that he'd even told me where he was going, and dumb old Blackstone hadn't a clue. Ah Mike,' I called out, hearing the sadness in my own voice, 'you always had to show off. You always had to try to be just that bit smarter than you really were. And you always had to try to be one up on me.

'I told the Dutch authorities about my guess. They checked

yesterday's flights out of Schiphol, and they came upon two UK males, Mr Michael Auden and Mr Stuart Dee – another poet and another river; another bloody Dylan joke, I'll bet – booked KLM to Singapore, then routed on to Bali.

'That was their getaway destination all along, and the cheeky sod even dropped me a hint, never thinking I'd work it out.

'He did it the day before yesterday, as well; when I called him to ask him to run those checks into abandoned production platforms – which of course he never did. The mad bugger practically told me, if I'd realised it at the time, to look at Dawn's e-mail. "If he phones . . ." he said, "if he uses the post . . ."

'The best of it is that he was right. I really am as dumb as he thought. I actually tipped him off that we had rumbled Donn when I asked him to do that. And later, I even mentioned the activating word for the account – code name "mother-in-law", I told him. That's how they were able to release the money without waiting for the deadline or for an e-mail from Miles. Mike knew your Mum's first name. He met her that time we all had dinner in Glasgow.

'Oh, love, I knew something was wrong, I knew there was someone else involved, but I never suspected it was Mike himself until we hit that platform and found that Donn had gone early. When I spilled the code, Dylan sent him an e-mail, then headed straight for Amsterdam, while his partner flew there in the Jet Ranger. The Dutch found it last night in a car park on the edge of the city.'

Prim was dry-eyed by now. 'How did they get together?' she asked.

'Superintendent Hennessy – that's Mike's boss; he was one of the guys who interviewed me in Amsterdam – thinks that he recruited Donn as an informant; around the time of that do at Gantry's, when the photo was taken. The guy had no record, but he did have shady connections in Scotland and in Holland. Interpol knew about him, apparently; they had him placed as one of the movers of big loads of Pakistani hashish from the Far East through Europe. The dates of those operations coincide with him working offshore in the area.

'Dylan's private notes in the office refer to him turning Donn. He didn't have the brains to do that, of course: what really happened was that Donn turned him, completely in the end. When Mike ran for it, he took two genuine passports, made up from blanks that had been stolen from an office in Liverpool, but recovered by the Glasgow police in a raid.

'We'll never know for sure whose idea it was to kidnap Dawn for ransom, as part of the vendetta against me, but I'm pretty sure that Mike came up with it and Stephen did the planning. Getting himself on to the movie crew was a brilliant idea, and as it turned out, so fucking simple. He does some research, knocks down the Szabo guy, then turns up next morning at his agency looking for movie work, with special experience on oil rigs as an added attraction.'

I looked sideways at Primavera. 'He was a really clever piece of work, was Stephen Donn, and like Myrtle Campbell said, vicious with it. I'm pretty certain that if the two of them had got to Bali, and had got to the money, not long afterwards Mike would have been found dead in a ditch.'

'What about the money?' Prim asked. 'Is it gone for good?'

'No. They'll get it back. Governments are involved now;

ours, the Dutch, the Swiss. Even as we speak, bankers are being leant on very hard. Your brother-in-law has some incredibly powerful friends, you know.'

'I know that, my love, just as you've had an extremely dangerous enemy. That's still the big unanswered question, isn't it. Why the hell did Stephen Donn have such a hatred of you?'

I smiled at her; the sort of grin that leaves smugness way behind and climbs to the upper reaches of self-satisfaction. 'Oh, I know that,' I told her, as casually as I could.

'I've been thinking about that from the very start; and I've had a wild idea about it. Thanks to a check that the MI5 man made for me tonight, I know for sure now. I'm not going to do anything about it though, not yet.

'The real life Oz Blackstone movie isn't over yet. There's still one last scene to be shot.' Primavera gasped with astonishment as I outlined the script.

57

The next few days were spectacular. The news blackout was lifted at two o'clock that afternoon, at a press conference in Whitehall no less, at which the star performers were Miles, Dawn, me . . . and the Prime Minister, determined to milk every last drop of publicity from the story.

He took the lead in telling the story of the kidnapping, of our turning to Detective Inspector Michael Dylan, a rogue Scottish policeman, only to be betrayed by him, of Miles turning in desperation to his Friend in a High Place, and of our insistence on being involved in the rescue mission ourselves.

He ended with an account of the confrontation in Amsterdam Airport, of the two fugitives' attempt to use human shields to escape, and of their being shot by a Dutch Special Forces officer.

A few of the details were a bit fudged up; I didn't like Mike's name being blackened any further, but I knew that the PM could hardly tell the world that he'd been executed, on his orders, to save embarrassment. I was pleased though, that no mention was made of earlier events.

As you can imagine, the media went absolutely apeshit. Questions flew at us from all corners of the room. Miles was asked about his feelings when he realised that his wife had been taken, and his relief when we found her safe. He dealt with them with dignity and with eloquence . . . although he said nothing about almost blowing Dawn's brains out, or even about shooting the shit out of the galley kitchen.

They asked me about Dylan, and about what happened in Amsterdam. I told them that he had been a good friend to me, that there had been many times in my past when he had been there for me when I had needed him, and that his betrayal of us all for nothing other than money was one of the saddest things I had ever known. I also asked everyone to spare a thought for his girlfriend, who was at that moment under sedation in Glasgow.

I went along with the official version of the events in the airport restaurant as best I could. I didn't say outright that Mike had threatened anyone, simply that 'they' had attempted to take a woman hostage, and that my Dutch companion had been left with no choice but to shoot them.

They asked me about Stephen Donn too; I told them that I had only ever known him as Stu Queen, movie electrician. I resisted the urge to add that Miles was disappointed that we hadn't found him on the rig, since he would have taken great satisfaction from shooting his lights out himself.

Dawn didn't take any questions. Miles told the crowd that she was still unable to speak about her ordeal, and they respected that. As our limo drove across Westminster Bridge on the start of the journey back to Surrey, he told me that their agent had sold the rights to a world exclusive interview to CNN for three million dollars.

Prim was with us in the car; she had stood at the back of the room during the press conference, unnoticed and anonymous.

'Poor Susie,' she said at last, as we headed south. 'I can't imagine what this will do to her.'

I looked at her. 'At a time like this,' I told her, 'a girl needs her father. Why don't you tell that to old Joe Donn?'

We drove back up to Scotland next morning. I had to team up with the GWA – for a trip to Amsterdam. You wouldn't believe the pop I got from those Dutch fans when I stepped up for my first announcement – and Prim wanted to spend the weekend with Susie.

Then on the following Monday, I was back at work on the movie. Miles did re-shoot the ending to make it more like our real-life adventure; we got into wetsuits again and filmed some scenes in a big tank. But Dawn and I were still the surprise bad guys, he still got zapped, and I still went to my fiery doom in the blazing chopper. All in a day's work – or in this case, a week, for by Friday we were finished, and *Snatch*, subject to editing, special effects, and adding the music score, was a wrap.

'What do you think?' I asked Miles, as he drove me to Heathrow to catch the shuttle to Glasgow. 'How's the movie going to do? Will I ruin it?'

He chuckled. 'Nothing and no one could ruin that now,' he said. 'You remember that half-point of yours.'

'How could I forget it?'

'Well, it's a point now. I owe you; that was a big thing you did, backing me up on that rig. In money terms, you can start thinking two million dollars and work up from there. Just one thing, though. Take my advice and don't say anything to that money-grabbing bastard of an agent of yours!'

He dropped me off at terminal one, and I rushed for the

plane. In the lounge and en route for Glasgow, I must have signed thirty autographs. Was this what life was going to be like from now on, I wondered? If so, I decided, it might be time for a sharp exit.

As I stepped off the 757, and out into the grey, drizzly Glasgow night, where Prim was waiting for me, I found, to my total surprise, that I was whistling *Bali Hai* – a bloody sight more tunefully than Dylan ever did, I might add.

58

Life was quiet for a few weeks after that. Just as well, for Primavera Phillips and I had a wedding to plan, with one enforced change in the cast; I needed a new best man. I wasn't sure what he would say when I asked him, but for the first time in over ten years, Miles Grayson agreed to accept a supporting role.

There was another change to the guest list too. We added Joe Donn. The old guy had taken Prim's advice and told Susie, who was left as bereaved as any widow by Mike's death, that he was her natural father, whatever the position was legally. She didn't believe him at first, but finally, when he offered to take a DNA test to prove it, she accepted that he was telling the truth. Just as well, for apart from a hated aunt, her father's sister, he was the only relative she had left in the world.

I stuck to my plan to spend the night before the wedding in a suite at Gleneagles. Miles and Dawn had elected to sleep at Semple House, but he and I arranged an impromptu stag night, in the very pub in which Stephen Donn had slipped his Mickey Finn into SuperDave's Guinness. To our surprise, Dad Phillips insisted on joining us; to our even greater surprise, Elanore didn't say a word.

Even although Mac the Dentist, who was stopping overnight at Gleneagles with Mary, Ellie and the boys, was there, it was a quiet do. Miles and Dave knew what their lives would be worth if I turned up for my wedding with a major hangover, so they made damn sure that I didn't step over the line.

My Dad, on the other hand, was halfway to being rat-arsed when our taxi dropped the two of us back at the hotel. He got a bit sentimental when I tried to put him into the lift.

Instead of stepping inside, he grabbed my shoulder. 'This has got to work this time, son,' he slurred. 'All your life you've been the luckiest bugger in the world, in every respect but one. But there's nothing you deserve more than a happy marriage, 'cos you know what? Son or no son, you're the best fucking man I know.'

I felt myself getting sentimental too, so I shoved him into the lift, pushed the button for his floor, then stepped out before the doors closed and walked up to my own.

I had been back in my suite for no more than five minutes when there was a soft knock at the door. I knew who it was even before I opened it.

'Come on in, Noosh,' I said to the slim figure in the corridor. 'I wish I could say I was sorry about your brother, but I'm not. I saw him die, and he bloody deserved it.'

She took a small silver automatic from her handbag as she stepped inside. I've no doubt she'd have shot me there and then, had Mark Kravitz not moved up behind her and ripped it from her hand.

'You don't know my friend,' I told her. 'It's time you did, though; he's had you under observation for weeks.' There was a sofa in the suite's sitting room. I pushed her gently down on to it. 'Come on,' I said. 'I can guess the story, but let's have it anyway.'

She looked up at me, and her narrow face took on the look

of the purest hatred I have ever seen. 'How did you know?' she hissed.

'Through your mother,' I told her.

'No one ever found out much about your brother; he was two people, Stephen Donn and Stu Queen, and he covered his tracks very well by moving from one personality to another. When he died, I thought at first that I'd never get to know why he held such a vicious grudge against me. As far as I could see the trail was as dead as him.

'Then I thought of his mother; she was the only link with him I had left. So I asked someone, one of the spooks who was around in Amsterdam, if they could find out more about her. It didn't take long at all. She's a naturalised British subject, so she has a file at the Home Office.

'That told me that she entered the UK in 1968, having escaped from Czechoslovakia a day or two before the Soviet invasion. In those days, her name was Mira Turkel, and she brought with her a five-year-old daughter, Anoushka.'

Her poisonous glare only made my smile wider. 'Sometimes, I'm as thick as two short planks, you know, Noosh.'

'Yes, I know,' she said, in a voice so acid that it should have melted her teeth.

'I should have smelled a rodent straight away up in Aberdeen, when you showed up in the Treetops, acting reasonably pally. But no, I'm loveable Oz, am I not? No one can stay mad at me for ever, so I fell for it, and I got you into that movie crowd scene next day. No wonder the Grampian police couldn't find a bullet. There never was one, was there? Stephen fired a blank from the back of that bloody motorcycle.

'If my brain had been working, I might have twigged it

right then. A series of attacks on people close to me; okay, vicious, twisted, but with a mad logic to it. But why were you one of the targets? Who could have known about the connection between you and me, unless they had heard it from you?

'You shouldn't have involved yourself, Noosh. I was too dumb to work it out until it was too late, but it was a huge risk.' To my complete surprise, I felt a gusher of rage blast up inside me. I had meant to play that final scene as Mr Cool; superior, dismissive, more in sorrow than in anger. But I wasn't that good an actor, nor will I be, ever. I hated that woman as much as she hated me, and I could not keep it from showing.

'You had to do it, though, hadn't you. You're better than the rest of us aren't you, and you have to let us know it. It's not enough for you to be in command of your own destiny, is it; you have to control other people, too. You're good at it too. God, you fooled Jan for long enough.'

'No, she fooled me,' Anoushka snarled, her accent becoming thicker. 'Both of you did. I loved her, I was good to her, and she said she loved me too. But all the time, all the time she lived with me, all the time I thought that we were a couple, you were playing with me, both of you.'

'Wrong,' I shouted at her. 'You're totally wrong. For a while Jan believed all that too; you had her fucking mesmerised. I'll tell you this, though. All that time, I hated you; I knew that inside yourself, you were an evil, corrupting influence. Jan never saw you that way; but she did realise eventually that she couldn't let you run her life any longer.'

She jumped up and spat in my face. I lost it; I hit her, backhanded, across the cheek, sending her sprawling back across the couch, as Mark Kravitz stepped between us.

'You're a liar,' she shouted. 'You used me, both of you, and you thought you could get away with it. But Jan didn't, did she? I punished her, just as I am punishing you.'

I yelled back at her. 'What the fuck do you mean, you crazy bitch?'

When she smiled at me, I wanted the hatred back, pronto. She really was crazy, and that look scared me stiff. 'You didn't really think that thug could have set such a trap on his own, did you?' she sneered. My blood ran cold. 'Stephen did that; he was with him, and he wired that machine. He made it lethal because he knew who Jan was, he knew what she had done to me, and he knew how much I wanted to punish her.'

I knew that I daren't touch the woman again, ever. But I wanted to mark her, in any way I could. 'And now he's fucking dead,' I said, sounding cold, and I admit it, as vicious as her. I touched the middle of my forehead. 'Right there, the Dutchman shot him; his brains were all over the carpet, and he pissed himself.

'Know what? Right now I feel just a bit sorry for the bastard. Because I'm sure you controlled your half-brother all his life, and that you turned him into your creature, the way you tried to turn Jan. Poor Stephen probably never had a chance.'

Finally, I got to her. 'No,' she protested. 'That's not true. I've loved two people in my life – Jan and my brother. No one else. My mother was always a weak woman, and when she married that pitiful Scotsman I gave up on her. My father, I never knew.

'They were my only two. Jan betrayed me, but Stephen never did. It was really me who brought him up; his parents would have held him back, but I showed him what he could be. He was my treasure and when he was older, my little secret. None of my acquaintances knew about him, not even Jan. But he has always been there for me, whenever I've needed him.'

And then the madness was back. 'He and I planned together how we would make you suffer; we had hoped that you would be arrested for poisoning that man, as almost you were. When you talked your way out, we knew we had to do more. Originally Stephen was simply going to kill Dawn Phillips, but then he saw the script, and had the wonderful idea of acting it out, and making himself rich.

'Your policeman friend was a big help, all the way along. He was corrupt; you know that, don't you. Stephen was supposed to be his informant, but it was the other way around. From time to time Dylan would give him money that was supposed to be for tips, but Stephen would give it back to him, and lots, lots more.

'He was included in the kidnap, because I thought it would be too dangerous to leave him behind in Glasgow. He would never have seen any of the money, of course. That was for Stephen . . . and eventually for me.'

She sneered at me again. 'You think now that it is over, Oz? No, it is not. Noosh will always be around. When you and your little Prim are married, I will always be there in your nightmares. When you have children, you will always be afraid that one day—'

Kravitz killed her then; he stepped up behind her and broke her neck. More orders, you see. Stephen had left nothing behind him, nothing to prove that Noosh was behind it all. But when I knew who she was, I knew she had to be. The powers that be decided that they couldn't pull her in and confront her with it, just in case I was wrong; so instead, they let me run with it, they set me up as live bait to see if she would bite.

What they didn't tell me was that she was going to die too, jumping off a cliff just south of Aberdeen in a grief-stricken suicide. But what the hell; she's best off with her murderous wee bastard of a brother.

She was right about one thing, though, was Anoushka Turkel. I still see her in my dreams; keep this to yourself but, occasionally, I wake up screaming.

Poisoned Cherries

Quintin Jardine

When Oz Blackstone is offered a major role in a cop movie shooting in Edinburgh, he cannot resist taking centre stage. And Oz has had a brief liaison with Susie Gantry, a beautiful and self-possessed business woman, that is turning into something much more long term.

It all looks like a bowl of cherries until ex-lover Alison Goodchild turns up asking for a favour. But when he finds Alison's business partner murdered in her flat, Oz can't help but suspect he's been set up. And when he discovers a trail of intrigue leading to the cast of the star-studded movie in which he is performing those cherries begin to taste very rancid indeed . . .

'Perfect plotting and convincing characterisation . . . Jardine manages to combine the picturesque with the thrilling and the dream-like with the coldly rational' *The Times*

'Jardine's plot is very cleverly constructed, every incident and every character has a justified place in the labyrinth of motives' Gerald Kaufman, *Scotsman*

0 7472 6472 4

headline

On Honeymoon
with Death

Quintin Jardine

Returning to L'Escala, the idyllic Spanish village where they were once so happy, Oz Blackstone and Primavera Phillips are looking to forget the past.

But old ghosts are not so easy to placate, and the shadow of Oz's childhood sweetheart Jan, now tragically dead, is threatening to turn their relationship into a seething cauldron of bitterness and recrimination.

Until a body turns up face down in the swimming pool of their new villa, and suddenly they are very much back in harness again. Faced with the indifference of the local police, Oz and Prim are forced to investigate the murder themselves, and soon they begin to uncover a nest of very dangerous vipers beneath L'Escala's sunny exterior.

Praise for Quintin Jardine's novels:

'Remarkably assured . . . a *tour de force*' *New York Times*

'More twists and turns than TV's *Taggart* at its best' *Stirling Observer*

'Deplorably readable' *Guardian*

0 7472 6471 6

headline

Autographs in the Rain

Quintin Jardine

As Bob Skinner takes an evening stroll with an old flame, glamorous film star Louise Bankier, a frightening shot-gun attack sends them diving for cover. Danger, it seems, has zeroed in on him once again.

Returning to her native Scotland to shoot her latest film, Louise Bankier is one of Scotland's most popular exports, except with the stalker who seems determined to scare her witless – and maybe worse. For Skinner, tracking down her tormentor isn't just business now. It's very personal indeed.

Meanwhile, the case of a pensioner found dead in his bath turns out to be anything but an open and shut case – especially when one of Skinner's closest staff is accused of murdering him. And a gang of thieves specialising in stealing items of a rather slippery nature is driving more than one police force to distraction.

On several fronts, Skinner is about to find out that nothing is quite what it seems . . .

Quintin Jardine is the author of ten previous acclaimed Bob Skinner novels: 'Remarkably assured . . . *a tour de force*' New York Times

0 7472 6387 6

headline

Head Shot

Quintin Jardine

DCC Bob Skinner has witnessed the aftermath of murder countless times. Yet nothing could have prepared him for identifying the strangled bodies of his wife's beloved parents, killed at their lakeside cabin in New York State. Driven by cold rage, Skinner quickly muscles in on the investigation, and soon he's found links with three other cases where the killing is too professional to be the result of a burglary gone wrong. But can he penetrate the multiple layers of intrigue to unearth the killer?

Quintin Jardine is the author of eleven previous highly acclaimed Bob Skinner novels:

'Remarkably assured . . . a *tour de force*' *New York Times*

'In Scotland, Jardine outsells Grisham' *Observer*

'If Ian Rankin is the Robert Carlyle of Scottish crime writing, then Jardine is surely its Sean Connery' *Glasgow Herald*

0 7472 6388 4

headline

Now you can buy any of these other bestselling books by **Quintin Jardine** from your bookshop or *direct from his publisher*.

FREE P&P AND UK DELIVERY
(Overseas and Ireland £3.50 per book)

Oz Blackstone series
Blackstone's Pursuits	£6.99
A Coffin for Two	£6.99
Wearing Purple	£5.99
Screen Savers	£6.99
On Honeymoon with Death	£6.99
Poisoned Cherries	£6.99

TO ORDER SIMPLY CALL THIS NUMBER

01235 400 414

or visit our website: www.madaboutbooks.com

Prices and availability subject to change without notice.